The Earl's Captive

The Earl's Captive

Lorna Read

Chapter One

"No! *Martin*, not the child, she's just a baby. I don't care what you do to me, but ... *leave* her, Martin. Oh Martin, *no!*"

Her mother's voice had risen to an agonized scream as a glancing blow from her father's tightly clenched fist caught her on the cheekbone and sent her reeling against the wooden dresser. A sturdy blue milk jug teetered and fell, smashing into irregular pieces on the tiled kitchen floor.

The moment was frozen forever into Lucy Swift's memory: the blow, the rocking jug, the white explosion on the floor, the sight of her mother on her knees, a crimson mark on her face already turning blue, sobbing as she picked up the sharp shards of pottery, and her father muttering an oath as he swayed unsteadily towards the door.

Looking at him now, hearing him whistle through his teeth as he brushed the bay mare into gleaming splendour with methodical, circular strokes, Lucy could hardly believe that the brutal drunkard and this careful, tender man were one and the same person – her father. Yet her earliest memory was no fantasy.

Similar scenes had been repeated time after time during the nineteen years of her life. They had driven her mother, Ann, into premature old age. At thirty-eight, she was grey-haired and haggard, her body shrunken as if by her efforts to protect herself from her husband's violent words and blows, her face lined and scarred from where he had once, during an exceptional bout of drunkenness, lashed her with a riding whip.

Lucy loved her mother with a fervour that had led her, from an early age, to stand up to Martin Swift. Once, at the age of four, she had rained blows on his knees with her childish fists as he sought to knock frail Ann aside, convinced that she was hiding a jug of ale from him. Her hot-blooded defence of her mother had often earned her a painful beating, but she knew she also had her father's grudging respect, especially where horses were concerned. Not like her brother, Geoffrey.

As if reading her thoughts, Martin Swift glanced from the fidgeting horse to his daughter.

"Bet Geoffrey wouldn't have made as good a job of it as this, eh?" he enquired, casting an admiring glance at his own handiwork. In the dusty yellow light of the stable, the pretty grey mare's hide gleamed like moonlight on snow. He didn't expect an answer, but dodged round to the other side of the horse and resumed his hypnotic brush strokes.

Lucy watched him while he worked. At forty-one years old, in spite of his over-indulgence in ale and spirits, Martin was in his prime, not a tall man, but wiry and strong, with the black hair and blue eyes that betrayed his Irish ancestry, although he, and his father before him, had been born in the same tiny Lancashire village where the Swifts still lived. Only his florid, weather-beaten complexion and broken nose bearing its route-map of tiny red veins gave a clue to his outdoor, rough-and-tumble life. Indoors, dressed up, with his body scrubbed clean of the smells of the stable, he could, in a low light, pass for the gentleman he thought himself to be.

Geoffrey was not a bit like his father, reflected Lucy, as she idly chewed on a piece of fresh straw. She missed her brother badly, even though it was three years since he had left Prebbledale, running away at fourteen to escape his father's bullying. She had aided his flight and she didn't regret it, even though she had, by this risky action, deprived herself of her staunchest supporter and closest confidant, probably for ever. For Geoffrey, dearest, kind, humorous Geoffrey, with his fair curls and poetic nature, was far more like his mother than either Lucy or Helen.

"That mewling little milksop," was his father's usual derisive way of describing him. Born with a deep-seated fear of all large animals, Geoffrey would scurry for the nearest hiding place whenever his father came looking for him to take him into the stables and try to teach him some horse-lore. Martin Swift was known and respected all over the county and beyond for his skill in breeding, handling, breaking-in and training horses. Dukes and earls would send for him and ask his advice before parting with their money for a thoroughbred racehorse or a pair of carriage horses, knowing that his judgement was sound and unerring.

"No-o-o," he would say slowly, shaking his head as some fine-looking specimen was paraded before him. "Not that one. Weak left hock. 'Twould let ye down over the half-mile." And Lord Highfalutin' would wave the animal away and slip Martin a sovereign for saving him fifty.

The grey mare, Beauty Fayre, stamped a hoof and snorted, breaking Lucy's reverie. Who knew where Geoffrey was now? In the East Indies, maybe, having worked his passage on a trading ship; or perhaps he was dressed in the uniform of a naval rating, keeping the look-out while he mentally composed an ode to the heaving sea. Unless he was … Lucy couldn't bring herself to consider the worst fate of all.

A sound behind her, like the scuffling of a dog in the straw, made her turn her head. One shoulder and half an anxious face were poking round the corner of the cobwebby door-jamb as Ann Swift attempted to catch her daughter's eye without attracting the attention of her husband. Giving an almost imperceptible nod, Lucy took two silent steps backward towards the door and spun quickly round the corner of the building, trying not to catch her skirt on a protruding nail.

She had totally forgotten that her sister, together with her husband John and twin sons, Toby and Alexander, were paying them a visit that afternoon. Her heart sank at the thought of having to play auntie to the toddlers, cudgel her brains to think of something to reply to

John's suggestive remarks and listen to her sister's predictable, boring grumbles about servants, children and the latest London fashions. It was always the same.

"Not married yet, our Lucy?" John would bark, in his brusque attempt at a jocular tone. She would wait to see the beads of sweat break out along his forehead as his eyes raked her lasciviously up and down.

"Really, Mother, I just cannot understand how Helen can put up with him. He's a *beast*," Lucy complained to her mother.

"Shush, girl. He's a good man. She could have done a lot worse," replied Ann in her quiet voice, like a defeated whisper. They'd had this conversation many times before. It was a ritual warm-up to all Helen's visits.

"But she'd never have married him, surely, if she hadn't wanted to get away from Father so badly," Lucy persisted. "She was only sixteen. Who knows who she might have fallen in love with if only she'd had the chance? She didn't even know John Masters. Father fixed it all up. I think it's disgusting – like bringing a stallion to a mare."

* * *

"Lucy!" Ann was shocked, but amused, too. Privately, she thought Lucy's outspoken opinion was quite correct. She reached out and straightened a roaming lock of Lucy's chestnut hair as the two of them sat side by side on the settle in the window, watching for the arrival of the visitors. How like her father Lucy was, with her straight back, her alert blue eyes, her plump, curving lips and her plain-speaking ways.

There was a vividness about Lucy that reminded Ann of her first-ever glimpse of Martin, as he stood in the marketplace of Weynford, her hometown, twenty-three years ago. To her, he had seemed to stand out from his companions as if surrounded by a kind of glow, undetectable to the human eye but nevertheless capable of being picked up by some sixth sense.

Even now, in spite of the years of torment and agony she had undergone at his hand, abuse that had caused her ill-health and a permanent nervous trembling, she was still in awe of him, still capable of feeling that same old wonderment whenever he looked at her kindly or gave her one of his special, half-cheeky, half-loving smiles. Whatever he possessed that gave him that unique power over people and animals, Lucy had inherited, and sometimes Ann feared for what life held in store for her younger daughter. Particularly now, with Martin so anxious about her unmarried state.

They had discussed it in bed just the previous night.

"Damn that kitchen maid!" Martin had expostulated, having sipped at his night-time beverage of warm ale only to find it stone cold. "Get rid of her, first thing tomorrow. And what are we going to do about Lucy?"

Ann, used to her husband's abrupt changes of subject, had sighed and withdrawn to the far side of the lumpy feather mattress, trying not to incur her husband's further wrath by drawing too many of the coverlets with her.

"Well?" he had snapped, reaching out in the darkness and digging his fingers painfully into her shoulder. "*Well*? Helen's twenty-one and she's got two fine sons already. I'm the laughing stock of the neighbourhood, having that strapping lass still on my hands at the age of nineteen. Why, only yesterday that cur Appleby had the damn' cheek to suggest that maybe nobody would have her because she was soiled goods. I whipped the blighter to teach him to hold his tongue. Still, an insult's an insult. She's been on our hands long enough, eating our food, taking up room about the place, striding round like a … like a great *lad.*"

Ann had felt a chuckle inside, knowing full well that Martin did treat his younger daughter almost exactly like a son. She knew, too, that Martin found Lucy a great help with the horses as she had inherited every bit of his own natural talent. Even unbroken horses calmed for her and let her approach them. It was as if some secret understanding passed between beast and girl. Sometimes she wished that Lucy had been born a boy. She would have gone far in life, of that Ann had no doubt – and that life would have been a lot easier, too.

Martin was continuing his monologue: "I've seen the way they all look at her – tradesmen, stable lads, respectable gentlemen. They'd all like to get their hands on her. We could have married her off twenty, thirty times already. If only I hadn't been so soft with her, giving in to her every time she said, 'No, Father, I won't marry him … No, Father, I don't like him …' Spoilt and wilful, that's what she is. Well, I've had enough. There's a good man I've got in mind for her. None better. She'll marry him and that'll be an end to it, even if I have to take the strap to her."

Ann, with much nervous clutching and kneading of the bedclothes, had found the breath to whisper, "Who could this be?"

His answer had given her very mixed feelings indeed and caused her to lie awake the best part of the night. "Old Holy Joe. The Reverend Pritt."

Chapter Two

"Here they come," said Lucy, as John Masters' coach swept down the lane, pulled by a pair of matching bays. Masters was a wealthy grain merchant and Helen, as she stepped from the carriage, was, if not perfectly suited to her middle-aged husband, at least perfectly dressed.

The two little boys followed, identically dressed in blue jerkins and knickerbockers, their brown hair combed and twisted neatly into shape.

Binns, the maid, announced them breathlessly at the door, "Mr and Mrs Masters and the two Master Masters," then flushed, as if realizing that what she'd said had sounded most peculiar.

"Thank you, Binns," said Ann, rising to her feet. "We'll take tea in the drawing-room. And bring some apple cider for the children – watered, if you please."

Ann was remembering one disastrous previous occasion when the maid before last had failed to water down the cider, resulting in two very dizzy small boys being sick all over the chaise longue.

"Yes, ma'am," said Binns, dropping a brief, awkward curtsey and hastening out of the room as fasts as her lumpish legs could carry her.

"My dear," breathed Ann, embracing Helen, who was taller than she was, and grazing her cheek on an amber brooch pinned to the shoulder of her daughter's short cape of the most fashionable shade of lavender blue.

Lucy felt her hackles rise as the portly figure of John Masters confronted her and she felt his hot gaze travel up and down her body. The crude sexuality of the man disgusted her. She was always having to dodge his groping hands and try not to blush at his suggestive remarks. She, who had never kissed a man except in polite greeting, could not conceive of her sister in the arms of this fat, ugly, lecherous old man, doing all the things you had to do in order to get with child.

Lucy's sexual knowledge was scanty but basic. Living in the country and working with horses as she did, she could hardly have avoided noticing the way they acted at certain times of the year. Her father always forbade her to leave the house when a stallion was put to one of his mares. What he didn't know, however, was that Lucy's bedroom was not the stronghold it appeared to be. An athletic person of either sex could, with a modicum of nimbleness, lower a leg from the windowsill, find a toehold in the crumbling, ivy-clad stone and from there, scramble sideways into the old oak tree, from whence it was a short and easy climb to the ground.

So, on more than one occasion, Lucy had heard the excited whinnying and snorting of the stallion and seen the mare, hump-backed and docile. Seen, too, the way in which her father and a helper aided the stallion by guiding that huge, terrifying, yet fascinating limb, thick as a man's leg, into the mare. Watching the frenzied couplings, Lucy had felt hot, breathless, faintly disgusted, yet tingling with strange sensations, much as she felt whenever a handsome man looked at her the way her brother-in-law did.

"I won't ask the usual question," John Masters said, by way of greeting.

Lucy was surprised by this change in his usual tactics. Motioning her to sit in one of the two high-backed chairs that stood on either side of the marble fireplace, empty and screened now as it was a warm September afternoon, he stood in front of her, swaying to and fro, his fat legs crammed obscenely into his tight, shiny black boots.

"There's no need, is there?" he added, giving her a sly, conspiratorial wink with one corner of a weak, grey, piggy eye.

Lucy sat bolt upright. She took a deep breath, feeling how her tight stays constrained her lungs. "What on earth do you mean, brother John?" she demanded. Her words, spoken too loudly, cut across the currents of other people's conversations and stopped them dead. Helen, her mother, her father, even little Toby and Alexander from the privacy of their den beneath a table, were all staring at her, aware of the first rumblings of an emotional storm.

Lucy gulped and toyed with a bow on her cream silk dress. She wished she hadn't opened her mouth. Probably John had only been making a joke. He could not really be privy to some information concerning her future, about which she knew nothing.

Her brother-in-law's boots creaked as he shifted position uncomfortably. "Nothing. Um … that is …" He shifted his gaze to Lucy's father and she intercepted his glance.

So there was a plan afoot. Of course, she could have taken his remark to mean that there was no need to ask her if she were engaged yet because she obviously wasn't. But John Masters was a creature of habit, a mortal blessed with not one iota of imagination. He would only have made such a comment, and accompanied it with such a look and a wink, if he knew something which she didn't. After his *There's no need, is there?*, there had been a silent, unvoiced, *Because it's all been settled.*

They were all waiting, her mother brushing crumbs off her lap, her father working his toe into the rug, Helen pretending to straighten her necklace. A muffled giggle from one of the twins broke Lucy's tense trance and gave her back her voice. She directed the full, undiluted power of her iciest blue gaze on her father, who returned it equally coldly.

"Father, if any plans for my future have been made, I think I have a right to know what they are."

"Very well, Lucy, but before you fly into one of your famous tempers –" *Tempers? You're the last person on earth who can accuse anyone else of having a bad temper*, thought Lucy furiously, wishing she were strong enough to pick her father up bodily and shake the truth out of him –

"remember I am your father and head of this household, and as such, my decisions are not to be argued with. You're nineteen years old now, my girl. Nineteen!"

He looked triumphantly at everyone in turn and, backed up by their encouraging nods, turned to face Lucy again. "I can't wait for you to choose a suitor for yourself. I don't hold with such liberated notions. Allow a girl to pick for herself and she'll choose some ragamuffin with a roving eye and no'but two brass farthings to rub together."

"Aye," interjected John Masters approvingly.

His wife glared at him, but Lucy's gaze rested unwaveringly on her father, daring him to be a traitor and bestow her very own birthright of freedom and choice on some man she did not wish to know, and would detest if he were the King himself. *Father*, she willed, trying to project her thoughts behind his eyes and into the farthest recesses of his misguided brain, *Father, I will not be married off. You can't do it. You will not do it*. Her jaw was clenched in a spasm of steely purpose as she poured her whole being into her gaze.

But Martin Swift was untouched by his daughter's silent message. "Your mother and I love you and wish to do our very best for you. If you agree to marry the man I have in mind, not only will you live in comfort with a good man, but you will hold a very honorable position in the community, far higher than your mother or I could ever have hoped for.

"I had no idea that my daughter had caught the eye of such an august man as the Reverend Pritt. To be the wife of a man of God, Lucy! When I informed your sister and her husband in the hallway – well, I couldn't keep such a compliment to the family to myself, could I? – they were so pleased for you that ..."

His voice seemed to be fading into the far distance, like the echo of a stone dropped into a dry well. At the same time, a mist formed in front of Lucy's eyes. She tried to pass her hand in front of her face, on which she could feel a cold, clammy perspiration forming, but her arm was like a lead weight and remained, unmoving, in her lap. Then a great lassitude overcame her and she felt her surroundings dissolve and her chair whirl like a spinning top.

Chapter Three

Lucy had never fainted before. She came to and found her mother hovering anxiously over her while her sister bathed her forehead in cool water from a basin held by Binns, the young maid.

"Don't you worry 'bout her, ma'am. She be herself right soon enough," said Binns reassuringly. Lucy could have embraced her for her honest country forthrightness, but Binns, for all her commonsense, could not smooth the worried furrows from her mother's brow.

"My dear, are you all right? It is very hot today. You're not catching a fever, I hope?"

Helen's small, square hand in its cuff of pale blue lace touched Lucy's forehead, then her temples, and finally pulled down the lower lids of her eyes, making Lucy jerk back and blink in alarm. "The boys had a summer sickness some weeks ago," Helen explained. "They went quite, quite pale under the lids. But there's nothing wrong with you."

"I wish there *was*," moaned Lucy fervently. "I'd sooner waste away and die than be married to that old ... *goat!*"

* * *

Ann Swift drew a deep breath and chewed her lower lip thoughtfully. How she wished her younger daughter was as docile as Helen had been. She had gone to the altar with John Masters without a murmur and, indeed, the marriage seemed to be working. Helen had her boys and a good allowance and a husband who didn't beat her, even if he did sometimes respond rather over-enthusiastically to attractive members of the opposite sex.

At least this philandering tendency kept him from eternally bothering Helen with his attentions. He had done his duty, fathered twin heirs, and now Helen was free to attend to her duties of lady of the house and follower of fashion, something that pleased her far more than her husband's twice-monthly drunken fumblings in her bedroom. Even love-matches couldn't be relied upon to be perfect, as Ann knew to her cost. Yet, for Lucy, that is exactly what she would have wished – the perfect love-match for her beautiful, unruly, headstrong younger daughter.

* * *

"I won't do it," announced Lucy, mutinously, waving away Binns's proffered glass of water. "I refuse to allow myself to be incarcerated in that damp prison of a rectory with that revolting, ugly, nasty-minded old man. 'Man of God' indeed! I would never take a young, sensitive child to hear one of our dear vicar's sermons. To hear him ranting about the terrible punishments God has in store for us all if we dare to defy His will or take His holy name in vain, makes me think that worshipping the Devil would be the easier option."

"Leave the room, Binns. See how Cook is faring with the roast pork," ordered Ann, terrified lest Lucy's blasphemies be prattled about all over the village.

But Lucy wasn't done. "Reverend Pritt has a very twisted idea of what God is really like. I think something very terrible must have happened to him in his life to make him turn his good Lord into the kind of enemy he would have us believe God is, someone who isn't kind and just and forgiving at all, but is a cruel tyrant – rather like Father."

Helen clutched her sister's arm in the hope of distracting her from her subject, as it was obviously upsetting their mother, who was standing by the window, fanning herself agitatedly. But Lucy was not so easily deterred.

"I am sorry, Mother," she continued, a softer note creeping into her voice. Lucy loved her mother dearly and the last thing she wanted to do was upset her, but, on the subject of her own life, with her whole future at stake, she felt she had to express her feelings, even if it meant coming out with a few home truths.

"I know you love Father, in spite of his vile temper and the anguish he's caused all of us. I am his dutiful daughter and have always done my best to obey him, but this is one thing that all the beatings on earth could not persuade me to do. He can beat me until I'm dead if he likes, but nobody will force me to share my life and, even worse, my bed, with that gospel-twisting, repellent old cadaver, Nathaniel Pritt!"

"Oh Lucy, see sense," put in Helen, stroking her sister's curly hair as if calming one of her toddlers. "He must be sixty if he's a day. One night with you and he'll probably drop dead of an apoplexy. I bet you he's never touched a woman in his life!"

"And he's certainly not going to touch *me!*" Lucy exclaimed, brushing aside her sister's hand and swinging her legs off the couch. Her head swam a little as she put her feet to the ground and stood up, but she ignored her lingering weakness. Appalled by the way both her mother and sister were calmly complying with Martin's wishes, Lucy turned to them, appeal in her eyes.

"Can't you see, either of you? Can't you understand?" She fixed her gaze on her sister. "I'm of the same blood as you, we're kin – who could be closer? Yet you seem to be made of totally different stuff. Why are you so meek? Why is it that you don't mind having to share a house and your body with an old, fat man whom you don't love?"

She was pleased to notice Helen's eyes blaze for an instant as the barb of truth stung home. Turning to her mother, Lucy continued, in impassioned tones, "I know you can't stand up to Father. I know that, if you had done, either you'd be dead by now, or he would have turned you out. But you're both trapped. *Trapped!*"

Her voice was rising on a note of hysteria. The whole room, with its pictures, hangings, heavy, cumbersome furniture and dark-coloured floor-coverings, seemed to be exuding waves of hostile oppression.

She paced the drawing-room carpet agitatedly. She had to make them *see*. What was wrong with them? Nobody, not even her father, had the right to do this to another human being, to order their life right down to whom they should marry and when.

She thought of Reverend Pritt, clutching his lectern and rocking back and forth while his congregation's ears were dinned with threats of being visited by plagues even unto the third and fourth generation, his gaunt face grey with stubble, his yellowed teeth spraying the unfortunates in the front pew with holy saliva. She imagined herself spread like a naked sacrifice on a white-sheeted bed surrounded by the mouldering walls and ragged tapestries of the vicarage, with the knobbly, grey, corpse-like body of Nathaniel Pritt kneeling over her, his fetid breath fanning her face, his obscene, maggot-like fingers about to touch her own warm, living flesh.

"No!" she screamed. "No! Mother, Helen, you've got to help me! Tell him it's impossible. I don't care that he's the vicar, I don't care about his position in society, I don't want to share it. I'd sooner marry an ostler, a highwayman, *anybody!* But I won't marry that... that ..."

Words came to her mind, words she'd heard her father and the grooms use. However, before she could say anything more, the door burst open and in strode her father, glowering like a thundercloud.

"Martin!" cried Ann, rushing towards him and catching his elbow in an attempt to halt a physical attack on his errant daughter.

"Woman, leave me be!" snarled her husband, his face suffused with scarlet anger. He shook off her restraining hand so violently that Ann lost her balance and fell, dashing her head against the ornately carved leg of a side table.

"Mother – oh, Mother!" wailed Helen, rushing to Ann in a crackle of starched petticoats and kneeling over her prostrate form. "You've killed her, Father!"

Chapter Four

Her mother lay as still as a corpse on the floor, yet Lucy made no move towards her. With her father charging towards her, she didn't dare and she dodged round the back of a damask-covered armchair for protection.

Martin took two more furious strides towards her then stopped, and Lucy felt as if her heart had stopped, too. How she hated and feared him! Suddenly, she was a child again, screaming at him not to hurt her mother. Then she was a young girl being slapped across the face for some minor misdemeanour such as not having bid him a polite enough 'good morning'.

Now, she was almost as tall as he was and her will was equally as strong, even if her muscles were not. In many disagreements in the past she had given way, but not this time. It meant far too much to her.

"Well, *madam*," hissed her father, with heavy sarcasm, "so we have a new head of the household, have we? One who thinks she can set rules for herself and all the other silly little bints in Christendom!"

Lucy noticed his fists spasmodically clenching and unclenching and steeled herself to expect the blow. Across the room, Helen was still kneeling and chafing her mother's temples, and against the tapestry-covered door, a silent observer, John Masters, was nonchalantly leaning, a smug leer plastered on his plump wet lips.

"So Miss High-and-Mighty thinks a vicar isn't good enough for her, is that it? She thinks to stamp her pretty foot and defy her father, who's only a stupid, tyrannical old man? 'Marry an ostler or a highwayman' indeed!"

Lucy's hand flew to her mouth. So he had overheard her incautious words. There was no escaping a punishment now. Her eyes flicked desperately round the room, to the door, the windows … Her long, full-skirted dress made it impossible to move fast enough to escape. Either he, or her brother-in-law, would stretch out a foot and trip her, or catch a handful of her dress and tear the delicate fabric. All she wanted to do was ascertain that her mother would recover and then fly out of the room, out of the house, to heaven-knows-where.

Across the room, Ann Swift made a low moaning noise and began to stir.

"Thanks be to God!" called Helen, tears streaming down her rouged and powdered face. "She's alive!"

Lucy unfroze and started to move towards her mother, but had scarcely taken two steps when her father grabbed her by the wrist and, with an adroit movement, thrust her face down across the arm of the armchair she been standing behind.

"Get off me!" Fury seethed in Lucy's brain. To be beaten by one's father in private was one thing, but here, front of her sister and her odious brother-in-law … Her father had his hand on her left shoulder and was forcing her painfully down. With a cat-like twist, she jerked her and sank her sharp teeth into his arm.

"Ouch!" Her father's cry of pain nearly deafened her as his mouth was so close to her ear.

The pressure on her shoulder was suddenly gone but as she made to spring to her feet, she heard a hated voice drawl laconically, "Whip the bitch."

"John!" replied Helen sharply. "This is none of your business. You keep out of this."

"Hold your tongue, wife, or you'll be getting a beating too. A good flogging never hurt a mare – aye, Martin?"

Lucy caught her breath in a sharp gasp as she saw the object that John was holding out to his father-in-law – a small riding switch with a thong made out of tough hide, knotted at the end. Before she could cry out in protest, her father stuck out his leg and upended her across it. In spite of her vigorous kicking, she felt her petticoats and skirt being hauled up.

How *could* he? Lucy had never felt so horrified and shamed in her life. The leather thong sang through the air three times, causing her to shudder in pain. The embroidery on the screen in front of the fireplace, of which she had an upside-down view, began to blur as tears misted her eyes. She hated her father. She would never forgive him for this.

She heard her mother's weak voice pleading, "That's enough, Martin."

Her mother's intervention stayed his hand. The whipping suddenly ceased and Lucy stood up shakily, smoothing her skirts and pushing back her tangled hair.

"If you'd have been a boy, I wouldn't have stopped at three strokes. You deserved a dozen at least for that show of defiance. Now, I hope we'll have a bit more obedience from you, my girl."

He paused to consult the French clock on the mantel-shelf. "I am expecting a visit from Reverend Pritt in just over an hour's time. He has already made it known to me that he is coming to ask for your hand in marriage. His own dear wife died many years ago, before he came to this parish, and he is a very lonely man who dearly wants children, which his first wife could not provide for him.

"Go and clean your face, girl. Helen can help you do your hair. I don't want the Reverend to think you are a slut with those unruly locks of yours. Put your best dress on, the blue one that makes you look like a girl rather than a stable-lad, and come downstairs when I call you. You are to behave to the vicar like a well-brought-up young lady. None of those bold stares, my lass, and no answering back. Just reply politely to any questions he may ask you – and of course you are to accept him. There is no question about that. Understood?"

"Yes, Father," whispered Lucy, frightened of the sarcasm that might creep into her voice if she spoke any louder. She bowed her head and inclined her knee, then stood up and took stock of the rest of her family: of her mother, crouched on the settle in the window, face in hands, weeping silently; of her sister, pausing in the act of comforting Ann to give her sister a look which said, 'I had to go through it and now it's your turn'.

To her surprise, her brother-in-law was nowhere to be seen. She reflected that he had probably gone to check up on the twins who were, no doubt, being plied with buns in the kitchen by Binns and Cook. With the exception of her ill-used mother, Lucy despised the lot of them. Giving them a contemptuous glance, she swept out of the room.

Once in the safety of her bedchamber, she paused. She had less than an hour in which to devise a plan. Maybe she could think up some way of putting Nathaniel Pritt off her, by saying or doing something so subtle that he, but not her father, would detect it. Maybe she could say something about religion which would show him that she was not in accordance with his own strong-held beliefs. He would not want to take for a wife a woman who was not totally committed to his own beliefs.

Yes, that was it! If she could let slip some pagan idea, or some comment that had more in common with the Church of Rome than England, maybe he would see at once that she was not the stuff vicar's wives are made of.

There was a knock at the door, and Lucy started guiltily, as if the visitor, whoever it was, had been able to read her thoughts and was coming to assure her that there was no escaping her fate. But it was only Binns with a basin of warm water, which she placed on the marble dresser. Lucy gave her a grateful smile and dismissed her.

Alone again, she sank down onto the gold-embroidered coverlet of her bed and instantly stood up as the pain in her buttocks was so bad. On the other side of the room, next to the cupboard where she kept her clothes, was a long mirror in which she could see her image reflected from head to toe. She had grumbled when it was installed, insisting that she didn't mind what she looked like. However, her mother had prophesied that, as she got older, she would mind, and so the thing stood there, in its heavy gold-leafed oak frame. Lucy stepped before it and examined her reflection. She saw a tall girl, whose naturally pink and white complexion had no need of rouge, with loose chestnut curls tumbling down to her breasts, wearing a rumpled dress of cream satin and ruffles which she'd always hated because it was feminine in such a silly way.

If I were a witch, she thought venomously, *I would take some witches' wax and, under a waning moon, I'd make a figurine of John Masters and stab it with a hatpin there* (she imagined the pleasure of spearing him through the groin) *and there* (now his heart was pierced by a silver barb).

Suddenly, Lucy started. Surely her imagination wasn't that strong? For a moment, she thought she'd glimpsed the face of John Masters in the mirror. Dropping her skirts, she whirled round – and did indeed find herself face to face with her loathsome brother-in-law.

"A pretty sight," he purred, his double chin sinking into his cream-coloured waistcoat. "But a few additions from myself would make it even prettier."

"Get out of my room!" yelled Lucy, furious that her most intimate, private moment had been invaded. She advanced on the interloper, not quite sure what to do, but determined to wreak some damage on him. Like a tigress unsheathing her claws, her fingernails lashed towards his eyes. His arms went up and caught her hands and squeezed them until she squealed. "Let me go, you're hurting!"

"All in good time, little sister."

"If I scream loud enough, Father, Mother, *someone* will hear," she warned him, and inhaled to fill her lungs for the effort.

"But you won't, will you, Lucy?" he informed her, his small eyes in their puffy surrounds of fat boring into hers.

Lucy stared at him in surprise. She had long thought her brother-in-law to be cunning, but she had no idea what devious scheme he was working on now.

"You can yell all you like, my dear, but I doubt if you'll be heard. Your mother and sister are at the other end of the house, supervising refreshment for your … *suitor*." He hissed the word with obvious enjoyment, reminding Lucy uncomfortably that time was running out for her.

"The children have been put to rest in the conservatory," he continued, "and as for your father, he's in the cellar tasting the wine to help him decide which to offer the dear Reverend. So you see, my sweet, we are all alone. I sympathize with you, my dear. Reverend Pritt is an old toad, about as lusty as one of the tombs in his graveyard. It would not be right for your pretty body to go to him without a full-blooded man having enjoyed it first."

"Let go of me!" Lucy demanded.

Pretending to swoon, she sagged limply onto the counterpane and then brought her knee up in one swift movement, but unfortunately missed the vital spot.

"You little bitch!" He gave her wrists a painful twist. "Give in gracefully, my girl, or I'll tell your father I saw you bare-arsed in the hayloft with one of the stable-lads."

"But I didn't… I've never …" Lucy began.

"Who d'you think he'll believe?" Masters cut in. "You, who he knows to be a cheeky, devious little hussy, or me, his well-intentioned, honorable son-in-law? Do you really think your life would be worth living then? Don't you think he'd treble his attempts to get you married off before your reputation was in question, or your waist started to swell?"

He transferred his grasp on her wrists to one hand and used the other to grope for her breasts. Lucy twisted to left and right, trying to deflect his podgy fingers.

"Be sensible, Lucy, there's a good girl."

Sensible? She would rather render him *insensible*!

"You're in a tight spot and maybe I'm the only one who can help you. Give yourself to me and I'll put in a good word with your father, try to convince him Pritt isn't the fellow for you, and that maybe I can find someone more suitable amongst my wealthy friends. I think the mention of money might make him see reason. And I know a lot of young studs who'd be a good match for a lusty young wench like you."

As he groped at the skirt of her dress, there was a knock on the door and Binns's flat country tones could be heard saying, "Your father wants to know if you're ready, miss. The Reverend is expected in fifteen minutes."

"Damn!" cursed Masters, swinging himself off the bed. "I never realized the old bastard would be here quite so soon. How long do you think he will stay? One hour? Two?"

"I don't know," Lucy said. Right then, a couple of hours spent in the Reverend's company felt like sweet relief compared to whatever Masters might have in store for her.

"Well, I'll stay the evening and come to your room later. Remember what I said, sister dear. I'll put in a word for you if ..."

Lucy nodded. Bending towards her, he pressed his lips on hers and Lucy shuddered in revulsion as it felt like kissing a slimy, dripping fish. Then he was out of her room with a wink and a leer, leaving her to collect her scattered wits.

Where was Helen, who was supposed to be helping her with her hair? Where, indeed, was Binns, who should have been dancing attendance on her, lacing her into her dress, proffering advice about this necklace or that, rather than just calling to her through the door? Lucy had never felt so alone, so abandoned, so confused.

Feeling dazed, she got up, reached in the cupboard for her blue dress and began, mechanically, to unfasten the cream one she was wearing. Then, struck by a sudden thought, she fastened it again and stepped quickly over to the window.

Outside, dusk was falling and low-flying swallows were dipping over the meadow at the back of the house. She had climbed out of the window before, but never in a dress as full as the one she was wearing. Still, she had no time to change.

Glancing up the hill, her eyes found, and rested on, the clump of sombre pine trees that surrounded the rambling old vicarage. It could have been her imagination, but she thought she spied a moving speck descending the hill path – Nathaniel Pritt on his trusty Welsh cob. There was no time to lose.

Pulling up her skirts and knotting them at the side, she unfastened the casement and swung her body out onto the ledge. She clung to the window sill as her feet found the familiar fork in the ivy. Then she was down it, on the tree branch, feeling her dress snagging on a hundred sharp twigs. She dropped lightly to the ground and glanced nervously all round her. She could hear distant voices from the parlour and the sound of her father shouting, but here, at the far corner of the house, all was quiet.

It grew darker still as she crept towards the high meadow, fervently wishing that she were dressed in dark clothing instead of the all-too-conspicuous cream dress. Reaching the fence, she lifted a halter off the gatepost and gave a low call to the bay stallion who was silently cropping the turf.

"Here, Emperor. Here, boy."

The horse pricked his ears in interest. Martin Swift's prize stallion was always willing to lower his noble pride and answer the call of a human if there was any hope of an apple or a handful of sugar. Obediently, he trotted towards Lucy, a tall shadow in the gathering darkness. Meanwhile, Lucy climbed onto the gate. As soon as the horse was close enough, she held out her hand and, while he was inspecting it for the hoped-for sugar, she slipped the halter over his ears and was on his back before the surprised animal could sense her intentions.

Emperor set off at an indignant gallop across the field and Lucy clung grimly onto his back, thanking God that she'd had the nerve to take moonlit, bareback rides in the past and accustom herself to doing without a saddle. It always felt strange to be riding astride a horse like a man, especially when wearing skirts of slippery silk, but she jammed her thighs and knees against the horse's polished hide and willed him not to stumble.

The far fence was looming up. Emperor made as if to swerve, but Lucy, by holding him in check with reins and calves, forced him to square up to it, then, giving him his head, she jabbed his flanks with her heels. He took off like an eagle and soared over, landing in the lane that led upwards, away from the town, towards the moors.

Lucy gave an anxious glance over her shoulder. The Reverend Pritt should be nearing the farm by now. Surely he would hear Emperor's hoofbeats and raise the alarm? Or maybe her disappearance from her room had already been noted.

"Come on, Emperor boy," she murmured encouragingly, giving his hard, muscular neck a pat. She had no regrets about stealing her father's prize beast. Not after all he'd done to her. She planned to get a safe distance from Prebbledale and then set him free, knowing he could find his own way home by equine instinct. Gripping tightly with her knees and crouching low over his neck, she dug him again with her heels. He obligingly set off at a fast canter, tackling the steep hill as if it were nothing but a gentle slope.

As they crested the summit, Lucy slowed her mount and looked round. The moon was out now, silvering the trees and fields and revealing the houses and outbuildings of the village in eerie silhouette. Her eyes picked out her own house and she noticed, to her alarm, several dark figures darting around: her family, looking for her. Soon, they would discover the theft of Emperor, and then horses would be saddled and searchers sent out with lanterns to look for her and bring her back.

Ahead stretched the moors, wild, rocky, deserted except for the occasional band of gypsies or robbers. She would take her chances with them, she decided. By tomorrow, she'd be far away. She'd disguise herself and maybe find employment in an inn, or perhaps some kind family would take her in and give her work as a housemaid.

She stirred the spirited horse into a gallop and felt the wind singing through her hair as Emperor's hooves struck sparks from the stony ground. The physical exertion of riding stripped the tension from her and she laughed out loud, the wind whipping the sound from her mouth before it could echo among the rocks. They would never find her. On she galloped, into the welcoming darkness.

Chapter Five

Lucy dreamt of snow. She was lying on an endless expanse of it and above her, from an inky sky, soft, white flakes were falling in their thousands and settling on her shivering body. Gradually, the shivering stopped and a kind of drowsy numbness took over.

She was almost warm now and a deep sleep was overcoming her. She had been told that this was how people died. She didn't mind dying this way, in comfortable, floating numbness. It was as if her body had already left her and only her spirit remained. Yet her senses were still working because she could hear the neighing of a horse.

The neighing grew louder, piercing her dream and forcing her awake. She had made her bed under an overhanging rock to protect her from the night dews and had pulled her skirt and top layer of petticoats around her shoulders and arms, to keep herself as warm as possible. Even so, the September night was chilly and the stony ground beneath her uncomfortably lumpy, and she wished she had brought a warm cloak to snuggle beneath.

She heard the neighing again and, in a sudden fear that Emperor might be under attack from some wild animal, crawled from her hiding place, stretched her stiff limbs and set out in her thin satin slippers across the damp, prickly heather to the place where she'd tethered him to a tree stump. The horse was standing, gazing at her. His ears were pricked and his stance suggested observant attention, but there was no sign of any marauding animal or bird. Nothing, not even a mouse or a hunting owl, stirred on this lonely stretch of high moorland.

Suddenly, without warning, something encircled her waist and gripped her tightly. She thought at first she had accidentally strayed into some kind of animal trap, and screamed out loud, but a man's coarse chuckle behind her told her the 'trap' was of human rather than mechanical origin.

The moon had tantalizingly hidden behind a cloud and, even if she had been able to twist round sufficiently to face her assailant, Lucy would have been unable to make out his features in the total darkness which now engulfed the moor. So much had happened to her during the last few hours that now, even at this terrifying moment, she felt numb rather than afraid.

Her mind was icy clear and her nerves steady. She knew that, realistically, she did not have the strength to attack and overpower her captor. She doubted if there was anyone within earshot but, with the small chance of there being a poacher or benighted traveller in the vicinity, she opened her mouth and let out a piercing scream using the full power of her lungs.

The man holding her seemed unimpressed. "Scream out, me darlin' girl. No one will hear you. There's only miles of hills and the night birds and the dark waters – and me an' me cronies."

Lucy's heart sank. So there was a whole band of them. No point, then, in fighting and screaming and risking physical damage to herself. She had nothing to give them apart from Emperor, and they would be foolish to steal him as he was a well-known horse who could be easily traced. Better, she thought, to go with the man willingly and calmly and keep her wits about her. Perhaps these 'cronies' of his would prove to be a blessing in disguise, for, if they took her along with them, she stood less chance of being found by her father.

"What do you want with me?" she asked the man, still unable to see his face.

He remained silent.

She tried again. "Who are you?"

"Me name's Rory McDonnell," he replied in his soft brogue, a mixture of Irish and North Country English.

"Then, Mr McDonnell, sir, kindly release me. You're holding me so tight that I can hardly breathe. I won't run away, I promise."

How *could* she run away? Once out of sight of the road, she knew she would only get lost among the rocks and lakes and, if she didn't have Emperor, she would stand little chance of reaching civilization.

"What name are ye havin'?" he asked her. His voice was soft and sounded young. Lucy wished the clouds would blow away to allow the moonlight to reveal his features. All she knew was that he was taller than she was.

There seemed no harm in revealing her name to him. "It's Lucy. Lucy Swift."

"Swift as the deer, me little white doe! I won't shoot you, my beauty, you're quite safe with Rory, but I'm afraid I have to do this, although I know you won't like it. It's for your own sake, mavourneen. You don't want to be after dashin' off and breakin' your pretty ankle on the wild moor, where no one will find ye."

Lucy flinched as a length of cord was wound tightly round her wrists. Then her captor stepped to one side, the end of the cord wrapped around his own hand. Once the pressure of his arms was gone, Lucy took several deep, thankful gulps of air, then regarded the man curiously. He stood a little above average height, his shoulders were broad and his face was half covered by a black beard. In the night gloom, she could not make out his features clearly, but she guessed he was nearing thirty. As she stood there regarding him, he tugged on the cord.

"Follow me," he ordered and set off purposefully towards Emperor. He made a clicking noise with his tongue, then stretched out a hand. To Lucy's amazement, the spirited stallion stepped docilely towards the stranger and allowed his muzzle to be stroked, whereupon Rory gripped his halter and set off down the hill leading his two prizes.

It was at this moment that the numbness that had settled on Lucy's thoughts lifted and she found herself seized by a surge of pure panic.

Where was he leading her? Who were his friends? Were they gypsies? She hoped so, because there would be women and children among them. She would be more inclined to trust and feel safe with a member of her own sex.

As she stumbled through stones and bracken, feeling sharp stalks and small pebbles working their way painfully into her flimsy shoes, Lucy longed for the comfort and safety of her home. She felt a rush of affection for her mother. Maybe she would never see her again!

Yet she could never go back to face the things her father had in store for her, especially now that she had stolen his finest horse. No, her home life was in the past. Yet the future, as it seemed right now, seemed to hold little better – more fear, more violence, more threats. She felt totally bewildered by the events that were carrying her along at such a breakneck pace, as an unwilling victim.

As they turned the corner, Lucy still being led by her captor, Emperor still following obediently without so much as a whinny, she noticed that the sky seemed to be getting lighter, lit by an orange glow. They rounded an outcrop of rock and the reason was immediately apparent; Rory's companions, whoever they were, had constructed a sizeable fire and she could make out two or three figures silhouetted against the flames. Rory gave a kind of hoot, like a hunting owl, and a huge figure uncoiled itself from a sitting position and approached them.

Lucy's spirits plummeted as the man swam into vision in the flickering orange light. He was a giant, bigger than anyone she'd ever seen before in her life. His cowhide coat was cracked and aged, his hair brindled like a dog's. He, too, sported a flourishing beard and his broad face displayed a mixture of dirt and scars. When he smiled, his teeth were black and brown like the stalks of rotten mushrooms. She had never seen anyone who looked so thoroughly a ruffian.

"We-e-ell," the giant drawled, pushing back his coat to hook his thumbs into his belt and revealing an all-black outfit that made him resemble an executioner. "What 'ave we 'ere, then? Let's see ... Hmm ..."

He walked in a wide circle round the trio, looking them up and down. "It's been good 'unting for you, Rory me lad. Two fine specimens, a thoroughbred stallion and –" bending his body at the shoulders, he brought his ugly face down so close to Lucy's that she almost reeled from the force of the liquor on his breath – "a thoroughbred brood mare, too, by the look of it!" Straightening up and towering against the sky, he let out a raucous laugh that caused Emperor to flinch nervously.

"Wouldn't mind doing a bit of breeding with her meself."

The new voice came from Lucy's left and she turned her head to see that a third man had joined them, unnoticed till this moment. He was a slight individual, old and unhealthy-looking, with hollow cheeks and sunken eye-sockets. From his upper lip sprouted a wispy moustache. Lucy thought he looked like a sick weasel. However, he appeared to be an expert on horseflesh. He ran his hand over Emperor's neck, across his withers, over his flanks, inspected his hocks and finally picked up each hoof in turn. At length, evidently satisfied, he turned to Lucy.

"He yours?" he enquired briefly, almost immediately entering into a spasm of coughing that made his weak frame tremble like breeze-buffeted reed.

"Yes, he's mine – or rather, my father's," answered Lucy, as sternly and boldly as she could. These men had to be shown that she was better than them. Yet in her heart she wondered if she really was. There, to one side of the fire, was a group of horses, roped to each other. The men were obviously horse traders, on their way to a fair. At worst, they could be thieves. Even this would make them no worse than herself, for hadn't she stolen a champion horse from under her own father's nose?

"Pay a good price to get him back, would he?" asked Weasel-face, having recovered from his coughing fit.

Lucy stifled a gasp. The last thing she wanted was for the men to drag both her and Emperor home to her father's house, delivering her back into the clutches of all she was fleeing to avoid, plus the added horror of her father's wrath, which was bound to be near-murderous.

Yet she couldn't really explain to men of this type that they could take the horse back, but not her. That would be inviting them to use her in ways she refused to imagine. Maybe the best way out was to tell them part of the truth: "No doubt. But, you see, I've already stolen him myself."

Her revelation evinced a shocked silence from all three men. Then, in unison, they broke into guffaws, Giant slapping Weasel-face on the back with a blow that sent him staggering, and even Rory at her side bellowing fit to burst.

Eventually Giant, wiping the tears from his eyes, bent down to Lucy again and chucked her under the chin. She resented such familiar treatment and, huge as he was, she glared at him as viciously as she could.

"Pretty little thing. A bit foolish and ill-mannered, though. Fancy stealing a horse from your own father!"

He started to laugh again, then checked himself. "I'm sure we can teach her a few manners, though, eh, lads?"

"I'll bet," agreed Weasel-face enthusiastically. The pointed tip of his tongue came out and wetted his lips, showing small yellow teeth.

Lucy shuddered. These men were bestial. She couldn't bear to be touched by them. But her intuition, sharpened by fear, was as keen as an animal's and she could feel a sensual charge in the air, the kind of electricity that is generated when lusty men, starved of female company, find themselves in the presence of an attractive woman. She stole a glance at Rory, the man who had initially captured her. He had remained silent all this time. She wondered if it could be that he didn't agree with the sentiments that were being bandied about – or was he, perhaps, worse than either of the others?

In the light from the fire, she could make out his features: a strong, well-shaped nose, a broad brow from which his unruly black hair sprang like uncontrollable weeds, and a chin hidden by his beard. He looked younger than she had first thought, maybe only three or four years older than her. He was certainly more agreeable-looking than his ugly, ragged companions.

But she had little time for reflection. Weasel-face began to whistle a tune which Lucy recognized as a crude ditty that she had sometimes caught her father's stable lads singing. Suddenly, she found herself wrenched from Rory's hold by the big man and whirled around in a kind of dance.

Within seconds they had drawn close to the fire. Lucy, her hands bound behind her back, lost her balance, staggered and would have tumbled into the flames had not Rory noticed in time and pushed her out of the way.

"Careful!" he yelled. "We don't want the little darlin' roasted, do we?"

Gasping, her lungs burning from inhaling the fire-smoke, Lucy collapsed onto her knees, only to be hauled to her feet again by Weasel-face, twirled round, caught by Rory and flung towards the giant. She felt as if she were being used in some perverted game of pass-the-parcel. With Rory joining in the fun and so obviously enjoying it, she was bereft of the one man she hoped would be her ally and at the mercy of these three ruffians, who seemed set to torment and abuse her in the worst possible way.

The left sleeve of her dress tore at the shoulder seam as she was spun wildly around. Soon, she was too dizzy and exhausted to notice whether her clothes were holding together or not. She felt fingers roughly tugging at her, foul breath on her face, hands fondling her breasts and buttocks and closed her eyes, praying to faint.

"Smithy – here, catch!" called Rory, delivering her with a sharp slap across the rump into the arms of the next man. Opening her eyes briefly, Lucy discovered that "Smithy" was the weasel-faced one. The sight of his grey face and jaundiced eyeballs revolted her.

She found herself in the arms of Rory again, who was grinning down at her, his teeth startlingly white and wholesome in comparison to those of his companions. "Please," she moaned, hoping that perhaps she could touch some core of compassion in him. "Please ... make them stop."

He didn't answer, just pushed her away from him, calling, "Pat! Your turn!"

Lucy felt herself reeling and landed with a hard thump on the ground and lay there, winded.

She was aware of someone crouching over her; male smells of sweat and spirits. Her face was tilted upwards and a prickly beard scratched her chin. A man, breathing hard, clamped his lips down onto hers so hard that her mouth was forced open. She didn't need to open her eyes to know who it was molesting her. It was the man from whom she stood the least chance of protecting herself – the giant, Pat.

Desperately, she moved her head from side to side, seeking refuge from his revolting kiss. Her arms were twisted beneath her, her hands trapped painfully between her body and the stony ground.

"Stop!" The word cut through the air like a whiplash. She felt the body above hers tense, the tongue withdraw from her mouth. "*I* found the bay stallion and the white mare! I know 'share and share alike' is our motto, but that's for the horses, not wenches. I'll do a deal with you. You can have the horse, sell it, split the money. But I saw the girl first. I captured her and brought her here.

"I've been telling you for a long time, I need a wife. Well, here she is. My wife, Lucy."

Chapter Six

Wife? Lucy's mind reeled. Only yesterday, she had run away from one unwanted suitor, yet now here she was, faced with another. How was she going to get out of it this time, with the odds so severely stacked against her? It was almost as if Fate had decreed that now was the time for Lucy Swift to get married and it didn't matter to whom.

Still panting from being used in a game of pass-the-human-parcel, she rubbed her bruised arms, brushed a cleansing hand over her lips and sat up, tossing her tumbled hair out of her eyes.

The bear-like figure of Pat was still looming over her, his eyes small and mean as they flicked over her in what seemed a mixture of lust and contempt. He gave Smithy a cuff on the side of the head, then turned to face Rory.

"Me Oirish friend," he said, his voice heavy with sarcasm, "pretty boy Rory. Always one for the ladies. I never thought you 'ad it in yer to get married."

His face lit up in a cunning smile. He came up to Rory and planted a fist like a joint of beef on his shoulder. Lucy gasped. He could kill Rory with one stroke. Yet Rory regarded him calmly and coolly, his body unmoving, his demeanour amiable.

"So it's marriage you want now, my green little leprechaun," the giant continued.

Lucy saw the corner of Rory's mouth twitch, as if he were suppressing anger. She had to admire his self-control. She was also impressed by the quick-thinking way in which, by bringing an element of something legal and sanctified like marriage into the midst of an ugly, base scene, he had saved her from violation.

Having feared for her own safety just minutes ago, now she was scared for him. If he were to pick a fight with Pat and be injured or killed, what would become of her then? There would be no one to stop the progress of the hideous giant's evil desires and she would sooner die than be forced to submit. But she couldn't understand the course the discussion was now taking. Rory had surely only suggested marrying her in order to save her, surely? Nobody could force him to carry out his inspired but impossible suggestion.

Pat was regarding Rory with an ugly glint in his eye. A cunning smile flicked across his ugly, begrimed face. "If you're going to be selfish about it and keep 'er all to yourself, then by God, you'll 'ave 'er properly and honestly. Smithy!"

The skinny little man scrambled to his feet, left the comfort of the fire and scampered to Pat's side.

"You'll be the witness," ordered the giant. "Now, fetch me 'oly book."

Lucy looked at them aghast. What on earth was going on? She shot a puzzled glance at Rory. He looked at her, unsmiling and then, with the same serious expression, took a knife from the pocket of his britches and sawed through the cord that bound her wrists. Her fingers were swollen and painful, her wrists marked with purple grooves where the twine had bitten into her delicate skin. She rubbed them ruefully, wincing as she touched the damaged flesh.

"Come 'ere," boomed the giant. "Let the service begin."

Lucy took a good look at the black book Smithy had brought, which now rested in Pat's hands. It was, indeed, marked *Holy Bible*. An uneasy shiver crawled down her spine. What was this mockery, this charade? The giant had a strange sense of humour. Perhaps it was better simply to let him act out his fantasy rather than risk incurring his fury and the possible resumption of his attack upon her virtue.

Lucy had attended her sister Helen's wedding. She knew the wording of the vows. To her horror, the giant reeled off exactly the same lines. Rory took her hand and was clasping it firmly. She gave an experimental tug and his grip immediately tightened, leaving her in no doubt that it would be impossible for her to break free and run away.

She struggled to catch Rory's attention. He was staring at Pat as if mesmerized, but, feeling the power of Lucy's gaze on him, he inclined his head to face her. There was so much she needed to say to him, so much she wanted to ask him.

"… any lawful impediment," intoned the giant.

Lucy did her best to whisper without letting her lips move, hoping that Pat wouldn't notice. "He can't do this, can he?"

A faint nod was her answer. Lucy felt the blood pound in her temples and her hands went icy cold. It was all a joke – it had to be. She must let Pat get this mock ceremony over with, let him firmly believe the fantasy that she and Rory were actually married, and then he would not try to molest her again. The words he was speaking would make her taboo to him and Smithy. But Rory? Surely he didn't believe these vows were legal?

She had to make doubly sure, so she nudged him and whispered out of the corner of her mouth, "He's not a real priest, is he?"

Another nod.

Lucy felt her heart hammer in panic. She had to get away, now, before it was too late – before these crazy men tried to make her believe she was married to a total stranger! Using her free hand, she tried to prise Rory's fingers off her other hand, but he just held onto her even more tightly. Emotions washed over her, each stronger than the one which preceded it; fear, pleading, fury, helplessness, hopelessness.

Suddenly her hand was squeezed. An urgent whisper sounded in her ear. "Go on. You must speak. He'll kill you if you don't."

She found herself being led forward and forced to kneel before the cracked boots of the 'vicar'.

Above her head, Pat asked, "What's her full name?"

"Lucy Swift," she heard Rory reply.

"Lucy Swift, will you have this man to be your husband …"

There was a roaring in her ears similar to that which she had experienced the previous day, just before she'd fainted. She felt herself starting to sway, but a sharp elbow prodded her urgently in the ribs.

"Say 'I do,'" begged Rory.

Groggy as she was, she still caught the warning tone in his voice. She had never before had to struggle with so many emotions all at once. How could she speak these two words, the most momentous words any woman ever speaks during her lifetime? For all she knew, she really was committing herself to something legal and binding.

The urgent whisper came again. "*Say* it."

"I do," murmured Lucy. Seconds later, or so it seemed, she heard Rory repeat the same words.

The huge bulk of the man above her shifted like a tree in a landslip. His booming voice declared, "You may now kiss your bride."

She was pulled to her feet and enveloped in Rory's embrace. She closed her eyes and puckered her lips, bracing herself for a mockery of a husband's kiss. Instead, Rory brushed her lips perfunctorily with his own and murmured, "Well done, girl. Don't worry."

"A drink! A toast to the bride and groom!" Smithy had a bottle of some kind of spirits in his hand, which he offered to Pat, who put it to his lips and took a deep draught.

"Aagh," Pat sighed, wiping his mouth with the back of his filthy hand. "'Aven't married anyone for a long time."

"Not since you were thrown out of St Barnabas's, I'll be bound," wheezed Smithy, chuckling catarrhally.

"For squeezing that old girl in the vestry? Oh-ho-ho, that was funny! You should 'ave seen the curate's face when 'e came in and caught me wiv me 'and down 'er front. Oh, the sin of fornication was never one *I* preached against, Smithy me boy!" Pat thumped his hand between Smithy's shoulder blades for emphasis, forcing the frail man into another of his terrible, rattling coughing fits.

Smithy was doubled up, his cheeks hollowing and puffing as he fought for breath. "'Ere, 'ave a drop of this." The big man thrust the bottle against Smithy's grey lips and, between spasms, Smith reached out a trembling hand, took the bottle and sucked hard from it. At last, the dreadful, bubbling spasm ceased.

"He's going to die!" observed Lucy worriedly, quite forgetting her own predicament in the face of the man's desperate state.

"Yes, probably. Aren't we all?" answered Rory.

Lucy, shocked by his callousness, gazed at him open-mouthed. "How can you be so cruel?" she demanded, ready to upbraid him for being so unconcerned about a fellow mortal.

"Smithy's had that cough for years. Never gets any worse, never gets any better. Sure, it's the cross he has to bear."

"And what's yours?"

"Hush up, wife!"

"*Wife?*"

Lucy rounded on him, feeling ready to strike him now that her hands were free again. The fire had died down now and the air was growing cold around them. She could hear the restless shifting and cropping as the horses moved over the ground, seeking grass blades among the prickly heather. Pat had guided Smithy to the fireside and was pulling a ragged blanket over him.

"I'm no more your wife than you are my –"

"Your husband," supplied Rory, placing an arm round her shoulders which Lucy angrily shrugged off. "That I am!"

"But you're *not* my husband!" Her shrill tone made Pat look up from his vigil by Smithy and the fire.

"He is, you know. And if you don't stop nagging him, woman, 'e'll take his belt to you!" A guffaw rumbled deep in the giant's chest as he sank down beside the dying embers and pulled a horse-blanket round himself. The sky was still clouded over and, apart from the area near the fire, their whole surroundings were in pitch darkness.

"You stay there. I'll fetch a blanket," said Rory, walking off towards a heap of bags and saddlery.

Lucy knew that if ever she was going to get a chance to escape, this was it. Yet something kept her rooted to the spot. She had no idea why she was staying and she examined her mind to see if it could be confusion at not knowing which way to run, or fear of retribution from the fearsome Pat.

As she watched Rory delving among the baggage, a realization came to her which she was at first tempted to dismiss as being not worthy of her. But the more she thought about it, the stronger the conviction grew. In the end, she knew for certain that the thing which stopped her running was curiosity. She needed to find out the truth about this bizarre ceremony which had just been performed, and the only person who could aid her was Rory.

Besides which – and this realization was even harder to come to terms with than the last – there was something about him that prompted her to stay. She needed to talk to him, to thank him for saving her from Pat – and maybe for saving her life, too. After she had spoken to him, after daylight had come and she had got her bearings, then perhaps she would look for some means of escape.

Yet part of her longed to feel the touch of his lips on hers. Not a perfunctory peck such as he had given her earlier, but a warm, full, lingering kiss. She smiled drowsily as she imagined herself on her wedding night, receiving her husband in clean, soft linen sheets, blushing coyly as he peeled down a strap of her white nightgown.

Chapter Seven

Her shoulder ached abominably. Lucy wriggled, seeking a comfortable indentation in her feather mattress. Her pillow, too, was lumpy and hard, unyielding to the butting of her head. She raised a fist to pound it and redistribute the goosefeather filling – and felt something stay her arm in its downward swing.

"Wisha, girl, ye'll hurt yeself."

That's not Geoffrey. What's he doing in my bedroom, anyway? No, Geoffrey left, he isn't at home any more. "Father?" Lucy's sleepy, inquiring tones met with silence.

She stretched out an arm and encountered not soft, warm coverlets but pebbles and sharp bracken stalks beneath her hand. Her eyelids blinked open. Her bedroom ceiling had lifted off. There was blue sky above her, with wispy white clouds like streaks of spilt milk. What had happened? Where was she?

Lucy's heart raced in panic and she sat bolt upright, feeling a breeze on her face. Immediately, her eyes fell on the face of a man who was lying next to her beneath a ragged blanket. He was staring at her, as if she were as much a stranger to him as he was to her. Scattered recollections came back to her – her flight, her capture, her ordeal round the fire. She remembered Pat holding a Bible, Smithy and his coughing fit and her terrible anxiety about whether or not the ceremony she had undergone had resulted in her being married to ... to whom, exactly?

She looked at Rory again. His long-lashed brown eyes met hers and he gave her a smile and touched her arm familiarly. No, it was all a joke. They were drunk, they had played tricks with her. Now, the fun was over and she would be able to explain her position and the true reason for her being alone on the moor. They would take her with them wherever they were going, help her get far away from Prebbledale.

The thought suddenly occurred to her that she had no recollection of having fallen asleep the previous night. Surely she couldn't have ...? Surely he ...? She scrambled half out of the blanket and drew a deep breath of relief at finding herself still fully dressed and, it seemed, untouched by the man who had shared her resting place.

She realized that she must have tumbled straight into a deep, exhausted slumber as soon as she had settled her head on the pillow. She felt beneath her and discovered that the 'pillow' was, in fact, a folded cloak: Rory's. She had no memory of his having placed it there.

He was still regarding her with an amused expression. Maybe he had saved her from a hideous fate the night before, but that didn't mean she owed him a place in her life or a share in her body. She pushed the blanket right back and started to get to her feet. Her mouth was dry, her head ached and she felt tired and bruised and was painfully aware of the scars left by her father's punishment.

As her feet touched the ground, she winced and discovered that the soles of her thin leather slippers were split and her feet lacerated and tender.

"Don't worry, Lucy. We shan't be movin' on today. It's the Sabbath and there's no markets or fairs on the holy day. You just take your rest and heal up. I'm sorry about the way me fine friends treated ye last night but ye don't have to bother about them ever again. Not now you're me wife."

The same cold dread that had afflicted Lucy the previous night washed over her again, clouding the fresh blue day with grey uncertainty, as if she'd just woken from a bad dream to find it still continuing in her waking hours.

"Rory McDonnell – if that's your real name …" She paused, but there was no reaction from the bearded young man who lay, fully dressed, propped on one elbow, grinning at her. "Tell me, what *are* you and your ill-mannered friends? Highwaymen? Gypsies? Are you on the run for some crime? You used me last night as some kind of plaything. I'm not used to that kind of treatment."

She frowned sternly down at her companion but found it impossible to be angry with someone who was looking so cheerful and friendly, so like a brother. "All right. So maybe you helped me. But it's daybreak now. They – my family, that is – will be searching for me. Remember I told you I had stolen a horse of my father's? It's true. But what you don't understand is why I did it, and …"

Lucy's voice trailed off. She wondered why she was bothering to try to explain all this to a common ruffian who had treated her no better than if she had been a slut from some low inn. Besides, he was making no attempt to answer any of her questions.

She stood looking at him indecisively. A glance over her shoulder showed her the ashes of last night's fire, the outlines of two slumbering bodies and a string of horses, some cropping, some standing idly, heads down, dozing in the early morning sun. Emperor was with them, his halter knotted to that of a sway-backed grey cob. If she were just to wander over, give him a pat, untie the rope …

A chuckle broke into her thoughts, hauling her back to the moment of her capture the previous evening. A hand sneaked out from beneath the blanket and gripped her ankle, making her squeal in protest. "I know what you're thinking, mavourneen. But it's no good. Pat wouldn't stand for it after what you deprived him of last night. Don't you remember the vow you gave, Lucy McDonnell?"

McDonnell? My name is Lucy Swift!

She froze. Why did he persist in perpetrating this myth? Couldn't he see she'd had enough? She spat out the words, "What do you mean?"

"Sit down," he said.

Maybe he was right about Pat. If so, she would be wise to obey. She straightened a corner of the blanket and sat on it, thinking that he had better make his explanation a good one. She could still hardly believe that she was several miles away from home, and that she had spent the night with an uncouth trio of men, and Rory's words did little to make her feel more at ease.

"I'll tell you about me, right? An' then you can begin about you. I'm Rory McDonnell – ye know that already. I'm twenty-three, coming up twenty-four in November, a fine age for a man. I've never been much good to no one, especially to meself. Me da' was a tinker; me ma ... well, you would have loved her, everyone did. But she's dead."

"An' as for the old man, I haven't seen him for more than seven year. Last time was at a fairground when he was just about to go into the ring – he was a boxer, you see, and a fair wrestler, too. He winked at me and said, 'Rory, me son, where there's money to be made and you have a talent, you must follow. Gold, that's what matters first, then your immortal soul.'

"I prayed for him, mavourneen, prayed for him, I did, but they carted him off."

"Dead?" Lucy whispered.

He had no background, no breeding, she thought. Most of her father's stable lads could claim better lineage than Rory. Even her father's family line went back to the great kings of Ireland, or so her father said. Yet, for some reason, she felt as if there was nothing she would rather do in the growing warmth of that autumn morning than sit listening to the vivid reminiscences spilling from the lips of this born storyteller, even if he wasn't directly answering her questions.

"No, bless you," he continued, "not dead. He was carried off to the gallows – or the transport ships, I don't know which."

"But why?"

"'Twasn't his fault he killed the nobleman who fought him, but he did. Milord was drunk, did it for a wager. Big hulking fellow he was, an' there's me old da', nigh on forty, slight and slippery as an eel and cunning with it. Milord's built like a beef bullock, punching the air, hoping to find a nose in it, and there's Father, calculating his moment and then, *oof*, a straight left to the point of the jaw.

"Feller's head snaps back, we all hear it, then down he goes, *crack*, and everyone fussing and shouting. Then they comes and takes him away. It were a fair fight, but Milord's father insists that because he's a gypsy, he's used some magic trick, and so he's accused of murder."

His father, a murderer? Lucy felt herself shiver. How could she be sure Rory was telling the truth? Maybe he was a maniac from a whole line of cut-throats! All she knew of him was what she could see with her own eyes, a young man, with tousled dark hair, talking animatedly, crouching and rocking back and forth on his heels, his brown britches and dark green jacket rumpled and dirt-streaked.

"Did you ever see him again?" she asked.

"Never. When they came to take him, I ran. Not that I was a coward, Lucy, but it was twenty of them against him and me, and he once said to me, 'Rory, son, if ever the Devil or the Law come, make sure they only take one of us, leaving one to carry on'."

"And your mother? What happened to her?" Lucy was shocked at her own curiosity. Nobody had ever told her their life story before and she would never have had the boldness to ask. But up here, in the hilltops, with a grouse squawking somewhere in the heather and the breeze ruffling her hair, normal etiquette seemed not to matter.

"My mother, Kathleen ... Pretty girl, so I'm told. Came over from Wexford to settle in Lancashire with her parents."

"I wonder if she ever knew my father?" burst in Lucy impulsively. "His family did the same thing – came from Ireland, took a boat over the sea to Liverpool. No, that was my great-grandad. It was long before your mother's time."

"Still, we might be related. Who knows?" smiled Rory. Lucy found herself smiling back.

Rory seemed anxious to complete his story. "Her family didn't approve of her marrying me da'. She gave birth to me, caught a chill and never recovered. Me father nursed her for two whole years after that, while she grew thinner and thinner, until... Well, that's the way of the world."

He gazed off into space, then pulled himself swiftly back to the present. "Us now? Horses is our game. We trade, buy, sell ... mark a few here and there."

Lucy knew from her father what 'marking' was – disguising a stolen horse so that it could be sold as a different and apparently legitimate animal.

"Now, take that fine animal of yours. All the dye in the world couldn't turn him brown or white. We might manage a sort of piebald, though."

Lucy giggled at the thought of Emperor painted like a circus pony. "It was my plan to turn him loose and send him home," she informed him.

"Maybe that's what we'll have to do, if you don't want your father to come looking for you," he replied.

So he had remembered what she had told him and his companions the night before. Obviously an alert mind was at work behind the casual, careless exterior. What, then, would he have to say on the subject of their mock marriage?

Before she could ask this all-important question, he sprang to his feet and held out a hand to her. "A walk? Just over the hill?" he invited.

Lucy didn't need to be asked twice. Her legs were cramped and aching from the dervish whirling of the previous night. Besides, she wanted to see what, if anything, was visible from the highest point. Maybe she was still close to Prebbledale. She had no way of telling how far she and Emperor had travelled in their wild flight.

The hillside was steep, the bracken turning the crisp, brittle brown of autumn. A curlew gargled querulously, trying to draw them away from its nest and Lucy gasped and jumped as a hare sprang up almost from under her feet and raced, ears flattened, through a tunnel of undergrowth.

As they drew higher and the rusty ridges of rocky ground folded away beneath them, a panorama gradually emerged and when Rory helped her clamber onto a rocky pinnacle, the view made Lucy gasp in wonderment. Undulating below her were acres of uncultivated land in shades of purple, tan and green; clusters of stunted trees, white blobs of cropping sheep; a lake grey and opaque in the shadow of an over-hanging rock face.

As far as she looked, she could see no sign of a rooftop or church steeple. Close by them, a stream splattered over gleaming rocks, drop-ping in twin waterfalls to descend into a fern-fringed crevice several feet below. Just before it curled creamily over the sharp drop, centuries of running water had gouged out a hollow in its bed, forming a pool of maybe three feet in depth. Lucy longed to step into it and bathe her dusty, aching body.

She mentioned her wish to Rory, who immediately told her to go ahead, promising to stand on the ridge and keep watch to make sure no one trespassed on her privacy. Gratefully, Lucy lifted the hem of her dress, which was badly torn from constant snagging on rocks and un-dergrowth. She glanced up at Rory to check that his back was turned, then gave a small shriek as her legs were suddenly enveloped in icy water up to her knees.

It was cleansing and revitalizing, reactivating her sluggish blood, clearing her aching head. Lucy crouched down and thrust her hands into the stinging chill of the pool, then splashed her face. Water dripped from her hair, soaking her clothes.

The autumn sun was warm on her face. *Why am I standing here fully dressed? I should be naked*, she thought.

Trusting Rory not to turn around, she quickly undressed and sank into the pool, where she sat on the water-smoothed pebbles and, cup-ping her hands, sent delicious sprays of water splashing over her shoulders and breasts. Forgetting herself, she began to sing, her head thrown back, her russet hair streaming in seaweed strands all around her.

It was a small sound, like the snapping of a twig, that made Lucy look up. She had been so absorbed in her task of washing herself and her hair that she had momentarily forgotten the existence of her male sentinel.

"*No!*" She cried out in shock and fear as she saw a naked Rory approaching, the virile, black, curly hair springing from his loins and chest, the powerfully-made thighs and shoulders, the soft, dark fuzz on his arms and legs. Despite herself, she felt a throb of desire.

She tried to leap out of the pool and make a dash for her clothes but the water dragged at her legs and impeded her progress. With a great splash that sent water cascading anew all over her drying body, Rory jumped into the pool and landed beside her.

She was almost out of the water when he hauled her back, his hands slipping on her wet skin. Summoning all her strength, Lucy directed a mighty kick at his shins, but the water slowed down the swing of her foot, giving him time to dodge.

His arms encircled her, crushing her against the shameless reminder of his maleness. Lucy sank her teeth into his shoulder and was pleased to hear him wince in pain. She was shocked and angry. She had thought she could trust him. He had given her his word that she could bathe in safety and privacy, and now he was taking advantage of her while she was totally unprotected and vulnerable.

She tried to bite him again, then felt her long, wet hair caught and tugged backwards, tilting her face up to his. His lips closed on hers, his tongue darting around the tip of her own tongue, then against the roof of her mouth, flickering like a snake. Then he slackened the terrible pressure of his mouth and his lips became soft, seeking, exploratory, until she found herself responding with a heavy, drugged sensation in her head, a dragging, swollen ache in her loins, hardening nipples and an urgent need to be fondled, stroked and pressed even harder against his powerful body.

She hardly knew what was happening to her. All she knew was that she didn't want to fight him any longer. Her mind screamed, *He's let you down, you trusted him, he's misused you. Kick! Bite! Run!*, but her body was reacting without any orders from her mind.

She didn't resist as he picked her up, carried her to the bank and laid her gently down on a patch of grass beneath a bush of some aromatic herb that tanged spicily in the sun. She was no longer conscious of her nakedness.

She felt her hand being taken and a hard object being firmly pressed down over one finger. She raised her finger to her eyes and saw the sun glinting on gold. She turned it round and saw the break in the metal and, acting on a sudden suspicion, looked at Rory's ears. One bore an identical ring and in the other was a small hole, empty of the ornament it had once borne.

"One for each of us," he said, smiling at her. "I'll see if I can't get you a better one at Pendleton Fair."

"Are we … are we truly married?"

She held her breath, waiting for his reply, aware only of the warmth, both physical and emotional, emanating from the man at her side and of the newly awakened, unfamiliar sensations deep within her.

His steady gaze never left her eyes. "Yes."

Her eyelids closed and her heart thundered in her chest as she tried to make sense of his words. He began to talk, in the air over her head.

"Patrick trained as a priest many years ago. He's the only one of us who can read and write. He gave it up in favour of the travelling life, ale, women, but he's still qualified to perform marriages and baptisms and officiate at a burial. Those vows we took last night were just as real as any taken in a church. You're me wife, Lucy, in the eyes of God and you're more beautiful to my eyes than the mountains, the sea and the dawn."

Rory's mouth once more engaged with her own. His body moved across hers and pressed her down, crushing the juice out of the grass blades and wild flowers beneath her. Her nipples tingled and hardened as they brushed against the soft, dark pelt on his chest and she clamped her thighs together, fearful of what was to come.

If she really were his wife, then this was what was expected of her. But she was afraid, so afraid, not only of the pain which her sister had told her every woman experienced the first time she lay with a man, but of the overwhelming power of her own desire. Surely it was wrong to want a man so badly?

She shivered as his strong hand reached down and parted her thighs. Her eyes widened at the sight of his tumescent manhood. Surely her body wasn't built to accommodate anything as large as that? Panic rose in her.

"Be gentle, please," she murmured. "I've never…"

"Hush, Lucy. I know how to break in a filly." His eyes danced and he kissed her and she tasted herself on his lips, a sweet, salt taste like a sugared oyster. "Just relax."

He kissed her again, a longer kiss this time, his tongue dancing with hers, then he crouched over her and she tensed as the blunt, smooth head of his hard maleness sought entry to her body.

There was a sudden sharp pain as he penetrated her, and she cried out, instinctively trying to pull away from him.

"There, mavourneen, there," he whispered, caressing her hair. His hands fluttered over her body, pausing here, stroking there, soothing and relaxing her until she felt as if she were floating sleepily on the edge of a dream.

Then, in an abrupt change of mood and tempo, his lips rained hard kisses on her face and neck, his teeth nipped her shoulder, bit at her ear. Her body was pulled up into his embrace, twisted around, pressed down, as, embedded deep within her, he rode the rhythmic surges of his own pleasure.

Lucy was caught up and carried along in the urgency of his desire. All pain had gone now and the strange pulsations inside her belly, which forced her to jerk her hips spasmodically upwards, made her groan with delight. Never had she experienced such piercing, poignant ecstasy. Her whole being was overtaken by a series of shuddering ripples which made her shake and tremble. She gave herself to them, tossing her head from side to side, flinging her arms out, crying aloud, and her moans were soon joined by Rory's hoarse cry of fulfillment.

Later, Lucy awoke from a refreshing doze and smiled softly to herself as her forefinger traced the outline of her slumbering partner's eyebrow, which felt like a strip of velvet. At last she had an ally, someone who cared for her, someone who pleasured her, a man whose poetic vision and way with words surprised and delighted her. Maybe now, her future path would not have to be travelled alone.

Husband ... The word was alien to her. She didn't feel like a wife. The perfect marriage she would have planned for herself was to a man who loved and desired her and awoke an answering passion in herself. But, she was forced to admit to herself, that was exactly what Rory had done. Maybe Fate had had to move in strange ways to bring about the things that were best for her, she mused.

Though she hated not being in control of her own destiny, she felt like blessing the unseen hand that had brought the two of them together. She still felt like Lucy Swift, and not a bit like the Lucy Mc-Donnell that the gold circlet on her finger now proclaimed her to be. But she knew it must surely take time to become part of anyone else's life – and, for now, her individuality lay submerged in the afterglow of union and sensual satisfaction.

Chapter Eight

Ever since she was a small child, Lucy had loved fairs. Her father had taken her to many and she had never failed to be fascinated by the clustering throngs of gaily dressed humanity, the merry-making, the excitement.

Pendleton Fair was only a small, local event, but the population of many surrounding villages seemed to have turned out in force. One had to be on one's guard against the bands of pick-pockets who roamed around, looking for a woman absorbed in gossip or a man the worse for ale, who would not feel the light, dexterous fingers in their pocket or see the hand creeping into their cloak or basket.

She had now spent five whole weeks with Rory, Smithy and Pat. The attitude of Rory's companions towards her had mellowed, especially when they discovered that she knew every bit as much about horses as they did, with the exception of the tricks they got up to which enabled them to pass off an unsound horse as healthy, or even, on occasion, to make a fit horse appear damaged so that they could buy it cheaply. She did not approve of these sharp practices and wondered if her father was aware of their existence.

Her father ... He was causing her endless worry. Every time they visited a fair, which was two or three times weekly, as different towns held their markets on different days, she was constantly on the lookout for him, especially as he would naturally make a bee-line for the horse-sales. Lucy could only pray that she would spot him before he caught sight of her.

Yet, she reflected, a market or fair would probably be the last place he would expect to find his missing daughter. Doubtless he was happy to have Emperor back. Pat and Smithy had reluctantly seen the sense in her suggestion that, as he was an easily recognizable horse, he should be set free and allowed to wander home, and so they had led him to the track that wound down from the moors to the valley and had left him to make use of his natural homing instinct.

Perhaps her family would assume that she had had a fall and died. Tears flooded her eyes at the thought of her mother's sorrow. If only there was some way of getting a message to Ann to let her know that she was alive and well ...

A group of half-grown lads jostled past her and Lucy flinched. But she had nothing to fear now from greedy thieves and pickpockets; she had no valuables they could want to snatch. At the first fair they had been to, she had replaced the hated cream satin gown with a sensible plain homespun dress and warm cloak. Reluctantly, she had parted with the gold necklace that had been a gift from her father to mark her sixteenth birthday.

The necklace had fetched a price well below its worth, but it had paid for her other purchases, a pair of strong leather boots for herself and a blue woven shirt for Rory and there had even been some money left over. But, during the past few weeks, the rain and cold had often obliged her and her companions to seek refuge in a series of inns, and Lucy's supply of coins had rapidly dwindled.

She paused as a scent of herbs and dried flowers wafted to her nostrils. It came from a large straw basket placed on the damp mud. Little dried bundles of thyme and rosemary and other species she couldn't name, were mingled with sprays of lavender and small muslin pouches containing the withered petals of summer roses which gave off a heady perfume.

On impulse, she bent down, picked up one of the fragrant bags and held it to her nose, inhaling deeply.

"Two for a farthing, only a farthing," a cracked voice intoned.

Lucy saw that it came from a wizened old woman who was bobbing behind the basket like a sparrow. She fished in the near-empty pouch beneath her cloak and produced the required sum, selecting a bag of rose petals and a sprig of lavender.

She had turned to leave when the dry, rasping voice called her back. "Here, lady ..."

Lucy ignored her at first, suspecting that the aged crone was about to accuse her of cheating or theft, a common fairground trick to extort more money from an innocent customer. But there was something in the hag's tones that made her obey.

The old woman hopped out from behind her basket and clutched at Lucy with a bony, spotted hand. Lucy drew back in alarm. She had no desire to catch any nasty disease that this ancient bone-bag might be carrying.

"Ye're not married, are you, me dear?" said the hag. It was a statement, not a question. Lucy was about to show her the hand bearing her gold ring, then changed her mind.

"I *am*, mother," she retorted.

"A pretty bride ye'll make, in a silk gown, with your husband at your side. A tall man with light brown hair. And such a beautiful emerald."

She pronounced 'beautiful' in such a way, giving it four syllables and implying a gloating covetousness, that Lucy thought the woman must be mad and seeing senile visions. Just as she was wondering how best to detach the scarecrow-like hand from her sleeve, she spied Rory looking for her.

She waved with her free hand and called his name.

"That's my husband," she informed the old woman, "that tall, dark man with the beard."

The old crone bobbed back behind her basket and squatted down, shaking her stringy white locks. She didn't say another word or even look at Lucy but, as Lucy pushed her way through the crowds to join Rory, she heard a laugh like a jackdaw's cackle following her and was glad when she could tuck her arm into his reassuring elbow.

"We've sold the chestnut and you'll never believe it, we've got rid of the old grey cob at last," he informed her, eyes sparkling and a high colour in his cheeks.

Lucy thought that he grew more handsome every day. He certainly grew more loving. He was possessed of a passionate nature, quick to express anger and impatience, quick to forgive and always ready to love. Lucy responded to his sexual demands with alacrity.

She had thought their love-making was wonderful that day on the moors, when he had first seduced her, but even this experience had paled into insignificance in the face of the many blissful occasions since. Even now, she felt a little thrill of desire as she moved her hip against his and lengthened her stride to match his.

She had surprised herself many times since meeting Rory. Hot as he was, she was always ready and burning for him. At first, she had worried in case there was something wrong with her. Surely it was only men who were supposed to feel this way?

Had her mother or her sister ever felt this aching need, this languorous melting, which she experienced whenever Rory looked at her or spoke to her a certain way? Whenever their bodies accidentally or deliberately touched? Rory said that he loved her. Well, maybe this was love. She must be the luckiest wife in the world to inhabit such a paradise of mutual feeling and shared happiness.

Her mind flickered to the previous day, when, giggling and protesting, she had allowed Rory to pull her into a patch of thick woodland. Before his hands had even reached to unfasten the bodice of her dress, she was already aflame for him, both hating herself for her body's quick response, which she felt sure placed her on the same level as any common slut, and loving the sensation of being so fully, vibrantly alive.

She feared getting with child. She wasn't ready. She hoped it wouldn't happen for a long time – a year, at least. In fact, she had secretly purchased a herbal tea which she sipped every morning and evening and which was meant to prevent her catching. She also had a phial of a special tincture which, if she did suspect that she was with child, she was to drink without delay. Yet she doubted if any preventative would work when sex with Rory was so sweet and her feelings so strong.

"You're looking very pretty today," Rory said, his voice hauling her out of her happy recollections. Lucy wondered if the warm flush on her cheeks was responsible for her radiance.

"Here, me darlin' girl, I bought you a present."

He fished in the pocket of his grey britches and brought out something that flashed golden. Could it be the long-promised wedding ring? Her heart leapt.

He placed it in her hand and, to her disappointment, it turned out to be nothing but a trinket, a mock-gold chain bearing a small green stone in a setting shaped like a flower. Lucy reflected ruefully that it wasn't quite the emerald the old woman had spoken of, then thrust the mad witch's words out of her mind. It might not be valuable, it might not be a gold wedding ring, but still it was a pretty trifle, and a present from the man she loved.

She thanked him, stood on tiptoe and kissed his cheek, then fastened the necklace around her throat.

"Someday, when I'm rich like your father, I'll buy you a sapphire to match your eyes," Rory promised.

He knew her father, Lucy had discovered, having met him at horse sales in the past. The world of horses was a small one. Lucy found that Rory had a lot of respect for Martin Swift, although at first, he hadn't connected him with Lucy.

She had never thought of her family as being rich, exactly, but to Rory, who was used to years of sleeping in the open or in rough inns, a large farmhouse with several acres of land, a collection of good horses and a couple of servants, to say nothing of hired field hands and stable boys, must have sounded like luxury indeed.

Lucy didn't like to think of the future, preferring to live from day to day, but she had to admit that it worried her. She certainly did not wish to spend the rest of her life wandering like a gypsy. What way was that to raise a family?

She knew full well what lovemaking led to and could only hope that the natural consequences would be delayed, at least until she had persuaded Rory to abandon Pat and Smithy and the roving life and either take a job on a farm, where a tied cottage would be at their disposal or, better, save enough to start his own smallholding.

Rory had a good eye for a horse and a few clever deals could do it. Why share the proceeds with Pat and Smithy? He didn't need them, especially now that he had her, with all her expertise.

As they passed a stall where a foolish volunteer with his head through a hole in a board was being pelted with rotten fruit, a prize being awarded according to how long he could endure such insulting treatment, Lucy lapsed into a daydream in which she was at a major race gathering, draped in furs, the owner of the best race-horses in the country.

As her streamlined thoroughbred sped past the winning post, the name of Lucy Swift was on everybody's lips. Champagne glasses were raised to her. Royalty invited her to dine. She would have a fine town house with her own carriage and servants, plus a mansion in the country where her horses would be kept and trained. Her racing colours would be emerald green and kingfisher blue, with her initials, LS intertwined, on the sleeve.

But I'm not LS any more, I'm LM, she reminded herself, mentally re-drawing her design. 'Lucy McDonnell' just didn't have the same ring to it.

She was still chiding herself for being a snob when Rory ducked into the doorway of a canvas tent where a cockfight was going on, pulling her in with him. Lucy couldn't bear seeing any creature hurt. She detested the way in which the birds were fitted with cruel spikes on their legs with which to tear their opponent to pieces, but Rory ignored her protests.

All the men in the audience, and the few women present, too, appeared to be drunk. Like a pack of wolves, they howled in glee as one unfortunate bird's belly was slit and, slipping in the slime of its own entrails, it was hacked to pieces while still alive by the fierce beak of an evil-looking red-eyed rooster whose black feathers dripped blood. Realizing its foe was vanquished, the bird opened its gory beak and crowed, and the whole audience, with the exception of Lucy, stamped on the ground and roared.

She felt sick and wanted to leave, but Rory informed her he had a bet on the next fight and promised to go as soon as it was over.

The handsome white fowl on which Rory had unwisely placed his money was soon reduced to raw meat and feathers. Cursing his ill-luck, Rory kept his word and led a grateful Lucy out into the fresh air again. These were sides of her husband she didn't like; the ease with which he gambled and his obvious enjoyment of blood sports. Dog fights, bull-baiting, cock-fighting, it was all the same to him.

He'd place a bet and watch the contest with mounting excitement, weaving this way and that as his body followed the movements of the animal that his money was on, yelling in delight at the sight of a spurting wound, groaning as his champion fell. After the contest, he would turn to Lucy and murmur something ardent in her ear, or give her a caress that would leave her in no doubt that he was feeling stimulated and lusty. And she would pretend to respond although she was feeling sickened and disgusted.

But men were like that. Would she be able to respect Rory if he turned pale and ill at the sight of blood, or if he preached sanctimoniously against the evils of drink and gambling? She knew, in her heart, what the answer was.

"Got to get back to Jamieson's Field, darlin', see how we're faring with the nags," said Rory, lengthening his stride.

He seemed to have put his gambling disappointment out of his mind already. His moods changed so rapidly that Lucy was hard-pressed to keep up with him. No sooner had she got used to the fact that he was cheerful and whistling, than his brow would crease and suddenly he would fly into a rage about the weather, the fact that Smithy had been late getting the horses watered, or about his way of life in general.

She would immediately adapt her mood to his and be about to say something consoling when, out of the blue, he would be joking and laughing again and asking why there was such a worried crease between her brows.

Lucy gave up. Rory was Rory and maybe she would never understand him.

"Pat's bidding for a dapple-grey that must be three-quarter bred or I'm a fiddler! Smithy tickled her near hind with me magic potion when he examined her feet and she should be limping by now. I've said to Pat, if we don't get rid of that chestnut mare today we'll all be starvin' men.

"She eats so much and bloats herself out with wind so, that she looks as if she's about to give birth to a whole herd. I think we could fool anyone that she's in foal. What say we give it a try, me darlin' lass?"

He was in irrepressible spirits and Lucy was longing for the fair to be over, so that he and she could be alone together. They were putting up that night in the Ram's Head, a bustling inn in the market square. They had been lucky to get a room to themselves, with accommodation on fair days always being in short supply. Often, Lucy had been forced to lie awake for half the night, scratching flea bites, her ears tormented by the sound of Smithy's cough and Pat's powerful snores emanating from their straw pallets.

Jamieson's Field was a small, fenced patch of grass where the horse traders always congregated. The animals were paraded one by one and the asking price given and greeted by guffaws, whereupon the seller's sights were sensibly lowered and the bidding started in earnest.

Lucy and Rory reached the spot and had to push their way through a crowd of coachmen, who had left the vehicles and were busily and noisily quaffing quantities of ale from cracked and battered tankards. A solid knot of men were shouting bids, each intent on snaring a bargain. A sale was agreed, a study hack led out, and it was the turn of their chestnut mare, led in by Pat.

Although a lot of people knew him by sight, his size and appearance still shocked the crowd into silence. Lucy had to admit that the mare certainly looked as if she were in foal. Her sides bulged and she walked with the splay-legged gait of an expectant mother, a kind of smug waddle. She was a handsome animal with strong quarters, a deep chest and a slightly dished nose that spoke of Arab blood.

Pat declaimed her falsified ancestry, told of the well-bred foal she was carrying, and asked for twenty guineas. To Lucy's great surprise, a man's voice answered, "Aye."

Rory gave a gasp of amazement and even Pat rolled his eyes, trying not to show how taken aback he was at this departure from the norm. The confidence of the unknown bidder prompted another man to offer twenty-five. The first man countered with thirty. The bidding rose in rapid leaps to the staggering sum of fifty guineas, whereupon the mare was knocked down to the man who had first spoken.

Rory and Lucy rushed up to Smithy, who was standing with the rest of their animals. The old man was wheezing with mirth.

"Heh-heh! To think 'e thought 'e was getting two for the price of one! Uh-oh, that's rich! Some people don't know anything about 'orses, do they? Heh-heh – should 'ave sent 'is ostler!" Smithy doubled up, gasping, clutching his thighs.

Rory slapped him on the shoulder. "Shush, ye fool. Hold your cackle. Here comes feller-me-lad now!"

Lucy could hear Pat's booming tones and a well-bred voice answering him.

"Yes, I know. Sired by Fleetwood out of Darley Court, eh? I don't believe it, but I'll take your word for it – and if she births a hairy jackass, I'll string you up personally!"

The voice was light, young, refined, and Lucy looked up in interest. The man walking beside Pat was tall, slimmer than Rory and dressed in a magnificent yellow brocade coat worn over a dove-grey waistcoat and britches, all exceedingly well cut. While Rory's thick, black locks tumbled wild around his shoulders, this man's dark, gleaming hair was tied back neatly with a black velvet ribbon.

His complexion was pale and his features finely chiselled and there was a haughty set to his bearing that made Lucy feel slightly insulted, as if he were implying that it was beneath him to mix with such riff-raff.

"I have some business to attend to today and won't be back till morning. See that the mare is delivered at eight o'clock sharp tomorrow morning. Darwell Manor – about three miles on the West Road, up on the hill. Ask anyone at the inn where you're staying. They'll give you directions."

"Yes, sir," said Pat, with a bob of his head. It was strange to see the giant deferring to a man a whole head shorter than he was.

"And who shall I deliver her to, sir?"

"Philip Darwell, the Earl of Darwell's son."

The haughty demeanor, the expensive clothes, the aristocratic tone of voice: Lucy had known he couldn't possibly have belonged to anything but the upper classes. As he turned to walk away, he paused and looked directly at Lucy and Rory. Rory was murmuring something to Smithy in a low voice and Lucy thought that maybe the horse's new owner was suspicious, imagining them to be talking about him.

Lucy glanced at Rory, then back at the stranger, and suddenly realized that it was at her that his clear grey gaze was directed. Embarrassed, she looked down at her feet, then at Rory again, then finally she returned the stranger's stare with a haughty one of her own. Two could play at that game!

A faint smile curved his lips. Then he gave her a brief nod, turned and went on his way.

Almost immediately, Rory rounded on her. "Hussy!" he hissed.

"What do you mean?" asked Lucy indignantly, feeling doubly wronged.

"I saw the way that fancy man looked at you, and how you looked back at him – in front of me, your own husband!"

Rory had never been angry with her before. Lucy felt desolate. This onslaught was extremely unfair of him; she had done nothing to invite the stranger to look at her other than blush in embarrassment. Maybe Rory had mistaken the pinkness in her cheeks for another kind of flush entirely. His brow was knotted in anger. He looked wild, handsome, feral. Lucy could hardly believe that he belonged to her, that he loved her. She must find some way of patching up this silly tiff.

But it was not to be. All the way back to the inn he argued and would not see reason. By the time they reached their small attic room with its rickety wooden bed and crudely fashioned table, Lucy felt weary and depressed. What had got into him that had sparked off this totally unfounded jealousy? She had eaten nothing all day, and her stomach rumbled from hunger. She was used to better care from him than this.

"Rory," she said, covering his hand with hers as it lay across his thigh. They were both sitting on the bed, she on the side nearest the window, he on the end facing the door. "Rory, I love you. I'd never look at another man. There's no one who can match up to you. You've got me, body and soul, for as long as you want me. And if ever you don't want me any more, just tell me and I'll go. I'd never bother you. All I want is for you to be happy."

It cost a lot for her to say these words, angry as she was with his unreasonable behaviour, but it was the truth. She couldn't imagine ever making love with another man. Nobody would be able to stir or satisfy her so. And nobody could be more interesting, unpredictable, ever-changing, or more loving and caring towards her, apart from at this very moment.

He looked away, ignoring her passionate confession.

"Rory," she begged, "please believe me, I didn't flirt with that stuck-up booby. It was all in your mind. I couldn't help it if he looked at me."

"Oh, stop whining, woman, you're making my head ache. Just be quiet, will you?"

Lucy flinched at his unkind, uncharacteristic words. This wasn't the Rory she knew. There seemed to be some bitterness, some canker inside him that was gnawing and disquieting him and forcing him into irritability. There was nothing she could do to make him reveal his thoughts, but she wished that he trusted her enough to share his worries with her. Was it a gambling debt, maybe?

She shifted uncomfortably on the hard bed and gazed out of the window to distract herself from the uncomfortable silence in the room. She couldn't believe that her marriage was going wrong already, after five short weeks. All those people walking by outside, going to visit friends, family, lovers, or strolling in twos; none of them looked as if they were burdened with as many problems as she.

All at once, Lucy caught sight of a familiar yellow coat and sent out a silent prayer for Rory not to turn round and spot his imagined rival. She dared not breathe until the young nobleman disappeared out of sight behind a line of carriages.

Behind her, Rory heaved a sigh, and the bed creaked as he stood up. He caught her shoulders and turned her round to face him, then planted his lips on hers. Lucy's spirits rebelled. How could he expect her to make love when he had made her so unhappy? Did he have no sensitivity at all? Now, if he were just to apologize, beg her forgiveness, tell her he loved her ...

Lucy had never refused Rory before, but now something inside her bridled at the thought of this man who had caused her so much upset, satisfying himself inside her body. She craved some time alone; time to think, time to forgive.

"No, Rory," she said, the words choking in her throat. "No!"

She flinched at the look of hot fury that flashed across his face.

"What do you mean, 'No'? You're me wife and I'll have me husband's rights. Some men would take the strap to you for this!"

Tears sprang to her eyes and his face softened. "I'm not going to force you," he said. "All I'm going to do is ask you to see reason, girl, and give yourself to me. Now. Come on, Lucy."

He tugged at her arm and she pulled away, cramming herself into the corner of the room nearest the door. His face reddened with anger. She knew he was going to beat her.

Sobbing, Lucy sank to the floor, hugging her knees against her chest, rocking, bending her head so that he couldn't slap her face or, worse, kick it. His moods were like gusts of wind, shaking her, blasting her so that she felt dizzy and drained. If only she could read him like she could read horses. Even with a skittish horse, you could predict its moves and react accordingly, but not with this man. He was as tempestuous as a storm-tossed sea.

She heard the door slam and looked up. He was gone.

Chapter Nine

Lucy awoke to find the skin on her face dry and tight from crying. She felt exhausted and emotionally drained. A wave of loneliness surged through her as she scanned the room and found it empty. Her side of the bed was rumpled but the other side was smooth, the sheet and pillow cold to the touch. She felt certain that Rory had not been back.

Pulling aside the fraying curtain, she saw that people were already going about their daily business in the damp street, their collars pulled up around their necks to protect them from the dank, curling fingers of the November mist. She was empty, numb, with no tears left to cry – and yet, looking back, their argument had seemed so trivial, a mere tiff over an imagined glance, a jealous fancy. Surely he wouldn't leave her because of it? It wasn't as if he had caught her in another man's arms.

Maybe he had gone off gambling somewhere, or had got drunk in some other inn and was even now sprawled on a bench or a pile of straw, sleeping it off. Reason with herself as she might, Lucy still felt a quiver of apprehension as she slid her stiff limbs off the lumpy straw mattress, splashed some ice cold water over her face from the cracked stone ewer on the table and prepared to go below in search of Pat and Smithy.

She remembered the horse that had to be delivered that morning to the man who was the cause of her marital trouble, and wondered who had taken it. The main room of the inn was empty of guests. A little girl was cleaning out the ashes from the grate and a man was whistling cheerfully as he wiped pots with a wet, grubby cloth. Lucy approached him, described her companions and asked if he knew of their whereabouts.

"The big feller? The one with the black outfit to match 'is teeth? Oh aye, I've seen 'im all right, and little old granddaddy, too – a right case of consumption, if ever I saw one."

He paused, wrung out the tattered cloth and put it down on the wooden bar top. He was a small, fat, bald man with bright red cheeks and narrow, cunning countryman's eyes. He continued, warming to his subject.

"I remember Samuel Smethwick. A good man, Samuel, but never strong, reet poorly 'e always were. Now, 'e grew thin and pale and coughed a lot, like that man o' yorn, coughed pink froth with blood in it, 'e did. Went on for 'baht a year, it did ..."

Lucy was fretting with impatience, but afraid to butt in and annoy this man who was obviously determined to tell his story, in case he refused to give her the information she so badly needed. So she curled her toes tight inside her boots and steeled herself to look interested.

"One day ..." His slow, monotonous voice seemed to chew forty times on each word before spitting it out. "One day, 'e were walking down the 'igh Street, like, when all of a sudden 'e coughed and a great fountain of blood spurted out of 'im, *whoosh*, all over the white cloak of this fine lady who was walking past. Drenched in blood she was, like a lamb at the slaughterhouse."

He paused and chuckled at his own wit. He had obviously related his gory tale many times before and he had Lucy trapped, shuddering, mentally urging him to get to the end and answer her questions. "Oh, ho-ho, it were a reet funny sight, 'er face all green, like, and 'er lovely clothes all covered in ..."

Lucy tried not to listen. "When we buried 'im, 'e were bleached out like there weren't a drop of red blood left in 'is veins. All grey and sunken 'e was. 'Orrible."

He looked at Lucy with a satisfied smirk, which promptly dissolved as he realized that she wasn't about to scream or grow pale like other ladies he'd told his gruesome tale to. He picked up his cloth again and started banging the pots around.

"Ahem." Lucy cleared her throat loudly. to regain his attention. "My friends. Where are they?"

He made a vague gesture which seemed to indicate that she should go out of the door and turn left. His directions led her to a rough wooden shed round the side of the inn. There was something about the deep rumbling noises coming from within that sounded very familiar. Ducking into the doorway, she peered into the gloomy interior and, once her eyes had accustomed themselves to the dimness, she made out the recumbent forms of several men, sprawled in careless attitudes on the heaps of straw that covered the rough earth floor.

One was Pat, without a doubt; his snores led her eyes straight to him. The giant was flat on his back, his cavernous mouth open, an empty beer tankard still clutched in his hand. Curled in a fetal position next to him was Smithy. Was Rory with them?

Silently, hardly daring to move in case she wakened anybody and incurred their ale-induced wrath, she inspected each figure in turn. One, whom she at first thought was Rory on account of his blue shirt and shock of dark hair, sighed and turned over and revealed himself to be a much older man.

Perhaps he had taken the horse to Darwell Manor. There was only one way to find out. Making her way to the field behind the inn, where they had left the animals in charge of a watchman, stabling being at a premium on a fair day with the winter weather setting in, she took stock of the animals present.

They were all there, including the chestnut mare with her falsely bloated stomach. Lucy's heart gave a little lurch. She had no idea what time of day it was and Philip Darwell didn't look like the kind of man who should be kept waiting.

She hurried back inside the inn and enquired the time of the pot-washer.

"Seven, miss," he replied.

She knew the use of the word 'miss' was a deliberate insult, implying that she wasn't a respectable married woman staying there with her husband, but a whore who had been picked up and passed off as a 'wife'. However, with so many more important matters on her mind, she couldn't afford to enter into an argument to defend her virtue.

She decided to come straight to the point.

"My husband, Rory McDonnell, a young man with a beard and one gold earring. Have you seen him?"

"Your *husband*?" sneered the man. A shifty look passed across his puffy features. "Nay, can't say I have. Must have got up early and gone out for a walk, like, after a night with a hot little lass like you!"

His revolting leer made Lucy's stomach heave. She found herself cursing Rory for forcing her to lead the kind of life where she was expected to mingle with scum like this man. Rory should be here beside her, standing up for her, hitting this rogue in his foul mouth and teaching him how to behave in the presence of ladies.

And then she turned and saw him – and he saw her. They both stood frozen like statues, he in an attitude of guilt, she in one of horror, disappointment and anguish. He was coming out of a room behind the bar, buttoning his shirt and adjusting his britches, while the naked form of the plump girl, her big, flaccid breasts dangling like lumps of uncooked dough, was clearly visible behind him.

Lucy tried to speak but her throat had closed up. She felt a clammy perspiration break out on her face and hands and her legs began to tremble. She heard the naked girl gasp and saw her push Rory out of her room so that she could close the door on Lucy's accusing eyes. Slowly, like a man in a trance, Rory moved towards her, refusing to look at her. Then, without a word, he broke into a stumbling run and bolted out of the door into the street.

On an impulse, not knowing what she would do or say, Lucy dashed after him, hearing the snigger of the pot man following her. Rory was running blindly, like a frightened animal, blundering into people and knocking them aside. Curses rang after him, then stopped as the jostled passers-by halted to watch the chase.

"Go on, lass – you'll get him," chuckled one old man as Lucy raced past, her skirts bunched up in her hand to prevent herself from tripping.

But it was no use. Rory was too quick for her. He vanished up a side street and she was left panting, leaning against a wall, wishing she could die right there, on that chill November morning, with nothing left in the whole world worth living for.

For a while, she remained there, head down, sobbing, but eventually the damp mist penetrated her clothes, setting her shivering and forcing her to start walking to warm her body up, although every step seemed useless progress to nowhere.

Suddenly, she remembered the horse, and the fifty guineas to be collected from Philip Darwell. *She* would have that money! Rory had cheated her, left her homeless and penniless. Pat and Smithy would be all right. They had the other horses which, although they could never fetch such a mighty sum, would at least allow them to carry on eating and travelling. She was the one who was in desperate need, and surely they would forgive her, if ever they found out the true facts?

As she made her way back to the inn, her arms wrapped round herself for warmth, she thought of her parents sitting round a roaring fire – her father who, for all his faults, was a loving, clever man; her faded, adorable mother; her pet cat, Ha'penny; Emperor; the clean, vibrant smell of the stables … Her heart reached out in longing for the nostalgic familiarity of all she had left so many miles behind.

Rory's face swam into her mind and, with a huge effort, she pushed the vision of him aside. She had trusted him, loved him, offered him her whole life if he wanted it, and he had chosen to reject her in the vilest way, by preferring the company and body of a grubby, coarse, alehouse whore to her own.

Oh, if only she wasn't tied to him by the bonds of marriage! He had captured her, forced his will on her. How could she have been so gullible as to believe he wanted her for a life-long companion? Why could he not simply have ravished her and left her to wander on the moors, with her innocence gone, but her body, her mind and heart still intact and free?

Pausing to check that she could still hear Pat's thunderous snores, Lucy opened the gate into the field and nodded to the young lad who stood guard over the animals. He knew she was one of the group who had left them there the previous day and he helped her to saddle up the chestnut, stretching the girth with difficulty over her rotund belly.

"Got to ride her gently, eh?" he remarked, with a knowing look.

"Yes, I'll do that," she murmured, so preoccupied that she was hardly aware that she had spoken.

Her mind was in a turmoil, in the midst of which only one thing stood clear – that she must take this horse to Darwell Manor and collect fifty guineas. And then? With that large sum jingling in her purse, she could go anywhere, do anything and she would start with buying her own horse.

Money and horses… That was all her life seemed to revolve around. It had been that way ever since she was a child, as far back as she could remember. Money and horses, and the unpredictable, unreliable ways of men.

As she took hold of the mare's bridle, she noticed the gleam of her makeshift wedding ring. A thick, choking lump of tears gathered in her throat as she looked at the gold hoop which had once adorned Rory's ear. In a surge of fury, she snatched it from her finger and hurled it into the field.

As she goaded the mare out into the lane, she saw the boy scrabbling among the grass. *Let him sell it if he wants to*, she thought, *it's far more use to him than it is to me.* The gold band had always felt temporary and meaningless, like the mockery of a marriage it symbolized. Now she had lost both, but she did not feel in the slightest bit free or light of heart as she set out in the rain in search of Darwell Manor.

Chapter Ten

Theodore, the ninth Earl of Darwell, raised his head weakly from his pillows when he heard hooves clattering into the courtyard. One yellowed, emaciated hand, bearing a heavy gold ring with the family crest engraved on it, stirred on the sheet, then reached waveringly towards the bell rope.

He pulled and a tolling sounded in the servants' quarters but, seeing that Darwell Manor was now reduced to a complement of three, a cook, a general housemaid, and a butler, who were all busy fulfilling the tasks of at least fifteen, nobody answered the old man's call.

"Damnable business," he muttered to himself, "damnable."

What made it worse was that he knew it was entirely his fault, and his alone, that the Darwell family were reduced to such penurious straits. The death of his young wife many years ago had turned what were formerly pleasurable activities, lightly partaken of, into a way of life. Drinking and gambling were the pastimes of many a gentleman of leisure, though few were as over-indulgent as Theodore Darwell, who had allowed both his fortune and his health to waste away until now there remained only the merest vestiges of either.

"Eleanor ... oh, my dear, beautiful Eleanor," mumbled the old man, allowing his filmy eyes to fill with tears. "You could have been such a comfort to your dying husband."

"Nonsense, Father!" rang out a cheerful voice. "You're not dying. Imbibing too much, perhaps, but your guts must be so well pickled by now that they'll find you in your grave two hundred years from now, looking as if you had just gone to sleep."

The old man's lips tightened in petulance. The one thing he couldn't bear was for anyone to remind him of his own mortality. Why wouldn't they let him achieve the one thing he wanted, which was to slide into the past and live alongside his memories?

"Do something for me, m'boy. Fetch me m'porter."

A deep sigh issued from his son, Philip, who was standing framed in the doorway. He looked at his father with a stern yet indulgent expression, as if about to remonstrate with a mischievous child.

"Now, Father, you heard what your physician said. Not more than two glasses may pass your lips in a day and, to my knowledge, you've had three already. Who do you think you are – King George?

"He may have the money to drink all day and eat pheasant and swan all night, but may I remind you, dear Father, that our cupboard is bare. When I heard your bell ring, I thought, 'Has Father found a ruby in the mattress? A store of doubloons in the panelling? Then I thought, 'No such luck, he just wants a drink.' "

Philip Darwell found his father exasperating and foolish. He had cursed him many times for losing the family money by allowing himself to be cheated by bastards like George Hardcastle of Rokeby Hall, who, Philip knew for a fact, carried a pack of marked cards always about his person. Yet he was sympathetic, too, sorry about the lonely life Theodore had led for so long, grieving so much over his lost Eleanor that he could not bring himself to marry again.

Philip had been brought up by a series of governesses and tutors, until the Earl had decided it was less costly to send him into the army for a spell. He had soon become a popular cavalry officer and his good judgement of people had led to several shrewd business deals which brought in enough capital to keep himself in clothes, pay the servants' wages and buy his father's beloved porter, though there wasn't enough left over to stop the walls of his ancestral seat from crumbling into disrepair.

Except that it was not his ancestral seat any more. Not since his father's last card game with Hardcastle, when the Earl had put up his last big stake, Darwell Manor, and lost it to that ... that trickster, that cheat and swindler.

Philip had offered to fight a duel to win back the deeds to his home, but Hardcastle – fat, purple-nosed, crude, cowardly Hardcastle, who lacked any trace of blue blood but had made his money in the cotton industry, using the local townsfolk as slave labour – had declined, citing a violent attack of indigestion as an excuse. Indigestion! Philip would have liked to have pricked him in the bloated belly with the tip of his sword to relieve the old windbag's internal pressure!

And as for his horse-faced daughter ... Philip just hoped he could carry off the wedding successfully. Once their marriage had brought Darwell Manor safely back into his hands, Philip would soon teach her her place, the haughty hussy. But for now, he would play the charming fiancé, all cooing flattery and honeyed words. Later on, once he had planted an heir in her stringy body and gone back to join his regiment, there would be plenty of time for love.

Then Philip heard the stamp of a hoof on the cobbles. Peering through a distorted diamond pane of the mullioned window, he made out a figure on a plump horse. This was the moment he had been waiting for. There might be a lot of unfair things in his own life, he reflected, but some of them he could do something about, and by Jove he was going to put paid to this one.

Rogues and tricksters of any sort would be better off leaving the country than coming up against Philip Darwell. It would give him immense satisfaction to see the hangman's noose biting into their necks.

* * *

Lucy thought she had never seen a place that looked so neglected and devoid of life. Yet it could have been a beautiful, graceful house, with flowered creepers twining up the walls, rich tapestries in the windows and smiling servants at the door. There should have been children's laughter, constant visitations of titled ladies and gentlemen in smart carriages, instead of this brooding air of silence and neglect that dripped from the broken guttering and rotted windowsills.

Perhaps she was too early and the occupants of the Manor were still abed. As the young gentleman had said the previous day, the great house was easy enough to find. Indeed, it would have been hard to miss, with its grey turrets sticking like jagged teeth out of the clump of trees that surrounded it, a patch of majesty and mystery set in the fair pastureland of the Pendleton Hills.

It had taken the lazy chestnut mare over an hour to toil up the long slope to the Manor. Lucy had expected some kind of welcome, even if only from the head stableman. Surely they were waiting for her? Or had Philip Darwell regretted his purchase already and gone into hiding in the far recesses of his grand house? Maybe his 'business' had kept him away longer than he had expected. After her recent experience, Lucy had grave doubts about the nature of any man's absence from home.

She had no intention of leaving the horse without collecting the payment for it. The nobility, Lucy knew only too well, could cheat as much as any common man, and think less of it. No, she would wait; all day, if necessary.

It was a cold, dank morning and the dawn drizzle was giving way to steady, soaking rain. The mare disliked it as much as Lucy did, and stood with her head drooping and her tail clamped to her hocks. A vivid memory of Philip Darwell came back to Lucy now, as she sat shivering in her saturated cloak. Those grey eyes, so haughty and aloof, had held a flicker of interest when they met Lucy's, which was not merely physical appraisal, but something more cerebral, a kind of recognition, as if he realized that Lucy was different from her companions and in some way superior.

Behind his aristocratic, commanding facade, Lucy had sensed gentleness and humour. Maybe it was intuition, or perhaps she was totally fooling herself, but she had felt there were some admirable qualities about the dashing young man, which was why she was feeling so guilty now about bringing him a horse with no pedigree, a mere mongrel, who was not even in foal.

She would not be trying to take his money under false pretences if she did not need it so much herself. Her natural honesty urged her to apologize, explain and refuse to sell the animal to him, even though it meant facing the fury of the others when she got back.

Yet, if this were just an ordinary day, she would not be sitting here now, wet, cold and confused. Instead, Pat or Smithy would have delivered the chestnut mare and she would be back at the inn with Rory, making preparations to move on to their next destination. Laughing, joshing, taking advantage of having the room to themselves, and making love.

Lucy felt a pang of emotion spear through her like a rapier. There would be no more intimate hours of laughter and love with her husband. It was over. Rory had gone. He had let her down in the worst way a man could ever betray a woman, through another woman.

That slut! Lucy thought of her now, the tousled brown hair, probably lousy, the blubbery, sensual lips, the lard-like skin and big, drooping dugs. A slow-witted, bovine animal, sensate only when brought to life by a glass of wine, a gold coin and a man between her floppy thighs. Ugh! Lucy wished she could have marked that dull, common face with her fingernails, torn her hair out, kicked her black and blue and sent her naked out into the rain and fog for daring to seduce her beloved Rory.

Yet, she thought, deliberately calming her thoughts, perhaps it was not totally the girl's fault. Maybe – no, it couldn't be true, surely he wouldn't? – maybe Rory had been attracted to the grubby drudge. If that were so, then Lucy could only be glad that he was gone, for how could she ever bear to let him near her own body again? And the strain of always having to watch him when he was in the company of other women, whether fine ladies or common wenches ... No, it would never have worked. She would have suffered years of misery.

The anger raised by her reminiscences fired her to dismount, place the reins around a mounting block to prevent the animal from wandering and walk round the side of the house to the great oak main door. Grasping the heavy iron knocker, she raised it, then let it fall with a ringing thud on the studded wood.

Almost immediately, as if someone had been lying in wait for her, the huge oaken structure creaked open to reveal a familiar figure standing inside. Clad in a ruffled white shirt, a lovat jacket over a grey waistcoat, cream britches and highly polished brown boots, Philip Darwell was a spectacle to set any maiden's heart fluttering.

Lucy, in her overwrought state, was in no mood to be impressed. Uncomfortably aware of her wet, bedraggled state, she hoped he might at least invite her in to dry her sopping clothes by the fire and take a warm drink.

But there was no friendliness or invitation in his face, just fathomless coldness which she didn't understand, and when he spoke, his tone was like splinters of ice.

"I suppose you were too ashamed to come straight to the door. I watched you from the window, sitting on that wretched nag, trying to pluck up the courage to rob me."

"I ... I d-don't understand," stammered Lucy.

The trouble was, she *did* understand. So Darwell wasn't a fool, after all. He did know horseflesh and now she was to suffer for his knowledge. She watched the cold glint in his eyes change and become purposeful, and she backed away, hoping she could scramble onto the mare and be gone before he could pursue her.

She turned, made a sudden dash and a spring and was across the chestnut's back, but Philip Darwell was right on her heels. Seizing her blue cloak, he tugged hard. Unable to keep her grip on the saddle, Lucy found herself tumbling towards him. She kicked out furiously, sending the mare shying away from beneath her. For a second she felt as if she were suspended in the air, then, with a painful thud, she landed on her hip and elbow on the hard, slippery cobbles.

Before she could scramble to her feet, Philip Darwell had bundled her up and was dragging her towards the open door of the stables.

"Let me go, do you hear? Take your hands off me, you –"

All the breath was knocked out of her as he curled his foot behind her ankle and sent her spinning into a large bale of straw at the back of the dark stable. Winded and breathless, Lucy raised her arms to protect herself as Philip, his eyes narrowed and cruel, stretched out a hand towards her.

In that instant, the memory of the beating she had received from her father the night she ran away from home came back to her in discomfiting detail. Then, she had fought, bitten, scratched and kicked, yet still she had been overpowered.

Perhaps there was another way of dealing with this kind of situation – with calm reason and cool logic. Philip didn't look like the kind of man to be swayed by a woman's pleas or tears, but perhaps, if she could stand up to him, win his respect …

She gazed at him and caught his attention so that his movement towards her was arrested in mid air.

"I understand why you are angry," she said.

She meant it. She would have been mad, too, in his position. Then she paused, thinking hard. If he already knew that he had been tricked and the mare was not in foal, he must have known at the very moment when he was bidding for the horse.

Or had somebody informed him later, Pat or Smithy perhaps, in return for a financial gift from Philip for exposing their trick? No, they would never do that. It would be the end of their livelihood if they did. They had to be careful, especially when so many of the horses they handled were stolen property. A man could be hanged for less than that.

Hanged! A sudden shudder possessed Lucy as she gazed into Philip's steely eyes. He was coming towards her again. He gripped her arm, twisting her flesh, making her cry out in pain.

Her face must have shown how much he was hurting her, because he suddenly smiled coldly and said, "Go on, you little thief, cry! There'll be time enough for tears when the hangman is marching you to the gallows!"

Lucy's mouth dropped open in disbelief. What had she done? She was innocent of everything. It hadn't been her idea to pass off the mare as being well-bred and in foal. It had unfortunately fallen to her to deliver it, that was all. Yet, even as she thought this, she blushed, remembering her plan to keep Philip's fifty guineas for herself.

He held her down on the prickly straw, his fingers digging cruelly into her upper arm. Lucy remained still. There seemed no point in crying out or struggling. No, her first idea was the best – to reason with him.

But she would have to choose her words very carefully for, if she failed to sway him, he might just fulfill his promise of throwing her into the lock-up, until she was taken before the magistrate and sentenced to death by hanging. The danger she was in served to sharpen her brain. She would listen very carefully to what he said, then try to counter his arguments with logic, if not the truth.

He started speaking, slowly, as if talking to himself. "Thieves, crooks, swindlers. They've taken so much from me."

Then, fixing Lucy with a glare that frightened her, he spoke directly to her, venom in his words. "I've been watching you lot. I've been following your progress, you know. Oh yes, you might have thought you'd got away with disguising Silver Maiden, that grey that went missing from Lady Pettigrew's orchard last June!"

"I had nothing to do with any of it," Lucy pointed out quietly, though her heart was hammering in her chest. "I didn't even know them then. If you would just let me explain –"

"Hold your tongue, wench!" snapped Philip, shaking her. "It's your misfortune to have fallen in with them and so, as far as I'm concerned, you're all as bad as each other. You know what the penalty is for stealing horses and cheating honest citizens. I've got you in my hands now, and you're going to lead me to the others. And then ... " He paused.

Lucy's heart was pounding so loudly that she could hardly hear his final words, which he spoke softly and sibilantly, with an air of smug triumph. "And then it will give me great satisfaction to watch you all hang together."

"*No!*" The word tore itself from Lucy's lips before she could check it. Suddenly, her calmness left her and she twisted herself violently round in order to try and escape from Philip's determined clutches.

At the same time, she calculated how far away his leg was, and landed a mighty kick in the centre of his left shin. But Philip's leather riding boots were of excellent quality, and he reacted no more than he would have done had a butterfly landed on him.

"You heard what I said, didn't you?" He moved so close to Lucy that she no longer had enough room to take a swing at him. "People like you are the scum of the earth. They don't deserve to live."

Hot anger beat in Lucy's throat. "Son of an earl you may be, but your manners are no better than a butcher boy's," she said, trying to match his cold, cutting tone. "I demand that you release me right now and, what's more, give me the apology that's due to me for your unforgivable behaviour towards a lady."

Philip's bark of laughter was so loud that at the far end of the stable, there was a sudden flutter of wings and a huge white barn owl swooped low over their heads and glided out of the door, causing Lucy to squeal in terror as she felt the wind of its flight ruffling her hair.

"Pretending to be a lady now, are we, now that the shadow of the noose is round your neck? You're going to recant, are you? Call a churchman and confess your sins? Well, maybe God will forgive you, but I'm not God and I have no intention of letting you get away with your theft and fraud one moment longer.

"I've been trying to track down your particular little group for a long time. There's that huge oaf who pretends he's of the church."

"But he *is!*" interjected Lucy vehemently.

Philip ignored her. "That shrivelled little rat with the consumptive cough, and that bearded lady's man."

Lucy's first instinct was to spring hotly to Rory's defence and tell him he was her husband and an honourable man. Then the events of earlier that morning came back to her and she held her tongue.

"And then there is *you*, my pretty one." He rolled his upper lip back from his teeth like a dog about to tear out her throat.

Lucy shrank back from him. Was he going to have a fit? She had heard that the aristocracy frequently had fits; something to do with inbreeding, she'd been told. Or was he going to strangle her there and then, to save her the public agony and humiliation of hanging?

It soon became obvious to her that he was going to do neither. Pinning her arms behind her back, he reached for the clasp of her cloak and unhooked it. The sodden garment fell from her shoulders and Lucy felt suddenly vulnerable, knowing there was nothing but her flimsy dress and her undergarments between his eyes and her bare skin.

It felt horribly like the situation she'd been in with Rory and his companions, but on that occasion she'd been saved by Rory's intervention – although, she reflected now, it hadn't exactly done her a lot of good.

She was beginning to learn a lot about men, to discover what motivated them: money and sex. With both, their instincts were acquisitive and urgent. She was no longer a virgin, it was true, but she still had no desire to be ravaged by anybody, least of all a cruel, unreasonable man who refused to let her explain her circumstances and seemed intent on taking not only her body, but her very life.

"Philip Darwell." She had to try reasoning with him again, to appeal to his better nature, if he had one. It was her only weapon. If rape was indeed what he had in mind, he was certainly taking his time, fingering the laces that held the front of her dress together.

Her body gave a sudden tingle and betrayed her. He really was very good-looking. What a pity they hadn't met in better circumstances.

"If you are a gentleman and an intelligent, fair-minded human being, then at least let me put my case before condemning me to be handed over to the authorities. I was not with that group of men of my own free will. I –"

Her words were cut short as Philip's hard lips closed on hers. He had been toying with her, like a cat plays with a mouse; now the game was over and the prey was to be devoured. The prickly straw scratched Lucy's back as he seized the neckline of her dress. It ripped at the side seam so that one of her shoulders was exposed.

Lucy kicked and twisted and panted. Despite her better judgement, the struggle was arousing her. The smell of Philip's fresh sweat was like an aphrodisiac. She realized she desired him. Even the smell of his sweat was like an aphrodisiac to her. *What's wrong with you?* she asked herself. No woman should be feeling this way when a man was trying to force himself on her. She should be looking for ways to disable him, rather than feeling her body throb and melt for him.

Suddenly, there was a piercing scream from the direction of the doorway. "Philip! What are doing with that girl?" The voice was female and sounded aghast and tearful. Then there was the sound of running footsteps across the yard.

"Rachel! Oh no – Rachel! Rachel, wait!" Philip released his grip on her and raced off in pursuit.

She was free! The miracle had happened after all. She could go now. Her mother had always said she had a guardian angel and, for the first time ever, Lucy thought she must have been right. Grimacing at the clammy feel of her wet cloak, she draped it once more around her shoulders and fastened the clasp to hide her torn dress.

She was just about to tiptoe out of the stable block when she heard voices approaching the door. They were arguing. Philip was pleading and apologetic, Rachel furious and unforgiving. Lucy shrank back into the shadows to listen.

"No, Philip, I won't forgive you! You heartless traitor! How could you do this to me? Two months before our wedding, and I catch you with ... with a trollop!" Her voice broke into sobs and Philip's took over.

"Rachel, my dearest love, it's not how it looks, I promise you. There's a good reason. I'll tell you if only you'll listen. It's nothing to do with you, or with love. It wasn't even a passing fancy. It's nothing. That girl – she cheated me, stole from me. She had to be punished, so –"

"A fine way of punishing her!" Rachel's tone was acid. Lucy felt a stirring of sympathy. She knew exactly how she must be feeling.

"My dearest sweet, this was an unfortunate, isolated incident."

Philip's voice was wheedling and persuasive and Lucy hated him for his attempts to extricate himself from his dilemma. She almost felt like stumbling out in her ragged, bruised state and showing the girl how her precious sweetheart had abused a total stranger, thus making her loathe him even more.

But Rachel's next words sent her mind and sympathies spinning in quite the opposite direction.

"Like father, like son," she sneered. "Your father was fool enough to lose your family money and your fine house to my father, on the turn of a card. And now his equally foolish son, you, Philip Darwell –" Lucy, from her hiding place in the stable, could imagine Rachel pointing an elegant finger at him, – "has thrown away his only chance to get some part of his inheritance back. I realize now that you never loved me, although I once stupidly imagined that you did."

"But Rachel ..."

"No, no excuses. Do you really think that I, Rachel Hardcastle, wish to be married to a penniless ne'er-do-well with a meaningless title, who courts sluts every moment my back is turned? Why, I'd be a laughing stock in my own house! I don't wish to hear your lying explanation.

"There will be no forgiveness, either from myself or from my father. I'm totally disgusted with what I've just been forced to witness. I don't want your title, I don't want you. I hope never to set eyes on you again. As soon as your father passes away, Darwell Manor becomes mine, as my father has made me a present of the deeds.

"As for what happens to you, well, doubtless you can find some little serving maid with an accommodating body who will be only too pleased to take you in. Goodbye, Philip."

Lucy heard the sound of a horse's hooves and risked a glance out of the stable doorway. She saw a stiff back clad in blue velvet, and a long skein of pale hair tied back with a brown ribbon, vanishing down the drive atop a roan gelding, with Philip rushing after her, calling her name.

This, at last, was the perfect opportunity to make her escape.

Chapter Eleven

It was her own fault. She could have run round the stable block and found some route to lead her away from the manor, but she dithered. What stopped her was the knowledge that she was in terrible danger, not only from Philip but from Pat and Smithy, too.

Maybe, right at this moment, they were discovering the theft of the mare and the disappearance of both herself and Rory. They would jump to the wrong conclusion, of course; they would assume that she and Rory had stolen the mare and run off together.

Darwell Manor would be the first place they would think to look, but if they came here, they would be walking straight into a trap. Yet there was no way she could warn them, and no way of explaining her actions to them. Philip expected her to lead him straight to the remaining members of the party.

If they had noticed anything the previous day – that look which Philip had given her, for instance – or if Rory had informed them of his jealous suspicions, they might think, quite naturally, that she was siding with Philip against them. Yet, if she refused to obey Philip, the situation was just as bad for her. Whichever way she looked at it, the outlook was equally bleak.

Now it really was too late, for she saw Philip silhouetted in the doorway, scanning the shadows for her.

"I know you're in there. Must I take a lantern and find you, or will you be a good girl and show yourself?"

Was she imagining things, or was his voice not quite as stern as it had been earlier, before his encounter with Rachel? The tone of icy accusation seemed to have gone.

A quick glance round assured Lucy that there was no other way out of the stable building. She was at a dead end, with nothing but a row of loose boxes between herself and Philip. Taking a step forward, she said softly, "I'm here."

He made no move to approach her, so Lucy walked up to him, still clutching her cloak tightly around her torn dress. Once again, she had an intuitive feeling that she should be reasonable with him, in spite of the way he had abused her.

"I couldn't help hearing what just took place between you and your betrothed. I'm sorry. But if you'll let a woman you don't even know give her opinion, I'd say it was for the best. She doesn't sound like the sort of girl who'd make a man very happy."

There! She'd tried her best to be consoling. Now, would he soften his feelings towards her?

To her amazement, Philip raised one fist and brought it smashing down against the doorframe. Beads of blood sprang out along his grazed knuckles but he made no attempt to rub or suck them, simply left his damaged hand dangling at his side. There seemed to be some kind of inner conflict going on inside him.

Patiently, Lucy waited for a response or an order.

"What's your name?" His voice seemed to come from far away, as if he were speaking in a trance.

"Lucy, er, Swift." She had been about to say 'McDonnell', but the thought of being known by that name made her stomach churn. She wanted no more to do with the name, or the man who bore it.

He made no comment about her hesitation, just looked down at the straw-littered stable floor and mumbled, "It's a disaster. If I've lost her, I've lost everything."

Lucy wanted to point out that it was his fault – that if only he had let her explain, none of this would have happened – but somehow she managed to hold her tongue and say, as soothingly as she could, "I gather there was more than simply love at stake."

Philip raised his head and looked at her, as if seeing her clearly for the first time.

"Look, I … that is …" he faltered, "… I want to say I'm sorry for what I did to you."

His words started coming out in a rush, tumbling over one another. A faint flush rose to his pale cheeks. "I was very angry. It was true that I had set out to put a stop to the horse-thievery and crooked trading that has been going on, but I shouldn't have treated you like that. I saw you only as a thief, not as a woman. A lady," he corrected himself.

"I suppose if I had been a man, you would have given me a good hiding?"

"Yes, of course, although I don't know what chance I would have stood against that giant of yours."

"And would you really have turned us over to the authorities, seen that we all hanged?"

He fell silent, biting his lower lip thoughtfully. Then he raised his chin defiantly and said, "I can't lie about it. Yes, that was my intention."

Feeling that the perfect moment had arrived, Lucy spoke up boldly. "I'd like you to know that I didn't fall in with the bunch of thieves, tricksters, horse traders, or whatever you like to call them, entirely of my own free will.

"I was riding alone at night and I was set upon in an isolated spot and captured. For various reasons, I could not get away from them. I was as much their victim as, now, I am yours."

She faced him as defiantly as he faced her. She tried hard not to blink or let her gaze waver as his grey, inscrutable eyes held hers.

Finally, he broke off the contest, looked away and said, thoughtfully, "I think I believe you."

Lucy felt weak with relief. So there was some hope for her. Maybe, if he would let her tell the full story, then perhaps there was some way in which he could help her.

All at once he seemed to notice it was raining, and stepped into the shelter of the stable, next to Lucy. He stayed a little apart from her, as if trying to retain some shreds of dignity. Taking his silence as encouragement to carry on, Lucy found herself explaining the events that had led up to her capture on the moor.

She deliberately withheld the information about the so-called wedding she had been forced to undergo. An inner voice was urging her not to reveal to Philip that she was soiled goods. Instead, she gave him the impression that she had remained virtuous despite Rory's constant pestering, and that it was relief, not jealousy, that she had felt that morning on discovering him with the girl in the inn.

When she told him of her plan to steal his fifty guineas and use it for lodgings and a horse, he let out a peal of laughter.

"You silly girl. Do you really think I would have given it to you? Did I really seem that much of an ass to you yesterday?"

Lucy didn't dare say "Yes," so she contented herself with the tactful, yet enigmatic, "I had my doubts."

Philip frowned. "I can see that you are in considerable distress and trouble, girl. Still, although your plight touches me, I feel I cannot go back on the solemn promise I made to myself to put an end to all this crooked horse dealing.

"It is still within my power to end not just the livelihood, but the lives of you and your cronies. However, I do believe, after what you have just said, that you are an innocent victim of circumstance."

Lucy felt enormous relief, yet instinctively she knew that there would be a price to pay. Philip Darwell was obviously no spineless, effete upper-class wastrel, whatever Rachel may have said. She had an idea that he was about to strike some kind of bargain with her. Would it mean giving her body to him? Would she be forced to betray Pat, Smithy and Rory? What was she going to have to do in return for his sparing her life?

But Lucy's curiosity was not to be assuaged. Philip Darwell seemed unwilling to reveal what was going on in his mind. Instead, he smiled grimly.

"Come with me," he said, propelling her out of the stables and across the courtyard. "You're going to stay a while at Darwell Manor."

Chapter Twelve

The ground floor room was almost bare. The carpet must have been at least a hundred years old, Lucy thought, and the scuffed floorboards beneath it could be glimpsed through the moth holes. The bed and the giant oak cabinet in one corner were ornately carved with a matching leaf pattern and the same family crest Lucy had noticed above the front doorway of the Manor. The whole house spoke not of austerity, but of grandeur faded to a genteel poverty.

A housemaid had brought in some logs and lit a fire and Lucy felt her convulsive shivering starting to ease. The window was set into two feet of solid grey stone and opened onto a balcony overlooking a stretch of parkland. Once, it must have been beautiful, for the trees outside were set in straight rows flanking a wide avenue, now a wilderness of fallen branches and tangled undergrowth. Through the driving rain, Lucy spied a glitter of water beyond the trees and some remnants of ancient statuary – or were they just tree stumps covered in ivy?

Once, she thought, fine lords and ladies must have strolled arm in arm down that avenue, to dawdle by the fountains while musicians played on the flat lawn outside the orangery. In her mind, she cleared the tangled weeds and dead branches, plucked the fallen leaves and coarse grasses from the lawn and restored the fallen masonry at the foot of the walls.

Then, having tidied the garden, she set about revitalizing the heart of the crumbling mansion in her imagination, covering the naked walls with paintings and tapestries, placing an ornamental table here, a vase there, adding carpets, cushions and brocades in rich, glowing colours. Then she peopled it, imagining the conversations, the intrigues and romances, the fine clothes, sweet music and rich, delicious food, food fit for their monarch George 1V himself.

So lost was she in her fantasies that she did not hear the maid re-enter the room and jumped when she felt the light touch on her elbow.

"Sorry, miss. The young master said I was to bring you dry clothes. I'm afraid it's not very fashionable, but then, you see, it's one of my own. Made it myself, miss."

Lucy stared at her, and at the simple grey dress lying over her arm, a cotton chemise draped beneath it. The woman was about sixty, with a lined face and thin, greying hair scraped into a bun. She looked as if she had seen hungry days, but there was an air of contented resignation about her and her seamed mouth was smiling with pride as she proffered the dress.

Lucy took the garment and examined it closely. Although the material was simple homespun wool, the stitching was so fine as to be almost invisible, the sleeves perfectly set into the armholes and the waist gathered into soft pleats that fell the full length of the skirt.

"It's beautiful."

A smile lit the woman's face, making her brown eyes dance. It was just like turning on a lamp. She must have been pretty once, thought Lucy.

"I shall be proud to wear it."

"The young master said that, after you were dressed, you should join him for luncheon in the banqueting hall. I will show you the way."

Lucy could not resist asking a question. "You said 'the young master'. Does this mean the old Earl is still alive?"

"Yes, miss, although he's failing. These days he never leaves his bed. Matthew – that's my husband – sees to him. He won't have a woman near him since the mistress passed away. My advice to you is stay on the ground floor of this house and never venture upstairs where he and the young master sleep."

"Why?"

"The Earl is frail. The shock of seeing a stranger would be bad for him. He was once such a fine man, but the death of his wife changed all that."

The maid's eyes darkened as though she were reliving a sad memory, then she resumed her composure and began assisting Lucy to remove her wet garments. When Lucy took off her cloak, revealing the ragged tears in the dress, the woman tutted and asked Lucy's permission to mend the damage, which Lucy gladly gave.

"Will you be staying long, miss?" she asked. "I'll try and finish the sewing tonight, but if Matthew insists we cannot spare the candle, I'll have to carry on tomorrow. I'll rise before dawn and –"

Lucy cut through her breathless promises. "I think I shall be here for a while, a few days at least. You will have plenty of time to finish the work. I'm very grateful."

The dress was a little large but at least it was warm, for which Lucy was grateful. She remembered that she was still wearing the trinket that Rory had bought her at the fair. She knew she should have hurled it across the field to follow the earring, but it was the only piece of jewellery she possessed, so she was loath to part with it. Not only that, but every time she touched it, she thought wistfully of how much she had loved Rory then. There were some memories that not even the cruellest treatment could destroy.

She was about to lift it from inside the dress and let it rest against the grey wool, to give her neckline a touch of decoration, when something stopped her. She was in an Earl's house. Even if he and his son were now living in reduced circumstances, there must have been a time when they had known real gold and real jewels. She didn't want to stand before them wearing the kind of bauble a scullery maid might have sported. Although she couldn't match the Darwells in lineage, her father was wealthier than they, and Lucy had a well-developed sense of good taste. So the necklace stayed hidden inside her bodice.

Now the maid was brushing her hair, trying to smooth out the wet tangles. Lucy bore the pain patiently as the woman tackled each knot in turn, knowing full well that she could do it much quicker herself. But the maid was a good woman and Lucy had no desire to hurt her or rob her of her pride in her handiwork.

As her chestnut ringlets were tugged this way and that, Lucy asked curiously, "What happened to the young Earl's mother?"

"It was when the baby was born, miss. She lost too much blood and wasted away. The master never got over it."

There was an odd restraint in her voice. Lucy wondered at it, but dismissed it as imagination.

"If he was motherless, who brought him up?" she asked.

"At first there was the Countess of Harringford, the Earl's sister. The Earl was overseas on a long campaign and she hired a wet nurse and took Philip to her own home for two whole years, until the Earl came back and she found herself with child.

"Then the young master was brought back here and Matthew and I did our best for him. He thought of me as his mother, until the Earl overheard him calling me Mama one day and forbade it. He had a governess and a nurse then, until the Earl started to lose his money and they had to leave. But I'm talking too much."

She looked at Lucy as if begging her forgiveness, then confessed, "I was a terrible chatterbox when I was young. Matthew could never get me to stop talking. And now, apart from Cook, it's so rare that I get the chance to talk to another woman."

She stopped, her hand flying to her mouth. "I do beg your pardon, miss. For all I know, you might be a lady yourself. The young master didn't tell me."

"Don't worry, er …" Lucy raised an enquiring eyebrow.

The grey-haired maid quickly provided the information: "It's Martha, miss. I'm the housekeeper, the maid and just about everything else, miss."

"Oh really, Martha. Call me 'miss' if you must, but I would prefer to be addressed as Lucy." She had warmed to this woman, who could possibly become both friend and ally to her. "Regrettably, I'm not a lady, a countess or even a duchess – I'm just plain Lucy Swift." Not McDonnell. Definitely not that.

The fire had dried her hair. Martha brought her a looking glass and Lucy was pleased to see the flush that the heat of the fire had brought to her cheeks and the gleam on her clean hair. The shade of the dress was maybe a little drab, but her own natural, vivid colouring overcame it. She now felt ready to face Philip and she asked Martha to lead the way.

The corridor was uncarpeted and Lucy's footsteps echoed until, in her heavy boots, she fancied she sounded like a whole army on the march. She told Martha and they both giggled, until the maid put a finger to her lips and intimated that they were drawing near the banqueting hall.

Martha went ahead and opened a door. Lucy walked past her and found herself standing at the top of a flight of wooden steps leading down to the scantily carpeted floor of a huge rectangular room. Tattered remnants of flags, along with the mounted heads of magnificently antlered deer, adorned the dark-panelled walls and at one end of the room was a long stained-glass window bearing the now familiar family crest. Below it, a collection of ancient lances were crisscrossed in an orderly pattern.

As she gazed round her, fascinated, she felt her eyes being drawn to the centre of the room, where an enormous wooden table bearing two branched candlesticks, their candles lit against the dimness of the day, dominated the floor. Two places were set, but no one was yet seated.

In the great hearth, a towering log fire roared and crackled, sending skeins of red sparks shooting up into the dark chimney. Lucy was surprised that there was no smell of dampness or mustiness in the vast hall and said as much to Martha, who informed her that keeping a fire burning in the hall throughout the winter was one of her master's few extravagances.

A faint creak sent Lucy's eyes scanning the room. She sensed a movement and found it. The tall figure of Philip was silently poised in a doorway at the far end of the hall, just to one side of the ornamental window.

As she watched, he descended a flight of stairs similar to the ones on which she was standing, stood by one of the set places at the table and beckoned to her. Feeling unaccountably nervous, Lucy began to descend the stairs.

Then Philip's voice rang out: "Stop!"

Lucy felt a hot blush mounting to her cheeks as she sensed his eyes inspecting her. His next words made her redden still more.

"That dress! Terrible! It just doesn't suit you. Martha!" The hunched woman scurried to Lucy's side. "You know where Mother's things are. Find her something better. She looks like a peasant in that rag of yours."

"Sorry," whispered Lucy in Martha's ear, as they retraced their earlier journey down the corridor. She was furious with Philip, not only for the way in which he had made her feel insulted, as if she were an object, an article of furniture maybe, which had to be draped to suit him, but also for upsetting the good-hearted Martha. She saw the stricken look on Martha's face and smarted for her. Why did Philip have to be so cruel?

A stirring of fear revisited her. If he could be this unkind to the woman who had brought him up from a small child, what could he have in mind for her? The memory of his behaviour in the stable came back to her and she shuddered, but then recalled how different he had been in those moments when he had dropped his guard. He was an enigma, a completely unpredictable man, and she was, unfortunately, absolutely at his mercy.

Back in her room, Lucy gave in to a bleak wave of loneliness, the first she had experienced since leaving home. She missed the cheery and loving company of Rory. Doubtless he was in some roadside inn by now, revelling in the company of a slut. Lucy winced and thrust the thought away. She was not going to think of him impressing another with his stories, pressing another with his body. An excruciating, infuriating pang of desire stabbed her at the thought of Rory's naked, virile body.

Luckily, at that moment there was a light tap at the door and Martha entered, carrying a swathe of blue material that brushed the floor. As she lifted it and shook it out, Lucy gasped at the magnificence of an old-fashioned but exquisite dress made of gleaming, light-catching silk draped with lace of a paler shade, and worked with beads and ruffles on the low-cut bodice.

"I can't wear that!" exclaimed Lucy worriedly. Not only was it too grand and too old for her, being more suited to a titled lady of at least twenty-five, but Lucy feared the effect on Philip of seeing her clad in a gown which had once graced his dead mother.

"But Master Philip said I was to give you –"

"I don't care what Master Philip says. I am not wearing that gown. Take it away. If he insists on lending me something that belonged to his mother, then please find me something simpler and more suitable. I may be dining in a grand house, but I'm just an ordinary young girl, not a dowager duchess! And anyway –" she lowered her tone confidingly – "I'd much rather wear that dress of yours than all this finery."

Martha looked pale and anxious. "Cook has the food all ready and the young master has a fine temper when he's aroused. You've no need to take my advice but I'm giving it with the best of intentions. Wear this one and keep Master Philip happy."

"Oh, all right, if I must," sighed Lucy wearily. She felt very hungry and if it meant gliding to the luncheon table in a twenty-year-old ball gown, then glide she would, although she would feel utterly ridiculous.

Martha had applied some powder to the bruises on her neck so that they no longer showed. Lucy knew she was curious as to how the injuries came about, but she felt that, at this stage in their short acquaintanceship, she could hardly tell her that they had been inflicted by Martha's "young master."

As Lucy descended the stairs into the banqueting hall for the second time, she felt the heat in Philip's eyes as they looked her up and down. She reached for the platter of freshly cooked lamb but the sound of someone clearing their throat just behind her caused her to withdraw her hand.

"Allow me, miss." A man in servant's uniform took the serving dish from her and, with impeccable manners, proceeded to serve meat, vegetables and gravy to both Philip and Lucy.

Bowing his head to his master, their serving man apologized for not having been there earlier, having been out chopping wood. Lucy realized that he must be Martha's husband Matthew, a pleasant-looking man with an erect bearing, silver hair and an engaging smile.

Philip forgave him and explained to Lucy that servants were in poor supply in their household due to the Darwells' straitened circumstances and that each was expected to do several jobs. So that was why the gardens looked so abandoned, Lucy thought. With so many roles to fulfill, Matthew had to neglect something as there simply weren't enough hours in the day. In any case, it would take a whole team of gardeners working full-time to keep the estate looking well-tended.

"I gathered that," she replied, "from what I overheard of the conversation between yourself and, er, Rachel."

She gave a sideways glance across the table. Philip's hair was glinting in the firelight. He caught her eye and remarked, rather bitterly, "Yes. Rachel. The girl I was to marry." He sighed heavily. "That's where you're going to help me."

A forkful of meat paused on its way to Lucy's mouth. Perhaps he wanted her to act as a go-between, passing messages and apologies to Rachel and negotiating between them. Alas, she was not destined to play Cupid, as Philip's explanation revealed.

"If you overheard our conversation, you will probably have gathered what has happened. My father was, as Rachel so rightly pointed out, extremely foolish. He had no talent with cards and he could easily be tricked by unscrupulous people like Rachel's father. I begged him to stop gambling but he wouldn't listen. He said gaming was his only pleasure in life now that my mother was gone."

"Why did he never marry again?" asked Lucy, thinking that a man with a title and a manor house and all the accoutrements the Earl of

Darwell must once have had, would have been a pretty catch for any young lady.

Philip sighed and she wondered if she had overstepped the mark with her question, but he was quick to answer. "He was devoted to my mother, Lady Eleanor," he explained. "She was very beautiful and, they say, gentle, kind and accomplished, too. Everyone loved her, as Martha will tell you.

"My father wrapped himself in a solitary world after she died. He didn't think of the future. Even now, his mind dwells in the past. I've heard him talk to my mother as if she is there with him in the room. That's why losing the money and the house didn't mean anything to him. He was an old man, destined to die soon. He didn't think about his son being left with nothing to inherit.

"The one thing I cannot understand is why he gambled my mother's jewels. I would have thought they would have been more precious to him than either money or property."

"Do you love Rachel?"

Philip froze in the act of helping himself to another potato, Matthew having left the room to fetch more firewood.

He sat in silence for a few moments, as if battling with his conscience, then answered finally, "No. I admire her, I respect her, but I don't love her. She's cold –" *As you are cold*, thought Lucy – "and she has a cruel, callous streak in her like her father has. I've seen him lash a dog to death with his riding crop just because it had chewed a boot.

"No, it would have been purely a marriage of convenience. Hardcastle desperately wants a title for his daughter. I will inherit my father's on his death, but that is when Hardcastle will seize Darwell Manor. He kindly allowed us to continue living here until that day arrives.

"I want to keep this house. I love it. It's been in my family for three hundred years, although it's been remodelled several times, and bits added here and there."

His eyes sparkled as he talked about his home, bringing a warmth to his expression which softened his angular features and made him look younger and slightly vulnerable. Lucy found herself reminded of her brother Geoffrey, who had possessed the same shade of hair, though his face was more rounded.

"So, by marrying Rachel, you would be able to carry on living here in perpetuity and she would have gained a title, thus pleasing everybody." Lucy's words were a statement of fact and Philip nodded. "By losing Rachel, you've lost Darwell Manor."

She pushed her plate aside, feeling replete. Philip had also stopped eating and was looking at Lucy as if trying to make up his mind whether or not to say something. Her stomach tensed as she remembered that she was not just his luncheon guest, but his prisoner.

Briefly, she wondered where Rory was, and whether Pat and Smithy had moved on to the next town yet. If only she could get a message to them, to warn them. Maybe Martha …

Then Philip spoke. "Lucy Swift, you have impressed me as a girl of courage and spirit."

Lucy looked at him, startled. What could this be leading up to?

"After my father played his last game of cards against Hardcastle, in which he lost Darwell Manor and was forced to hand the deeds over to that obscene old ale-sack, I went into the study where they had been playing and I found –" he fished around in a pocket and brought out an object that looked like a playing card, – "this."

He handed it to Lucy. In the gloomy room, it looked just like an ordinary ace of clubs with a pattern on the back.

She handed it back to Philip with a puzzled expression. "I can't see anything odd about it."

He rose from his seat and came round the table to Lucy's side.

"Here," he said, turning the card over. "You'll have to look extremely closely but, just by this red design in the corner … Can you see it?"

His index finger pointed to the spot and Lucy bent her head to examine it. There, to one side of the swirling pattern, was a tiny marking in a different shade of red. She looked up at Philip, sudden comprehension in her eyes. "You mean …?"

"Yes. Every single one of his cards is marked in some way. I have visited his house since and stolen a good look at each of his packs of cards. If you didn't know what you were looking for, you'd miss it, but I knew what to expect and this is what I found. I'm surprised the old cheat has got away with it for so long. Yet he boxes clever and makes sure his phenomenal wins are sprinkled with a few losses, so that his successes could, by a slight stretch of the imagination, be attributed to luck."

"Isn't there anything you can do? I mean, is there no one to whom you could expose this trickery?"

Philip shook his head. Striding to and fro in front of the fire, his hands clasped behind his back, he seemed to be considering how to reply.

"This is a private matter," he said at length. "Hardcastle has many influential friends. All I want is to recover what is rightfully mine. And I want you to help me do it."

"How?" Lucy half rose in her chair, gripping the edge of the table. A pang of anxiety stabbed her and she tightened her grip on the table. "What is it you want me to do?"

He paused in his stride. "It won't be easy," he said, looking at her warningly.

"It has to be easier than the alternative," muttered Lucy drily, picturing herself swinging from a gallows.

"I want the deeds to the house back," he announced abruptly. His chin came up and he stared at Lucy almost defiantly, as if challenging her to play the weak woman and whimper that it was too much to ask of her.

He looked surprised when she responded quite calmly, "And how do you propose I do that?"

Philip fetched a wine decanter from a side table and filled the two glasses that were standing by their plates. Lucy reached her hand halfway to her glass, then withdrew it as she saw that Philip was not yet drinking.

"In answer to your question," he replied, his face resuming its usual stern expression which reminded Lucy once more of her precarious position in his household, "what I propose is this – that you take up the position of personal maid to Rachel Hardcastle, then find a way of stealing back the deeds."

Chapter Thirteen

If a battalion of mounted cavalry had, at that moment, ridden their horses right through the wall and into the banqueting hall, Lucy could not have been more thunderstruck. To steal into somebody's house and take something was one thing. That quite appealed to her sense of daring. But what he was proposing was, quite frankly, outrageous and, she felt, way beyond her powers to carry out.

"I ... a maid?" It was an insulting suggestion, implying that he thought her of lowly birth and that this position was befitting of her station in life. "I can't... I wouldn't know how." She bit her lip in anger.

"Don't forget, it's that or your life," reminded Philip.

At his sharp words, Lucy's wits returned. "Have you thought that perhaps she saw enough in the stable to be able to recognize me?"

"It was dark in there and besides, you were struggling and your hair was all over your face. The only thing she got a good view of was my back."

"How do you know she is even in need of a personal maid?"

Philip flung back his head and laughed, showing even white teeth. "Rachel is always in need of a maid. It's no sinecure working for Rachel Hardcastle. The duties are, to say the least, arduous.

"But you shouldn't have to stay for long. If you leave after four weeks, you'll be just another in a long succession of girls who, unable to stand working for Rachel, have done precisely the same thing.

Rachel's mother is a kind woman; she always gives them a reference. She knows only too well what her daughter is like."

"But I've never been a maid before. How am I supposed to get a reference saying I'm a good, honest, trustworthy lady's maid? And what if someone has heard of my father and recognizes my name?"

The more Lucy thought about it, and the more she recalled Rachel's imperious tones, the less she liked the idea. As for stealing ... Suddenly, she remembered Emperor and was forced to admit to herself that she was quite capable of theft so long as her conscience was clear.

"Leave the arrangements to me," said Philip. "I am quite sure my aunt in London, Lady Clarence, will oblige. She is in my confidence and is quite *au fait* with the situation."

"Just supposing for a minute that I am given the position, which I think is highly unlikely ..."

"Nonsense, they're desperate for someone," put in Philip.

"As I was saying," continued Lucy, "supposing they do take me on. What then? I have no idea of what these deeds look like or where the papers are kept, so how am I supposed to get them back?"

Philip pulled his chair out from the table and carried it round, replacing it next to Lucy's.

He pushed aside the dishes and cleared a space and then, dipping his finger in his untouched wine, began to draw on the table top the interior layout of Rokeby Hall.

"Here is the entrance and here, the corridors leading to the drawing-room. The dining-room is there. Here's the study, and there, to the right of the study door, is the main staircase."

Lucy nodded. She had a good visual memory and was already picturing herself walking towards those stairs, which would be broad and curving to allow the graceful passage of a wide, flowing ball gown. She forced herself out of her fantasy as Philip started to draw a different plan.

"Now, this is the map of the upstairs rooms. The servants' quarters are all at the back, over here. This fork represents the main corridor on the first floor. Rachel's bedroom is here."

He picked up a silver salt cellar and placed it close to the edge of the table. Lucy wondered how many times he had entered that room himself – if the frosty-sounding Rachel had permitted him to, which Lucy doubted very much.

"There is an empty guest room here, next to Rachel's. There is Rachel's mother's dressing-room and bedroom and here –" he dropped a fresh blob of wine onto the table-top – "is the master bedroom where George Hardcastle sleeps. His dressing-room connects with his wife's."

His sleeve touched her arm as he made some additions to his diagram. She gave a slight shiver and wasn't sure why. Philip took a handkerchief and mopped up his tracings. Dipping his finger in the glass once more, he began a fresh drawing.

"This is Hardcastle's bedroom. Bed here, dresser there, bureau, chest, door leading to dressing-room here. He keeps the key to the bureau in the oak chest over here by the window. There is a small ledge inside and the key is on it."

"How do you know that?" asked Lucy wonderingly. Philip just smiled and continued.

"Inside the bureau on the right-hand side there is a small drawer with a brass handle. That is where he keeps the deeds, not only to his own house, but to some farm cottages he owns, a property in London and ..." he paused, "Darwell Manor."

"And does he keep this drawer locked?" inquired Lucy, thinking how very complicated it all seemed.

"Unfortunately, yes. He always carried the key about his person, usually in a pocket inside his waistcoat."

"How am I supposed to get hold of it?" Stealing a key out of a chest was one thing, but having to be a pickpocket required a sleight of hand which Lucy didn't possess.

"That, my dear, is a problem you will have to solve. All I can do is get you into the house. Once you are there, you will have to think up your own plan for acquiring the key and the deeds."

"And once I have given you the deeds, will you let me walk out of this house a free woman? If I am to go to so much trouble for you, I don't want to think that you are likely to change your mind and hand me over to be hanged!"

This awful thought had only just occurred to her, together with the remembrance of that cold side of Philip's personality which she knew was never far from the surface. Perhaps he was not to be trusted at all. Then she felt a sudden soft touch on her hair. She flinched in shock and he immediately pulled his hand away as if from a scorching candle flame.

"Forgive me," he muttered. "Those ringlets of yours are so tempting, especially with the firelight shining on them, turning them into copper flames and that blue becomes you."

Furious about her sudden desire to be kissed by him, Lucy dismissed the thought and scowled. He wasn't going to get round her with sweet, poetic words. "And I suppose my body looked tempting to you in the stable this morning!" she snapped.

She regretted her words immediately when she saw the expression that came over Philip's face; that closed, cold, disdainful look she was getting to know so well.

He got to his feet. "This is a business transaction, Miss Swift. You fulfill your side of the bargain and I shall fulfill mine. And if you fail ... "

Leaving this unvoiced threat echoing through the lofty hall, he bounded up the staircase, slammed the door and was gone, leaving Lucy sitting there alone in her borrowed finery, wondering what she should do now.

Her solitude lasted a mere few seconds before Matthew appeared, silently as ever, and began to clear away the dishes. Lucy suddenly remembered the mare she had brought with her that morning and asked Matthew if he knew anything about it.

"She's been stabled, miss. Saw to it myself. She in foal?"

His honest brown eyes gazed searchingly at Lucy, making her wonder just how much he knew. Deciding that honesty was the best policy, she shook her head.

"Didn't think so. Way she bolts her food, she be just filled up with air, like. Had 'un like that myself – oh, near twenty years ago now.

Used to bloat out like a nine-month-gone woman. Ye'd fasten the girth, like, then be reet sorry ye did, for half an hour later, ye'd find your saddle slipping round her belly and yourself on the floor!"

Lucy joined in his chuckles. She had witnessed the mare play precisely that trick on Rory. He had landed with a crash on his backside in a patch of nettles, amidst guffaws from Pat and Smithy.

She wondered if Philip really was going to try and find them and expose their trickery. Maybe he was riding down to Pendleton at this very moment. Part of her, the bitter, hurt side, wanted to see Rory punished. How did any man deserve to live after what he had done? But not hanging; that was too slow and too cruel.

Matthew cleared his throat. He had finished tidying the table and was asking Lucy if she wished to be escorted to her room. She accepted gratefully.

It was only late afternoon, but she felt heavy-headed and sleepy, although neither she nor Philip had drunk their wine. Had he poured it out intending to toast the success of her mission? If so, her hasty words had spoiled the moment. She hoped her flash of temperament had not persuaded him to change his mind. She would sooner act the part of a maid and a thief than lose her life, even if that life hardly seemed worth the living any more.

* * *

Lucy awoke to find Martha tending the fire. She had dozed off lying on top of the bed and her beautiful dress was crushed out of shape.

Martha glanced at it disapprovingly. "If you were planning a rest, miss, you should have told Matthew to ask me for a nightgown," she said.

"I'm sorry," Lucy replied. "I didn't mean to. It's just that … well, I had a rather bad experience earlier today which upset me a lot and I think I must be quite exhausted."

Martha shot her a sharp look. "Is that how you came by those bruises?"

"No. Well, actually, I had two unfortunate experiences this morning …"

Lucy suddenly wondered what Martha must think of her. She had come into the house a total stranger, ragged as a tinker, bruised like a slut – and, for all Martha knew, that was precisely what she was. Perhaps she should explain.

"I'm not what you think I am, Martha. I come from a good family," she began.

"I never doubted it, Lucy." Martha spoke kindly. She reached out and patted Lucy's hand. "You're young enough to be my daughter, you know. You don't have to tell me anything, but if you want to, you'll find I have a sympathetic ear."

Lucy gestured to her to come and sit beside her on the bed. Martha obeyed and soon Lucy found herself confiding everything about her home life, about how she had come to run away and be captured by the horse traders.

The only thing she found herself unable to tell Martha about was her moorland marriage to Rory. She felt the older woman would be unable to understand how she had accepted it so willingly, or how attracted she had been to Rory. Better to let her think him a vagabond who had abducted her and then betrayed her with another woman. Let the sacred ritual remain her own secret.

As she had expected, Martha's eyes flashed with fury when Lucy described how she had seen Rory coming out of the tavern whore's room.

"Did you go for him? Is that how you came by those marks?" she asked eagerly.

Lucy shook her head.

Suddenly, a look of understanding dawned in Martha's eyes. "Master Philip was angry about the mare?"

Lucy nodded gratefully. So they did know. This would save her a lot of awkward explaining. "It wasn't my idea to sell him that horse. It shouldn't have been my job to deliver it, but there was nobody else."

"Yet you knew the horse was not in foal?" Martha's inquiring glance was keen.

"Yes," Lucy said gently, "I knew. But there was nothing I could do – and besides, with no home to go back to and Rory gone, I needed the money." She gave a guilty smile.

"I see." For a moment Lucy thought Martha was about to censure her. She was relieved when the housemaid put a hand on her arm and said, "You poor lamb."

Something broke inside Lucy then. Maybe it was Martha's gentleness, which reminded her of her own mother, or her warm, sympathetic tone of voice. Whatever it was, she suddenly found herself sobbing uncontrollably and turning blindly to Martha for comfort. The motherly woman wrapped her arms around Lucy and rocked her, while all the grief and shock she had suffered welled up and poured out of her in a series of racking sobs and flooding tears.

When she could cry no more, Martha offered her a handkerchief and Lucy blew her nose hard and mumbled her thanks.

"You stay here and rest," ordered Martha. "I'll fetch you up a nice, refreshing drink from the kitchen." Lucy smiled weakly at her and slumped back against the pillows. "I'll find you a nightgown, too."

"And would it be too much if I asked to borrow that dress again, the one you made?"

The delight in Martha's face made her request truly worthwhile.

Martha was gone a long time. When she returned, bearing the clothing she had promised, she informed Lucy that the "young master" had gone out and that she would be dining alone that evening.

"Couldn't I eat with you and Matthew? I'd like that," Lucy asked.

But Martha immediately rejected this idea, telling her that if Philip were to find out, he would be angry. "Walls have ears," she added darkly and Lucy felt it best not to press the subject, while wondering what she meant.

So, clad in the warm, homespun dress, she ate a modest repast of chicken, vegetables and fruit in her room, worrying all the while about

Philip. She knew she shouldn't care about the fate of her erstwhile companions, but they had been quite kind to her and she wished them no harm, even Rory.

She asked Martha for something to read to pass the time and Martha confessed that, as she herself couldn't read, she didn't know one book from another.

"Just fetch me anything," Lucy informed her and Martha reappeared after a short while with a leather-bound volume which turned out to be most entertaining as it dealt with local myths and folklore and even had a chapter about witches, which interested Lucy greatly.

She had no idea how much time had elapsed, but the candles in her room had burned low by the time she heard voices coming from somewhere near her door. She recognized them as Philip's and Matthew's, but, strain her ears as she might, she could not make out what they were saying. Shortly after that, she blew out all but one candle, donned her nightgown and prepared herself for bed.

No sooner had she snuggled down beneath the warm covers than she was roused by a tapping at her door. She held her breath, frightened to utter a sound and checked the whereabouts of the nearest candlestick in case she needed to beat an intruder about the head.

The tapping sounded again and then, to her horror, the door slowly began to creak open. Lucy gasped as a faint, spectral glow shone through the increasing gap in the doorway. She thought back to the book she had been reading earlier, about ghosts and corpse candles and was on the point of screaming.

Then she heard a voice calling in a low tone, "Lucy?" and saw the tall figure of Philip hovering in the doorway, a lantern in his hand. "Are you awake?" he added, in the same undertone.

"Yes," said Lucy, louder and more firmly than she had intended, causing Philip to start so that his lantern swung and sent shadows flickering across the ceiling.

"I just wanted to inform you that a messenger is at this moment on his way to my aunt in London. He should return with the reference within ten days."

Why had he disturbed her at night to tell her this? It could have waited until the morning. Lucy felt the flesh on the back of her neck begin to crawl with unease. He must have something else to tell her, something unpleasant. People were only roused from their beds at night for the delivery of bad news.

Her presentiment proved correct.

"I also think you should know," announced Philip formally, "that your old friend Rory McDonnell is dead."

Chapter Fourteen

They were all being so kind to her, Martha, Matthew, even Philip. For three days, Lucy could not get up at all and when she rose on the fourth day, Martha fussed round her, making sure she wrapped up warmly and drank a bowl of nourishing broth.

Philip had called in to see her several times on that dreadful first day, but she had been so lost in grief that she could not speak to him and, after several vain attempts at cheering her up, he had left, perhaps feeling helpless in the face of a woman's tears.

It wasn't until the third day that Lucy had felt sufficiently in command of herself to ask him to describe the circumstances of Rory's death. She wondered if Philip himself had killed him as part of his campaign to stamp out crooked dealings, but when Philip unfolded his tale, she felt that she believed him.

"I was down in Dudcott, doing some business there, when I heard a terrible commotion coming from an inn. All the townsfolk flocked to see what the fuss was, and I went along with them. I could hear a woman screaming, 'Murder, murder!' Then out rushed that giant of yours, blood all down his coat. Three men were hanging onto him, trying to restrain him.

"I called to a couple of soldiers who were shopping for supplies, to help halt the giant and they put down their kitbags and brought him to a stop, not without having to draw their swords. Once he was secured, I pushed through the crowd and went into the inn."

Lucy wasn't sure if she could bear to hear the next part of the story. To think of the man she had once loved so dearly lying dead, even his friends not having been able to protect him!

"The innkeeper was bending over the figure of a man lying on the floor," Philip continued. "It was the bearded young man I saw you with that day at Pendleton, without a doubt. Do you really want the details? They're not very pleasant."

"I want to hear everything – *everything*," pressed Lucy and without thinking, she added, "After all, he was my husband."

"Your *what*?" Philip's eyebrows shot up and she wished she could take her foolish, impulsive confession back. He stared at her and she remained silent, her heart hammering.

A masked look fell over his face as he continued. "He was sprawled on the floor as I said, and a knife was sticking from his back, an unusual-looking knife with a carved wooden handle."

"That's Pat's!" Lucy had seen that knife often during the weeks she had spent with the group. He took it everywhere with him, not just for protection but to use for cutting rope for halters, working stones out of the horses' hooves, even for spearing his food and eating it. But surely Pat wouldn't have … ?

Philip answered her question for her. "The innkeeper told me there had been a fight between Rory McDonnell and the big man."

"Pat," Lucy interrupted. "He's the one you call the giant. But why were they fighting?"

"If you'll just let me continue. It seems the disagreement concerned a horse and from what I gather, it was about that old nag you brought me. Pat accused Rory of delivering the mare as arranged and pocketing the money for himself."

"But the lad who was looking after the horses knows it was me who took her! Surely he would have told them?"

Suddenly, a terrible thought occurred to Lucy. Supposing the boy *had* told Rory? Rory might have felt guilty about his earlier behaviour and lied to Pat that it was he who had taken the horse. Rory might have died trying to protect her. She had as good as killed him with her own two hands!

She felt the blood drain from her face and the room started to spin around her.

"Lucy? Lucy, are you all right?" He was peering into her face.

"Yes, I'm all right," she replied woodenly. How could this cold, arrogant man understand the way she felt? Rory had been so full of life and laughter – and now he was dead. All because of her.

"What will happen now?" she whispered through numb lips.

"Pat will be hanged for murder, I expect. He has been taken off to prison in Manchester already. As for his accomplice, Smithy ... Well, he still has the remaining horses, I suppose, and could carry on the business, if it could be called that, on his own, or else he could join forces with some other rogues like himself. Though, from what I've witnessed, he isn't in the best of health."

"No," agreed Lucy, wondering if the frail little man would survive the winter.

Philip tactfully left her at this point and, once alone, Lucy sank into a dull torpor of misery, her hand clutching the little necklace Rory had given her as if it were a talisman which could erase the past and protect her from the events of the present. If only ...

* * *

By the fifth day, Lucy felt well enough to accept Philip's invitation to ride round his estate. Martha produced a faded green riding habit, another item from the wardrobe of the late Lady Eleanor, and lent Lucy her own warm cloak and, thus attired, Lucy mounted a chestnut hunter belonging to Philip and they set out to ride the boundary.

The horse gave Lucy a spirited ride, bucking and skittering in the freezing air, shying every time a bird or rodent rustled in the bushes. Several times Philip complimented her on her riding skill, and the exercise and the chill, windy weather brought a glow to her face which she knew became her. She thoroughly enjoyed the ride. Philip pointed out the local landmarks which could be viewed from the hill and talked about everything he would do with the grounds if he had enough money.

Finally, they paused by the ornamental lake and Lucy saw that the impression she had had on her first day had been correct; there were statues around the lake, badly in need of cleaning and repairing. She would have loved to tackle the job herself and mentioned this to Philip, who just laughed and said it was a job for a workman who didn't mind getting filthy.

The next few days were spent in similar fashion, riding, talking and dining together in the evening. Tactfully, Philip didn't mention Rory or the subject of their marriage and gradually, her grief lessened and she found herself enjoying Philip's company now that he had dropped his guard of icy formality.

On several occasions she caught herself looking at him admiringly. He was a good-looking man in a clean-cut, very English way which was so unlike Rory's unruly image and ruddy, outdoor complexion. He was an amusing, witty companion and his stories about London society and his cavalry experiences had her convulsed with mirth and almost forgetting both her recent bereavement and Philip's cruel treatment of her on their first meeting.

It was at night, when she was alone in bed, that sorrow and loneliness would steal over her. She would thresh around in what seemed like acres of empty space, longing for Rory's warm, strong arms to take her and hold her.

Sometimes she would imagine him lying next to her in the darkness. Her hand would trace his outline, her lips move towards the place where his lips should be and find nothing except unsettling emptiness. Then the tears would come again. She would cry herself to sleep and next morning, Martha would tut at the dampness of the pillow and the blotchiness of Lucy's face, and bring her warm water to which she had added a few drops of essence of rosemary, to soothe and clear Lucy's skin.

One morning she awoke to find a strange, cold, white light in the room. Pulling back the curtains she found the whole world covered in crisp snow. A blackbird was trilling on the tree outside her window, the only sound in a muffled, dead universe. Then, with a harsh, warning *chak-chak*, the bird flew off and Lucy heard men's voices downstairs.

Dressing quickly, in case the disturbance concerned her, she lingered in her room until Martha knocked to bring her some breakfast – new-laid eggs lightly scrambled, fresh-baked bread and a glass of warm milk, which Lucy demolished ravenously. She always seemed to have a greater appetite in winter.

After finishing her meal, she wandered round the house. All thoughts of running away had left her now, although she could easily have done so. But that would have meant stealing another horse and heading who-knows-where, for Manchester or Liverpool maybe, with no money in her pocket and snow on the ground. Darwell Manor was beginning to feel almost like home and every day, she was relying more and more on Martha's friendship and Philip's company.

She paused by the door of the library, where the voices were coming from, and was about to walk by when the door was suddenly flung open. Lucy flattened herself against the wall, half hidden by a large cupboard. Through the gap between the back of the cupboard and the panelled wall, she could see Philip escorting another man in the direction of the vast marble hallway.

The library door had been left open and she could see a sheet of paper lying on the table. Calculating that it would be several minutes before Philip returned, she darted into the room and snatched it up. The beautiful script that covered the page in swirls of black ink was her false reference from Philip's aunt which declared that Lucy Skinner – *Skinner?* – had been an excellent and skilled maidservant.

With the shock of Rory's death and her depression of the last few days, plus her growing, grudging liking for Philip and their rides together, Lucy had completely forgotten about the purpose for which she was being kept at Darwell Manor, and she found she didn't at all like being reminded.

Passing her eye quickly down the page, she noted that the reason for her leaving was an inability to settle down in London, Lucy being country-born and bred. However, Lady Clarence had added, she was honest and dutiful, clean and trustworthy and could be relied upon to perform her tasks with speed and industry.

The reference was such a fanciful embroidery that Lucy found herself admiring the lady's artistry and regretting that she could not meet her, as she seemed highly intelligent and in possession of a lively sense of humour.

Replacing the letter exactly where she had found it, Lucy left the library and wandered on down the corridor, through the banqueting hall and into the long-neglected ballroom with its faded, cobwebbed hangings. Filled with spectral light reflected from the snowy ground outside, the ballroom was a haunted place of half-glimpsed figures, unfinished romances and a tingle in the air like the vibration from unheard violins.

Lucy knew it was only her imagination at work, but she loved to linger in the ballroom, looking out at the park from the huge windows which ran the whole length of one wall and opened onto a long, covered balcony from which one could descend, by way of stone steps, to the sloping lawn below.

As she stood dreaming by the window, shivering slightly in air that was so cold that she could see her breath floating before her, the sound of the imaginary violins in her head grew louder. Humming to herself, she began to move her body, letting her feet carry her in a waltz tempo out into the middle of the dusty floor. Closing her eyes, she imagined a partner guiding her, and she dipped and swayed and twirled until she had made a complete circuit of the room and found herself by the windows once more, whereupon she halted, panting and chiding herself for being silly.

She could still hear the echoing strings playing the dreamy, slightly wistful melody and she shook her head to wake herself up, but the sound carried on. It was only one violin, not many, and she had no idea where the music was coming from, but it filled her with terror.

Lucy had never seen a ghost but she believed in them all the same; and now it looked as if she was in the company of a shade from the past. She couldn't see anything, but at any moment she expected a man from another century to materialize, wearing strange, old-fashioned garb. Perhaps it was the Devil himself! The book she had read several nights earlier had mentioned that the Devil sometimes prefaced his appearance with the sound of a violin.

She began to tremble. What would she do if she were suddenly faced with a satanic vision? Make the sign of the cross? Recite the Lord's Prayer?

Speaking aloud, with all the conviction she could muster, Lucy began the first few words: "Our Father, who art in Heaven ..."

She had got as far as "Thy will be done ..." her voice growing shakier with every syllable, when peals of demonic-sounding laughter rang out and echoed around the empty room. He was here! The Devil! Any second now, she would see him, red-eyed and fork-tailed, and he would drag her off to his sulphurous underground pit to wreak terrible tortures on her!

No! He would not get her. Life suddenly returned to her limbs and, with a piercing shriek, Lucy flung herself towards the door, tearing her fingernails painfully in her efforts to wrench open the unyielding barrier between nightmare and safety. She scrabbled, pushed and pulled with all her strength, but it was jammed, or else locked from the other side, or perhaps held fast by some supernatural power.

When she realized she was trapped, she sank to the floor, eyes fixed in a challenging stare, willing whatever was in the room to go away and leave her alone. There was no sound at all now save that of the spasmodic rattling of the windows as they were buffeted by gusts of snow-bearing wind, but still Lucy remained there, tense and alert.

And then she heard it; a slow, muffled creak, followed by another, slightly louder. Footsteps ... but where were they coming from? A grey mist of terror formed in front of Lucy's eyes and the room seemed to recede and then return in waves of dimness and clarity. Still she could see no one and yet she felt as if she were being watched, an uncomfortable sensation which made her scalp crawl and the tiny hairs along her arms bristle like the fur of an angry cat.

The footsteps stopped, and the feeling of being observed grew stronger. Lucy's heart was thudding so hard that she could see the tiny, rhythmic movements of its palpitation in the fluttering material stretched across her breast. Out of the corner of her eye she glimpsed a movement. One of the frayed wall coverings was wafting as if in a draught – and a dark-clad man was standing in the centre of the ballroom floor, surveying her!

All she glimpsed before the rushing noise in her ears overwhelmed her like a dark tide, was his vague outline and the violin he held in one hand.

Slowly, dazedly, she became aware of a warm pressure against her lips and forehead. Then she heard her name being repeated over and over again. "Lucy, wake up. Lucy Swift, are you all right? Please wake up, Lucy."

She wasn't conscious of having willed her eyelids to open, but they did and she found she was gazing directly into the concerned grey eyes of Philip Darwell. As soon as he saw that she had recovered consciousness, a look of relief came over him and he placed an arm under hers to help her to her feet.

"I'm so sorry," he said. "I really do beg your pardon. I had no idea you would wander into this particular room when you did and I had no intention of scaring you."

"I – I thought you were a g-ghost," stammered Lucy, shivering with a mixture of fright and cold.

"Here, let me help you to the drawing-room. Martha can fetch you a drink to warm you up and steady those nerves of yours."

The Darwell Manor drawing-room had once been elegant and attractive. The room, of noble proportions like the rest of the house, was at the rear and looked out over an exquisitely laid-out rose garden which now, like the rest of Lancashire, lay hidden beneath a blanket of snow. A warm fire was crackling in the hearth and the heat of the mulled wine which Matthew had brought sent threads of fire burning through her right down to her toes.

She thanked Philip gratefully, then asked, out of sheer curiosity, "Do you often spend time in the ballroom?"

"Yes, as a matter of fact I do. I love the atmosphere there. Years ago, when my father still had money, we had some glorious times. Apparently, when my mother was still alive, the Darwell Manor balls were talked about all over the county. Relatives would come all the way from London specially to attend.

"My father carried on the tradition for a while after my mother's death, because everyone hoped it would help take his mind off his grief – and I think some hoped he would find himself a second wife from among the guests – but when I was about four or five, entertaining in our house gradually dwindled, partly through lack of money and partly because my father grew tired of the endless matchmaking that was being done on his account. However, I think my love of music dates back to those happy times."

"You play the violin very well," Lucy informed him, privately thinking that he could express his feelings far better through the well-tuned strings of the instrument than he could through his own vocal chords. "I couldn't see you when you were playing. Where were you?"

"Next time you enter the room, look way up towards the ceiling at the far end. You'll spot a small gallery there – 'the kissing gallery,' we used to call it, because couples would stray there from the dance floor and conduct their courting high up over the heads of their mothers and fathers and sometimes even their wives and husbands.

"There's a narrow staircase leading up to it which is concealed behind the tapestry next to the big, gilt-framed mirror. It's not a place you would find by accident. I, of course, have always known of it."

"I suppose there are a lot of hidden tunnels and secret hidey-holes in an old house like this?" Ever since childhood Lucy had nourished a secret dream in which she would discover such a passage and find hidden treasure at the end, but alas, the Swifts' farmhouse, being a mere sixty years old, held no such surprises.

"Yes, there are one or two," replied Philip, smiling at her sudden enthusiasm. "However, I hardly think you'll have time to explore them. I received the reference from Lady Clarence this morning."

Although she had already seen it for herself, she flinched inwardly. Did that mean he wanted her to leave immediately? She wasn't in the least bit prepared and she felt sad at having to terminate what was fast becoming a very pleasant existence. Everything seemed to be happening far too quickly.

Philip must have informed Martha already of Lucy's imminent departure, because the maid was waiting in her room with the dress in which Lucy had arrived, now neatly mended. It was wrapped up in a small bundle, from which protruded a scrap of brown material that Lucy recognized – it was the homely garment which Martha had made herself, the one Lucy had so admired.

"Martha! I can't take that, I mustn't. You've put so much work into it, so much love," Lucy exclaimed.

"That's why I want you to have it, my dove. You'll need it over at Rokeby Hall. It's a cold house, so they say."

The maid's slight wink indicated that her words held more than one meaning.

Feeling a rush of gratitude, Lucy hugged her. "Oh Martha, dear Martha, you've been so good to me all the time I've been here. I really don't want to leave in the slightest!"

"Then why must you? It's bitter weather. It must be something really important to force you out on such a day." The maid's flat statement held an unspoken question.

"It is," Lucy told her. "It's something I have to do for the young master. It must be done right away."

"I see. Well, I hope some good comes of it, for it's a bad day for a journey."

Martha resumed her bustling about and resisted Lucy's offer to change back into her old dress and return the velvet gown of Lady Eleanor's which she was wearing.

"The young master said as how you were to take it. We don't want Miss Rachel looking down that snooty nose of hers, do we?"

Martha hardly needed to spell out her obvious dislike of Philip's former betrothed. As Martha had met Rachel, Lucy ventured to ask, "What's she like?"

"Your face and figure would beat hers into a cocked hat. She's cold – cold as that snow outside and hard as an iron horse-shoe. The young master would have had full hands and an empty heart if he'd married that girl. I've not time for any of that Hardcastle crew, nor has my Matthew. They're mean and devious, sneaky as foxes in a thicket. Have as little to do with them as possible, that's my advice."

Lucy longed to be able to tell Martha the truth about her mission to Rokeby Hall, but she refrained, partly from fear in case Philip found out she'd been prattling his secrets to the maid, and partly because she knew the warm-hearted woman would be horrified and upset at the thought of her having to work for Rachel Hardcastle.

When at length she stepped into the trap driven by Matthew, which was to convey her down the snow-covered lanes to Rokeby Hall, Lucy felt like a martyr going to the stake. Her final vision of Darwell Manor was of a towering grey building, with Philip standing, dwarfed by the huge doorway, and Martha's anxious face peering from the library window.

Chapter Fifteen

"You little cat. You did that deliberately!"

Rachel pushed her face close to Lucy's and there was a mad, yellowish glint in her narrowed eyes. Suddenly, her hand lashed out and struck Lucy on the cheek. The force of the blow was, in itself, not so painful but the large emerald ring Rachel was wearing caught her on the cheekbone, drawing blood, as Lucy discovered when she raised a hand to her stinging face.

The girl was of an age with Lucy and, if it hadn't been for the mission she had given her word to fulfil (how could she forget Philip's dark words, "It's that or your life"?) Lucy would have struck her back. The girl was so coldly, deliberately spiteful and cruel that Lucy wondered if she were possessed by an evil spirit.

She had been there only three days and already they had been the longest, most unpleasant three days in her whole life. Nothing she could do was right in Rachel's eyes. No sooner had Lucy brushed her hair into shining golden splendour and twined it into ringlets with heated irons, than Rachel would twist her wrist painfully, as if trying to make her burn herself on the hot tongs, then rake her fingers through her locks, undoing all Lucy's careful work and insisting it was exactly the opposite to what she wanted.

She was the same over her clothes. "Fetch me my green dress," she would order imperiously. Lucy would go dutifully to the closet and bring Rachel the required garment, whereupon she would tear the dress from Lucy's hands, throw it on the floor like a child in a tantrum and fume, "Not that one, stupid, the peacock blue one."

"But you said ..." Lucy had soon learned not to use these words or, indeed, to argue with Rachel in any way. For disagreeing with the pale-eyed girl would bring an instant tongue-lashing down on Lucy's head, or even painful physical punishment; Rachel was not above picking up a riding whip and slashing at Lucy in fury for the slightest mistake.

Lucy stared at her bloodied fingers. She did not have the temperament to bear much of this kind of treatment, but ... *it's that or my life!*

Biting back words of reproof, Lucy picked up the hairbrush which she had dropped when Rachel hit her and recommenced dressing her hated mistress's hair. How she loathed her! The closer Christmas loomed, the more irritable Rachel appeared to become. Christmas Eve was in three days' time and on that night, a major ball was due to be held at Rokeby Hall, to which the gentry of many surrounding towns and villages had been invited.

As far as Lucy could ascertain, the main thing that was preying on Rachel's selfish mind was the wintry weather, which was preventing the best young beaux and dandies from coming up from London and spending the festive season at Rokeby Hall. She had done nothing but moan ever since the snow had set in and Lucy dreaded the thought of having to spend that most precious time of year, Christmas, in her disagreeable company.

As she brushed – as gently as possible so that Rachel couldn't accuse her again of pulling her hair – Lucy thought about her mother, all alone with nobody except Lucy's father to prepare the Christmas goose for. Even he would probably be drunk and unappreciative. For the first time since leaving home three months earlier, Lucy felt a sharp pang of homesickness and Rachel's golden hair blurred into a haze before her eyes as she thought of the sorrow and loneliness which must be eating at her mother's heart.

First her brother Geoffrey, and now herself. How could her mother bear it? Maybe she was ill, pining for her two missing children. Lucy longed with all her heart to be able to knock on that familiar door on

Christmas Day and bring a glow of happiness to her mother's care-worn features.

"Bitch! I've told you not to do that!" Rachel's elbow shot out and dug Lucy sharply in the midriff.

She felt she would reach forward and strangle the girl if she kept on at her in this way. No wonder all Rachel's other maids had given their notice, or else run away. Lucy hoped they had found better positions with kinder mistresses. At least they were properly trained maids. What was she to do, with no home to go to and nothing but a forged reference to her name?

By the time she slumped onto her hard, narrow bed that evening, Lucy felt weak and dizzy from exhaustion. Not content merely with striking and insulting her, Rachel had, in a fit of pique, hurled a small glass vase across the room. It had hit the wall, smashed to smithereens and Lucy had been required to get down on her hands and knees and pick up every sliver of glass so that Rachel would not cut her feet when walking about her room.

Lucy, however, had cut her finger painfully, whereupon Rachel had laughed and taunted her. She longed to be able to lay her hands on Philip's precious deeds so that she could walk away from Rachel's tyranny into freedom, but Hardcastle, with the vital key in his pocket, had been away on business in Manchester and was not expected home until Christmas Eve.

Lucy had not yet set eyes on Rachel's father but she had spoken briefly to her mother, meeting her first of all when she was interviewed for the position of lady's-maid. Lucy had been impressed by her. She was a tiny, dark-haired woman, as delicately made as a doll, totally different to her rangy, blonde daughter who, Lucy guessed, must surely take after her father.

Harriet Hardcastle spoke in a thin, silvery voice which was in perfect keeping with her dainty appearance.

"So you are Lucy. Lady Clarence speaks very highly of you. She sent me a letter to say she was giving you a good reference, and her recommendation is certainly good enough for me. I hope you will settle in well with us and join in the Christmas festivities we always provide for the servants. Maud will show you to your room, which you will share with Daisy, the assistant cook."

She had given Lucy a charming smile and passed her over to Maud who, Lucy guessed, was around thirty, with an unremarkable face and figure and kind brown eyes.

In turn, Maud had introduced Lucy to her roommate, Daisy, who was portly, greasy-haired and spotty and was possessed of a snore every bit the equal of Pat's, so Lucy could only snatch brief moments of slumber before being awoken by yet another gargantuan rumbling. Daisy was fussy, and a grumbler – and she also, Lucy discovered, had a liking for the bottle, which no doubt accounted for her surplus weight and the fumes of stout that hung heavily on the bedroom's air each night.

She was suddenly exposed to the chilly night air as Daisy turned over in bed with a great lurch and a loud belch, taking all the covers with her. She sighed resignedly and filched the counterpane which was lying loosely on the top of Daisy's heap of blankets and wound herself tightly in it. Before she fell into a dreamless sleep, she sent out a silent prayer that, over the festive period, an opportunity would present itself to acquire the deeds and free herself both from her slavery to Rachel and her obligation to Philip.

* * *

The following day Maud fell ill with a heavy cold and a fever. Harriet Hardcastle declared that she could not bear to have her near, not only because of her unsightly red eyes and streaming nose, but also because she had a dread of catching it, too. So Lucy was summoned at dawn to attend her.

When Rachel discovered that Lucy was not free to receive her orders and torments that day, she flounced into her mother's room and complained, "Really, Mother, I think this is very selfish of you. I need Lucy more than you do."

Then, apparently realizing that her mother was not at all impressed with her show of temperament, her sly personality at once underwent an astonishing change from spoilt child to honey-voiced wheedler.

"I do want to find myself another beau soon. Dear Mother, I know you want me to make a good marriage. Father told me that he might be bringing Lord Emmett back from London with him. You know how much I liked him when he visited us last Christmas, only he was betrothed to that dreadful woman Cecilia Monotony, or whatever her name was."

"Countess Monatova," put in her mother gently. "A very charming girl, as I recall, even if her English was not perfect."

"I didn't like her," continued Rachel, compressing her lips.

Had Lucy known Mrs Hardcastle better, she would have shot her a sympathetic look because she felt sure Rachel's mother found her only daughter a trial at times. However, feeling unsure of her ground, she kept her eyes modestly applied to her task of hunting for a missing garnet earring in one of Harriet's overflowing jewellery cases.

"I never cared a fig for Philip Darwell, anyway." Rachel's attempt to worm her way round her mother by sweet talk had obviously been abandoned. "He's got no money, and what use is an empty title? I never wanted to live in that crumbling mausoleum Darwell Manor, either. It's like a ... a ... " Rachel's feeble imagination groped for a simile and failed to find one.

Warming to the subject of Philip, Rachel proceeded to express her feelings about the way Philip Darwell had treated her. "Finding him in the stable with that – that twopenny slut! The shame of it!"

Lucy felt her face beginning to burn. How much had Rachel seen? If she put her mind to it, would she find something familiar about Lucy, something which would connect her to that particular incident?

"I have never been treated so grossly," Rachel continued. "It was not just the mere fact that he was being unfaithful to me, but she wasn't even a woman of quality! I could see that from her dress and from the broken-down nag she had for a mount."

A smouldering nugget of hatred flared in Lucy's heart.

"But Rachel dear, he wasn't expecting you. Men will be men, after all," protested her mother mildly, giving Lucy the impression that she had liked and sided with Philip.

"That's not the sort of man I want," Rachel retorted, with a flounce. "I want one who can think of no other woman but me!"

Lucy had found the missing earring but was delaying announcing the fact in order to hear anything else Rachel had to say about Philip. Not that she cared, she told herself, but it was, after all, quite fascinating to hear somebody one knew being gossiped about – quite apart from the fact that Rachel's remarks added yet more fuel to Lucy's loathing of the spoilt, spiteful girl who was continuing to extol her own virtues.

"I want a man who worships me, who will dote on me and give me everything I want and deserve. I want him to be completely satisfied with me so that he will have no need to seek another woman. That's the only reason they do it, you know, Mother," Rachel announced, fixing Harriet with gimlet stare. "Look at Father, for instance."

"Rachel! Mind your tongue." For such a frail-looking woman, Harriet could, when aroused, produce a sharp, stabbing tone of voice.

"It's what I think, so I'm going to say it. If you had not stopped sharing Father's bed all those years ago, he would have had no need to go galloping off to London and Manchester and all those other places he goes to."

"It's business, Rachel, purely business."

"That's what he tells *you*!" retorted Rachel impudently, not letting her mother butt in. "I know all about Susan in Liverpool, Ellen in St. Albans, Ettie in Covent Garden ... "

Lucy watched Harriet's face pale to a waxen shade and then flush with a crimson tide of fury. "Rachel! Cease these poisonous aspersions at once! If you were younger, I'd send you to your father for a good whipping!

"I would be pleased if you would keep your fantastical ideas to yourself and refrained from speaking of them in front of either myself or my servants. Go to your room." Harriet's slender frame was quivering with rage and nervous shock.

"I've seen the letters, the gifts, the bills, they're all among his papers. You can go and look too, Mother. *'To my dear Ellen, one hundred pounds in payment for the generosity of her warm heart.'* I saw that written down in his ledger, and lots more besides. Go and look, go and look!"

Rachel's strident, vinegary voice rose to a crescendo and she pirouetted triumphantly around her mother's room while Harriet clutched a chair-back, looking close to collapse. In the doorway, Rachel paused, looked expectantly at Lucy and commanded, "You! Come with me at once and do my hair."

"I'm sorry, I am under Madam Hardcastle's orders today. I am not free to serve you unless she gives me permission," said Lucy, politely but firmly, hoping her tone of voice would give Harriet courage and let her know she had an ally.

It seemed to work, for Harriet withdrew to her toilet table, took the earring which Lucy was proffering and informed her daughter that this was quite correct and that she would send Lucy to her later if she could spare her.

Rachel shot Lucy such a venomous look that she almost flinched. Had Rachel been one of the Pendle Witches, Lucy was convinced that she would have died on the spot from such a dagger-thrust of a glance.

She ignored her, however, and proceeded to affix the earrings to Harriet's tiny, almost translucent ears. When she next looked up, Rachel had gone.

"Thank you, Lucy," said Harriet.

The remark could have been related to the finding of the missing earring, but Lucy thought she detected something extra, perhaps gratitude for helping give her the strength to stand up to her evil-spirited daughter.

Not another word was spoken as Lucy powdered and rouged the older woman's delicate face and arranged the lace at her collar and cuffs. When she had finished, she stepped back, regarded her handiwork and announced, with a certain amount of pride in her voice, "You look just like a princess, ma'am."

Harriet, obviously pleased with her appearance, smiled kindly at Lucy and replied, "You do your job very well, child. Lady Clarence must have been sorry to lose you."

Lucy smiled deferentially back. She could understand now why so many girls from lower stations in life aspired to a position such as this. Attending a grateful, pleasant person made earning one's keep seem worthwhile and, if one's mistress was attractive, too, as Harriet undoubtedly was despite her age, it also gave one a good deal of creative satisfaction.

Lucy herself had picked out the gown from among Harriet's sizeable collection as being one that would greatly suit her. Harriet had admitted that she had never worn it, thinking that the deep wine shade of the expensive brocade was unbecoming to her pale complexion, but now she could see in the glass which Lucy held in front of her, that her complexion gained from the colour. Her lips and cheeks looked redder, her teeth whiter and Lucy had arranged her hair in a younger, prettier style than the more severe one she normally adopted.

As Lucy watched Harriet gazing dreamily at her reflection in the looking glass, she could see five, ten years slipping away. With her doll-like looks, she was almost a young girl again and Lucy was thrilled for her. Maybe, when her husband next saw her, he would realize what his bed had been lacking all these years; maybe their marriage would start afresh, revitalized by this new, attractive change in his wife.

When Lucy actually laid eyes on George Hardcastle for the first time, she wished such thoughts had never crossed her mind. She would not have visited the attentions of this ugly, loud-mouthed, porcine boor on any woman. He strode into Rokeby Hall, flinging doors open on all sides, letting great clods of mud and melting snow from his boots fall all over the carpets instead of scraping them off on the iron boot-scraper by the door, as any civilized man would have done.

He bawled for his family and his servants and when the latter appeared, he immediately had them dancing attendance on him, bringing him dry clothes, pouring him mulled wine, removing his boots, offering him food and giving his companion, an effete-looking young man in foppish clothes, the same treatment.

While this commotion was going on, Lucy lingered on the landing. So that weak, dandified youth was the beau on whom the fiery Rachel had set her heart! Lucy felt sorry for him. Doubtless, if Hardcastle could buy Philip and his title for Rachel, he could buy this pretentious popinjay, too, with his ruffles and jewels and affected lisp.

"You, girl! I've caught you slacking! Come here at once and I'll give you plenty to do!" The imperious tones cut through Lucy's thoughts and she turned to face her hated enemy, who was beckoning triumphantly from the doorway of her bedroom.

"Yes, Mistress Rachel," said Lucy dully, wondering what kind of tortures this female fiend had in store for her now.

"That man in the hall with Father is Lord Emmett, the man I intend to marry. You will dress me in a way that will appeal to him. I want to look like one of the court ladies, fashionable and alluring. I know you're only a country bumpkin with no taste, but do try to find something among my awful, outdated collection of gowns that will be suitable for the occasion."

Dress after dress was brought and refused, with mounting impatience, by Rachel. Finally, she slapped Lucy's arm, called her "a stupid numbskull," and sailed to the capacious wardrobe herself, whereupon she pulled furiously at a dress and suffered a near smothering as a heap of heavy costumes descended onto her and knocked her to the floor.

Lucy could hardly hold back a loud laugh as Rachel kicked and writhed beneath the heap of dresses.

"Help me, you oaf! Get them off me!" Rachel screamed. She delivered an extra hard kick to Lucy's shins for her pains, as if the avalanche of silks and satins had been caused by her maid's carelessness rather than her own.

Rachel finally settled on a dress of yellow silk with an overskirt of cream lace. Lucy thought privately that it caused her to resemble a milkmaid rather than the great lady she imagined herself to be. The shade drained the gold sheen from her hair, leaving it looking like a hayfield after the harvest.

It also added an unhealthy liverishness to her complexion, but Lucy knew that it was definitely not her place to point out, no matter how tactfully, that perhaps the dress wasn't such a good choice after all. At least Rachel seemed reasonably satisfied, although she grumbled about the neckline not being revealing enough.

"Shall I alter it for you, mistress?" offered Lucy.

"What? Allow you to lay your clumsy fingers on one of my best gowns? Thank you, no. I'll wear it as it is. Maybe Lord Emmett will appreciate a girl who is rather more demure than the ladies he's been used to. He may find me a trifle refreshing, don't you think?"

With a flounce of her petticoats, Rachel simpered at Lucy, who had no intention of pandering to her colossal vanity and merely nodded. Instantly, a dark cloud crossed Rachel's features and she reached towards her dressing table as if about to hurl something at Lucy's head.

"I can hear Madam Hardcastle calling me. If that will be all, mistress …?"

Lucy ducked out of the door and was convinced she could hear Rachel swearing like a trooper behind her. Where could she have picked up such foul language? As she passed the door of the library wherein George Hardcastle was engaging Lord Emmett in some kind of guessing game involving the names of women and horses, she learned the answer to her question.

She didn't linger, however, for now it was her turn to don her best dress and try to prettify herself in order to attend the Christmas party which the Hardcastles provided annually for their servants.

Chapter Sixteen

"Well now, you're a pretty little thing, aren't you, m'dear? C'mon, your master won't bite you. Come over here where I can see you in the light."

Obediently, Lucy edged forward towards the pool of light cast by the oil lamp which was placed in the centre of the library table.

She had been quite looking forward to relaxing in the company of Daisy, Maud and the other staff of Rokeby Hall, many of whom she hadn't even met yet, and it was her bad luck to be passing the library door just as Hardcastle lurched unsteadily out in search of a fresh supply of liquor. The lamplight illuminated the dress borrowed from the late Lady Eleanor, so that Lucy looked as if she were clad from shoulder to foot in drapes of shimmering gold.

"*Parfait!*"

The affected voice made her turn her head, to see Lord Emmett draped languorously across a chaise longue, licking a sugared plum with a bored expression.

"Happen she's new. Haven't seen her before myself."

"Your wife made a good choice." Emmett's lips curled sardonically.

"C-can I go now, sir?" Lucy bobbed a quick curtsey and scuttled for the door, but her exit was barred by Hardcastle's foot.

"Not so fast, not so fast. Stay and sup some wine with us."

His crimson-veined nose spoke of much imbibing over many years and, to her disgust, he simultaneously winked lecherously and broke wind. As she looked at him, she was reminded, rather horribly, of the incident that had taken place what seemed like years previously but that was, in fact, only a few months in the past, between herself and her equally boorish brother-in-law.

Her quick brain sought a way out of her dilemma. "But ... the party. They are expecting me."

"Party? Humph!" Hardcastle snorted and turned to his companion. "Little minx thinks a servants' party is more important than being invited to join her betters!"

"Don't aspire to the court, do you, Hettie?" The bored aristocrat seemed to speak without moving his lips.

"Beg pardon, sir, my name's Lucy."

"Hettie. Maidservants are all called Hettie," lisped Emmet.

"Come here, Lucy," ordered Hardcastle, patting his fleshy lap, while Lucy tried her best to suppress a shudder. "Here, I said," repeated Hardcastle, a slight edge entering his voice.

She glanced towards the door. Why did these things always happen to her? What was it about her that made men, particularly old, ugly ones, feel they had to entice and seduce and manhandle her? If it wasn't for the mission she had to undertake for Philip, she would leave Rokeby Hall right now, even if she ended up perishing in the snow. Indeed, that might be a better ending for her than the gallows.

"Here, puss, puss, puss!" mocked Emmett, rubbing his thumb and index finger together.

"But sir, the party ..." Lucy faltered.

"Do as your master tells you!" thundered Hardcastle, his bushy eyebrows meeting across the top of his bulbous nose.

"Like animals. Have to show 'em who's master," simpered Emmett.

With compressed lips, seething with anger, Lucy approached Hardcastle, who was sitting in a deep armchair by the fire. As soon as she was within reach, he grabbed her around the waist and pulled her roughly onto his lap.

"Give her a good frigging, I say, George. Let's have a bit of Christmas sport around here."

Emmett's face showed its first sign of animation as Hardcastle's hand pushed at Lucy's bodice, seeking the warm mounds of her breasts. "Wouldn't mind giving the fire a poke myself."

"Seems she's my property, so I claim first go," announced Hardcastle, his wet, blubbery lips seeking Lucy's.

Instinctively, she shrank away from his kiss and was rewarded with a sharp rap across the cheek from the back of his hand.

"Naughty, naughty. Must do what your master says," intoned Emmett, then added, "What say you we play forfeits for her?"

"How do you mean?" grunted Hardcastle. His fingers had entered Lucy's bodice and were now probing beneath her shift. The touch of his clumsy fingers made her flesh crawl. This was a real dilemma. She daren't risk dismissal before fulfilling her quest, but she simply could not put up with being treated like a plaything by a succession of revolting men. She reflected wryly that she didn't include Philip on that list.

"Sirs, I beg of you!" she pleaded, looking from one to the other, deciding to play the innocent. "I'm only new here. I came but four days ago. I want to do a good job as Miss Rachel's maid. I don't want to do anything that might affect my position in the household."

Both men burst out laughing, Hardcastle wheezing until the tears ran down his bloated red cheeks.

"Position – humph! Haw, haw! The only position for you, m'dear, is on your back with your legs spread!"

"No, round your neck, George, your *neck*! Have you no imagination?"

It was then Lucy realized that, with both men egging each other on and neither wishing to lose face with the other, her chances of escape were slim.

Hardcastle, still wheezing and puffing, yanked at Lucy's bodice, exposing her cleavage.

Emmett applauded his feat with slow handclaps. "You've opened the chest, now let's see the treasure!" he quipped.

"*No*! How dare you?" Lucy protested as Hardcastle plunged his hand inside her dress.

"Mmm, mmm," murmured Emmett, making a loud sucking noise on the plum and taking another from the bowl.

"Put those fruits away, these are sweeter," joked Hardcastle.

"Please, sir, you're hurting me!" How she hated feeling so powerless. At moments like these, she loathed the male sex. If only all women could rise up and band together and turn the tables, and torment men the way they mishandled women!

"*Please, sir, you're hurting me,*" mimicked the odious Emmett, in a falsetto voice. "'*Please, sir, hurt me*' – that's what you'll be begging in a minute! You love it, you little minx. Look at you, giving him suck like a wet nurse! I've got something I'd like you to suck …"

Lucy wished she could stop her ears to protect herself from his crude words. Hardcastle was worrying her breast with his teeth like an unruly puppy, scraping the tender skin. She didn't dare try to pull away from him in case he bit her even harder.

Emmett, still reclining on the damask-covered chaise-longue, was languidly stroking his fingers up the inside of his thigh, caressing himself, although his features betrayed not one trace of arousal.

As Hardcastle fumbled with his britches, Lucy discovered that she possessed an ability of which she had not previously been aware. The only way she could describe it to herself was as a feeling of being detached from what was happening to her; as if her body were doing things but she herself were not involved. It was like the sensation she experienced just before falling asleep or collapsing in a faint; a dream-like feeling, as if it were all happening to somebody else.

"There, my little maid. Be a good girl and –"

Lucy had guessed what he was about to say, but before she could react, there was the sound of footsteps approaching the door.

"Quick – it might be my wife! Over here!"

Hardcastle bundled her behind a screen to one side of the fireplace and Lucy could hear men's voices and a clinking of glasses as a servant provided fresh victuals. She also discovered the reason for the screen – it hid a chamber pot which was already half full of malodorous liquid.

Lucy quickly sidestepped it and stumbled. As her shoulder touched the oak paneling behind her, she heard a whirring sound and found herself tumbling backwards into what felt like empty space.

Stifling a scream, she flung out her arms and found she was in some kind of narrow passageway. In the orange glow from the fire and the library's lamp and candles, Lucy spotted the first two in a flight of wooden stairs leading up and away from the library.

Without a second's hesitation, she began to climb, knowing she had no time to lose, for Hardcastle would soon summon her back. She prayed that he would be too fat and drunk to mount the steep narrow staircase in pursuit.

She could imagine Emmett's affected drawl informing Hardcastle that there were "plenty more Hetties."

The shaft of light from the library was soon far behind her. She had no idea how many steps she had climbed, fumbling for each one with her foot to make sure she didn't fall into some yawning chasm or come up against a blank wall. At least the passageway was dry, although the stone walls were freezing cold and festooned in spider webs and in some places the ceiling was so low that she had to bend and duck.

Suddenly, she heard the sound that she feared – Hardcastle's distant, drunken bellowing.

"Lucy? Lucy! Come back here. Confound the girl!"

She heard a mumbled conversation between Hardcastle and Emmett, then the sounds dwindled as she climbed even higher, feeling her way up and up. She wished there had been some way of securing the panelling behind her to hide the secret of her escape route. It would have been far better if he had thought she was a witch who had rendered herself invisible or flow away on a broomstick! Wherever this stairway led, it would be of no help to her in the future, now that Hardcastle had discovered it.

She raised her foot to take the next step and found that the regularity of the treads had ceased. She prodded the darkness with her toe and examined the walls with both hands, her fingers encountering a thick cobweb that made her shudder. The passageway was now taking a turn to the right. Fumbling her way round the bend, she readjusted her steps as the stairway began to ascend once more.

Panting with exertion and fear, Lucy at last reached the very top step and founded herself up against another expanse of panelling in total darkness. Somewhere on it, there had to be a release catch which would open a door, if only she could press or twist the right spot.

But where would she find herself when she got out? Would she fetch up in some deserted store room, long boarded up, the only exit from which would be back down the passageway and straight into the triumphant arms of the men she sought to escape? What if she found herself in, say, Rachel's bedroom or that of one of the servants? Particularly if the inhabitant was male!

Then she reminded herself that they would all be attending the party and if she didn't show her face there soon, there would be mutterings that the new lady's-maid was too hoity-toity and above herself to attend. That must not be allowed to happen. She dare not risk drawing attention to herself in any way. It was vital that she should find a way out of this cramped, cold, cobwebby passage as soon as possible.

Starting at the top left-hand corner, her fingers systematically examined every panel, tapping over the surface from corner to corner, left to right, top to bottom. Nothing. She began again, but still there was no welcome click of a catch or sign of any indentation in the obstinate wood.

Tired and thwarted, she slumped down onto the top step – and as she did so, her hip caught against a lever of some sort which was sticking out of the wall. With a great grating and creaking, as of a rusty castle portcullis being raised, a complete section of wall opened up.

With a gasp of relief, Lucy practically fell out. Her feet met thick carpet and she was aware of the dull glimmer of a window somewhere to her right. No abandoned room, this! It was obviously in frequent, if not daily use.

She paused for a moment, listening. No voice or footfall came to her, but she noticed a shaft of light gleaming from beneath a door and realized she must be somewhere in the main part of the house. If this was so, she had no time to lose. At any moment, the occupant of the room might return and she would be discovered.

Wishing that she had a candle to see by, Lucy sought for some means of closing the entrance to her secret tunnel. As she prodded and pushed, she remembered the conversation she had had with Philip on that very subject. Now, her childhood dream had come true; she had stumbled on a secret passageway, but there had been no leisure time in which to seek for treasure, no time to feel thrilled and excited.

She pressed something which looked like a knot in the wood and, to her relief, the panel slid shut with another protesting creak. Now, all that remained was for her to leave the room as unnoticed as she had entered it.

First, she knotted the broken lace on her bodice and pulled it tight, making herself as tidy as she could without a glass to aid her. Next, she took several bold strides in the direction of the door and had almost reached it when something made her turn back. There was something nagging at the back of her brain, something she had remembered, or else noticed, about the room she was in.

She traced her thoughts back. The first thing she had seen had been the window. She turned her eyes towards it. There, below it, was the bulky outline of a large wooden chest. An oak chest, by a window. Why should that seem familiar to her? None of the rooms at home had contained a chest in such a position, apart from the settle in the window of the drawing-room. Perhaps that was what she was thinking of.

Her hand reached for the door latch, yet still the uneasy memory plagued her. She was standing by a carved wooden bureau. Behind her was a four-poster bed with a dresser next to it, bearing a water bowl and jug. The positioning of all these objects seemed so familiar.

Lucy's hand flew to her mouth. Of course they seemed familiar! She had seen them before in her mind's eye, their shapes and positions having been suggested by a diagram drawn in wine on a table-top. She was in the bedroom of the very devil whose attentions she had so recently fled, George Hardcastle!

Lucy's heart thumped in panic. Did he already know where the secret staircase ended? Was he, right now, waiting on the landing to pounce on her as she emerged from his bedroom door, thinking herself safe? Was he – and here a pang of horror stabbed through her – was he already in the room, smiling sardonically to himself as he watched her blunder around in the gloom?

She probed every shadowy corner with her eyes. No, there was nobody there. She did not have that prickling sensation of being watched that she had experienced in the Darwell Manor ballroom. Taking courage from the knowledge that here, at least, she was alone, she walked over to the oak chest and lifted the lid.

There, just as Philip had predicted, was the ledge and on it a single key. Should she pocket it now? No, Hardcastle might miss it and raise an outcry before she had had a chance to secure the other key, the one which opened the drawer inside the bureau. Closing the heavy lid, she tiptoed to the door. There was nobody around. Breathing a sigh of relief, she stepped out into the corridor.

As she descended the back stairs that the servants used, she heard a woman's voice call her name. Composing her face so as to show no traces of anxiety or guilt, Lucy looked over the banister. There, standing at the foot of the stairs, was Maud.

"Where on earth 'ave you been? I've searched everywhere. We've all started without you, I'm afraid, but, if you come quick, there'll still be some left."

Lucy smiled at her gladly. "I was on my way when the master called me and then I had a duty to perform for Miss Rachel." That would explain what she was doing on the first floor.

Maud looked at her suspiciously. "But Miss Rachel has gone over to visit the Squire, accompanied by Lord Emmett."

"I know," Lucy lied glibly. "But she had spilt some powder in her room and wanted me to clear up the mess."

Maud accepted this explanation and rolled her eyes in sympathy. She, too, had borne the vituperative force of Rachel's tongue in the past and didn't in the least envy Lucy her position as Rachel's personal maid.

"Come along with me now. You won't escape this time. There are several nice young men all dyin' to meet you!" She sneezed and mopped at her nose.

"Bless you!" exclaimed Lucy. Although she'd only known the older housemaid for a few days, she was already fond of her. Broad-faced and plain, she loved her work in the big house and, while allowing herself to exchange badinage and gibes with the male servants, readily admitted that she preferred to keep her own company, having, in her own words, "twice the nous" of any of the males who had ever paid her court.

As Lucy followed her into the servants' dining-room, a wave of heat and a cheerful hubbub greeted her and she felt herself beginning to perspire beneath the heavy stuff of her gown. She had had no idea Rokeby Hall employed so many servants. There seemed to be scores of them, the familiar house servants plus coachmen, gardeners and stable boys.

She already knew several of them by sight, including the cook, Mrs Ramsbottom, a huge woman with arms like sides of beef; the butler, Hawkins; the little scullion, Teresa, or "Tree" as she was nicknamed; and Hardcastle's personal manservant, Jamieson, whom Lucy had hated on sight almost as much as his master, owing to his expression that was permanently set in a sneer, and his flat, shiny hair, so sleek and dark that it looked as if it was covered in boot blacking.

Maud, snuffling and coughing from her cold, introduced her to the head groom, who was named, most inappropriately, Adam Redhead, in spite of his mop of brown curls. Then there were the two stable boys, Davey and Jim; Dickon the gardener, a grizzle-haired elderly man; his young assistant Tom, a lad of about Lucy's own age and finally, the coachmen, brothers Nat and Josiah.

So many names and faces made Lucy's head whirl as if she had partaken of too much ale. Indeed, a great deal of it had already been consumed by everyone else, leaving Lucy feeling far too sober to enter into the spirit of the occasion.

She lingered with Maud and Daisy, until the latter slumped into a snoring heap across the table, to the great amusement of all. The food which Mrs Ramsbottom had provided was plentiful and delicious. Lucy ate slices of pheasant and venison and dainty pieces of spiced pie, and sipped at a tankard of ale which Maud thrust into her hand.

She could sense the eyes of the other women on her gown. No doubt they were wondering how she came to be in possession of such a grand, if old-fashioned and dusty, garment. Let them think what they wished. She would not be here much longer and their tongues could wag all they liked once she was safely back at Darwell Manor.

Gnarled old Dickon produced a wooden flute from his pocket. He proceeded to play a merry tune and some of the servants started to dance. Maud, in spite of her cold, was pulled to her feet by Nat, the elder of the two coachmen and whirled round the table in a fast jig.

Lucy sat there in the steamy room, mind roaming, idly drumming her fingers to the rhythm. Was this what Christmas used to be like for the servants of Darwell Manor, in the days when Lady Eleanor was alive and Philip still unborn?

She tried to picture Philip in his father's place, as Earl and head of the household. Somehow, she couldn't see him as a benevolent master, or even as a gentle, loving husband who would grieve over the loss of his wife to the point of driving himself demented, as the old Earl had obviously done.

Leaving aside the incident in the stable, her subsequent knowledge of Philip had only strengthened the first impression she'd gained of him at Pendleton Fair, as arrogant, self-opinionated, intelligent and cold. Though there were odd moments when he said something humorous, or behaved in a kinder way, so perhaps there was a warmer, more sensitive spirit lurking inside the chilly exterior. She hoped there was.

She gazed vacantly at the gyrating figures who were laughing, tripping, seizing mugs of ale as they passed the table, and listened with half an ear to the reedy music. If Rory had been here, he would have transformed the whole room with his larger-than-life personality, his singing, his joking, his ability to hold a group of people spellbound with his stories. She would not have had to return to her room lonely and uncomforted, for he would have held her close, murmured compliments to her beauty, assured her that she was loved and desired.

To have been married for so short a time, a marriage with so much potential for happiness, and have it end so abruptly – why, it was like crushing a chrysalis and depriving a beautiful butterfly of life! Already, Lucy was beginning to forgive her dead husband for his infidelity.

Something on his mind had been worrying him for some time, she had seen that, and it certainly wasn't the tavern slut. He had told Lucy he hadn't visited Pendleton for a year, and that bloated hussy certainly wasn't the sort of girl a man would have on his mind for twelve months.

No, something much more important than that must have been eating away at him, and it seemed so unbearably cruel that now, she would never find out what it had been. She would never be able to soothe him, love him, bear his children, a thing they had often talked about.

No other man would ever blaze with Rory's fiery zest for life, nor awaken the searing flames of desire deep within her which he had awoken. The vague stirrings she had felt when Philip touched her were nothing in comparison.

These dancing, happy, carefree people – how she envied them! They looked as if they had never known loss or heartache. Yet how could one ever tell?

"Why so sad, Lucy?"

The pleasant male voice with its soft local accent shattered her introspection. Men! Why wouldn't they ever leave her alone? Couldn't they see that she wasn't interested in them? That, for her, love had died along with Rory?

She found herself looking into the green eyes of Adam Redhead, the man in charge of the Hardcastle horses and couldn't even bring herself to smile.

"Are you homesick because it's Christmas? You don't come from these parts, do you?" he persisted.

She sighed. He seemed determined to engage her in conversation, so she would have to show some semblance of friendliness if she didn't want to be described as stand-offish behind her back. Later, when she was alone, she would have time enough for her memories.

"No. I come from further west, Prebbledale way. That's where my parents live."

"D'you like it here at Rokeby Hall? I've heard Miss Rachel is a hand-ful."

This was one topic on which Lucy could wax most eloquently. She proceeded to tell Adam about some of the things Rachel had said and done in the few days she had been working for her. When she had finished, she found Adam gazing at her in admiration.

"You must be a girl of spirit and determination, to put up with that. Did she give you that mark, the one on your cheekbone?"

Lucy put her hand up to her cheek and felt the hard, dry ridge of a scab. Of course! It was the place where Rachel's emerald ring had caught her. She had quite forgotten about it but, as she pressed it gingerly, it felt quite sore. She told Adam how she had incurred the wound and his brow furrowed with concern.

"That one girl could so mar another's beauty! She's probably jealous of you because you are so much finer looking than she is."

Was he being impertinent, or had he got too much drink inside him? Lucy withdrew a little and refused to respond to the compliment.

Adam appeared not to notice. "Come and dance. That'll soon cheer you up and put you in the Christmas spirit."

Lucy declined, pleading the fact that she was far too hot, but still the man would not leave her alone. Maud caught her eye and winked at her. Doubtless there would be gossip and innuendos the following day. She wasn't sure if she could stand it.

"If you won't dance, at least have a Christmas drink with me, Lucy. Here, give me your cup."

Without any compliance on Lucy's part, Adam seized her pewter beaker, poured the remaining two inches of ale onto the floor, fished around inside his waistcoat and produced a small flask which he proceeded to open. He poured a trickle of amber liquid into Lucy's cup, then took a deep draught from the flask, wiped his lips with the back of his hand and replaced the vessel in its hiding place.

He pushed the mug across the table towards Lucy. "Go on. This'll warm the cockles o' your heart."

She felt she couldn't very well refuse him. He wasn't being unpleasant in the way Hardcastle and Emmett were unpleasant; he was just a nice, ordinary man of twenty-six or so who was trying to welcome her into the servants' community and make it easier for her to mix with them.

She raised the cup to her lips and spluttered as the pungent spirit burned its way down her throat. It was neat brandy. She had only tasted brandy once before and that had been several years ago, when her father, in one of his drunken sprees, had offered her a nip and had laughed uproariously at her grimaces.

She bravely swallowed the mouthful she had taken, and a few moments later found she was indeed feeling more relaxed and sociable, having begun to tap her foot to the piper's tune and smile at the whirling, staggering couples all around her.

"Now, how about that dance?" Adam invited, holding out his hand to her.

Lucy grasped it and was soon weaving in and out among the other couples, steered by Adam, who proved to be a fine dancer. She careered past Maud, who was now in the arms of Josiah, whose wife was in the throes of a most remarkable dance with young Tom, the under-gardener, which called for much whooping and kicking-up of feet.

When the kitchen clock struck midnight, Hawkins, the butler, called for a toast to King George and then another to their master, George

Hardcastle, and all his family. On both occasions, Lucy downed more brandy and felt as if she were floating an inch or two above the floor.

Abbie, one of the kitchen girls, had produced some mistletoe from somewhere and was going around holding it over couples' heads and exhorting them to kiss, which they all did with gusto. Then it was the turn of herself and Adam.

His curly hair was plastered to his face with the sweat of his exertions and a broad smile wreathed his lips as his face bore down on Lucy's. She made no move to stop him. Indeed, she felt so deliriously happy that she responded to his kiss with far more enthusiasm than the occasion demanded and was suddenly aware of giggles and guffaws from all around, as the other servants stopped whatever else they were doing to nudge each other and remark on the length of the kiss.

She realized that she was rather drunk and would need to keep a tight hold on herself, so she pulled herself from Adam's embrace, found a stool and sat down. Not everybody was behaving with as much propriety as she was. Old Dickon's twig-like fingers were clawing at Daisy's ample bosom, and two pairs of feet, one pair pointing upwards and the other down, could be glimpsed round the pantry door.

Tom had Kitty, one of the dairymaids, spread along a bench, his hands vigorously exploring beneath her skirts, and even the sensible Maud had been pressed up against the wall and was allowing herself to be kissed and fondled by one of the stable lads.

Lucy did not feel at all shocked at this libidinous spectacle. It just served to emphasize her feeling of not belonging. She could summon up no enthusiasm for such licentious behaviour, although she certainly did not condemn it in others. She just felt distanced from them all, and rather wistful. How Rory would have loved this night.

Adam stood next to her, his hand on her shoulder, his fingers entwined in her hair. She looked up at him and he bent his face down to hers, meaning to kiss her.

She turned aside. "I am sorry. I have a headache coming on. I think I need to retire,"

A spasm of disappointment twisted his features. "But a few moments ago you were dancing and laughing. What's wrong? Have I done something, or said anything, to upset you?"

"No," replied Lucy softly, sensing his bewilderment. "It's just that I'm not used to strong liquor. I don't feel very well. Miss Rachel will chide me viciously tomorrow if I lack the energy to run round for her and do her bidding. You see ..."

She paused and smiled. She was about to impart a secret which she knew would set the whole household humming with gossip. She didn't care, for why should she feel any loyalty towards the girl who had treated her so badly? "You see," she continued, "Miss Rachel is husband-hunting and her quarry is Lord Emmett."

There was no slipping off to bed for her now. The female servants clustered round her, demanding to know more, and there was much screeching, guffawing and slapping of thighs. But when they noticed how very pale and Lucy had gone and how she was having to resort to frequent blinking to keep her heavy eyelids open, they at last agreed to let her go and Maud accompanied her up the back stairs, having noticed that she was swaying.

Lucy was grateful for the older maid's company as it prevented Adam from following her. However, she was not pleased to find, on entering the room, that Daisy was sprawled in a snoring heap right in the middle of the bed, leaving Lucy a mere few inches of space to curl up in.

Her head was spinning and Maud helped her undress, then took the stone bowl from the dresser and placed it strategically close to the side of the bed.

Fortunately, Lucy had no need of the bowl for sleep overtook her the moment her head touched the bolster. She awoke next morning to a blinding headache and the sound of Daisy coughing and groaning and bemoaning her own excesses of the night before. It was Christmas Eve and the day of the Hardcastle's ball at Rokeby Hall.

Chapter Seventeen

At first, Lucy feared that perhaps Hardcastle, with even more Christmas spirit inside his bulging belly than the previous night, might attempt to waylay her, but the ball passed without incident, the Hardcastles being much too busy entertaining their guests to dally with the servants.

Lucy lost count of the number of times either Rachel or Harriet asked her to fetch this or do that, or escort one of their fatigued female guests to a retiring room. By the time the musicians had packed up their instruments, Lucy felt almost dead on her feet, especially with her head still throbbing from the previous night's over-consumption of brandy.

She knew she ought to be thinking up some way of carrying out Philip's order but, the more she thought about it, the more she was forced to accept that there was only one way of obtaining the vital key and that was to take it while Hardcastle slept.

The only way of ensuring that he slept heavily enough not to awaken at the entry of an intruder into his bedchamber, was to see that he consumed plenty of ale and wine, with the addition of an extra ingredient. A pinch of spice in the form of a sleeping draught. Maud had a stock of it for her own use, made last summer from medicinal herbs and stored in a jar in a kitchen cupboard and Lucy had begged some, citing Daisy's snoring as her reason.

This meant that she would have to oversee Hardcastle's liquor consumption herself. What that might entail, she knew only too well.

* * *

Christmas Day seemed to last for ever. There were several guests for the Christmas feast. There were those who had stayed over after the ball, plus other friends and relatives of the Hardcastles, who had avoided an accident in the snow by wrapping the hooves of their carriage horses in felt to lessen the chances of slipping on the ice.

Lucy couldn't stop thinking of her mother, alone on Christmas Day, ignored by her husband who would have drunk himself into a stupor with the stable lads by midday. If only she could have been there to keep her company and make her life a little more pleasant.

Even the presentation of two surprise gifts – a tiny phial of lavender water from Maud and an embroidered wristlet from Daisy – did little to lift her gloomy spirits. She imagined Philip striding up and down the draughty corridors of Darwell Manor, wondering how close she was to accomplishing of her task.

Rachel was in a spitting, snarling mood, having failed to make much progress with Emmett during the ball, and Lucy was forced to suffer having her hair pulled and being struck with a hair brush as she sought to appease her ill-tempered mistress. She couldn't wait to complete her task and leave.

Every time she laid eyes on Hardcastle, he had a glass or a tankard somewhere near his lips and Jamieson hovering nearby to provide constant replenishment. Perhaps today was the day, Lucy thought, excitement starting to bubble inside her. Christmas night would be the ideal occasion on which to carry out her mission as, with luck, Jamieson, too, would drink too much and retire early.

That morning, Lucy had found an opportunity to steal into the library and peer behind the screen next to the fireplace. The panel was closed. Even if she needed to use this escape route a second time, she doubted if she could remember exactly what she had done to release the hidden spring.

Something else occurred to Lucy. How was she to get back to Darwell Manor? That was something that had featured in Philip's plan and it was something she should have asked him, as the manor was nigh on twenty miles away, over a snow-covered moor piled with drifts and veiled hollows into which she might fall and freeze to death.

How clever he had been in explaining his plan and instructing her in the lay-out of the interior of the hall – yet how remiss in failing to devise the successful delivery of that prized treasure! She was angry both with him and with herself.

As she ran the flat-iron over the bundle of petticoats that Rachel had thrust into her arms, demanding that they be quickly returned freshened and smoothed, Lucy wondered if there was any way of getting a message to the Manor so that Matthew, or even Philip himself, could wait for her somewhere and convey her to safety.

But that would mean stating an exact time, for she could hardly expect anybody to linger in the freezing cold. In any case, it would take several hours for her message to get there – that was, if she could find anyone to take it without arousing the suspicions of all and sundry. She could hardly steal a carriage, or even a horse, from under the vigilant eye of Adam Redhead and his fellows.

The problem of how to get the deeds back to Philip seemed insurmountable, yet this particular worry seemed minor when compared to the sheer horror of what she would have to accomplish first. Because it was fast dawning on her that there was only one reliable way of getting herself inside George Hardcastle's bedchamber legitimately, and that was for her to pretend to submit to his lecherous desires.

She hoped the sleeping draught would work, because the alternative was far too repulsive to contemplate.

* * *

"So, you little minx ..." Hardcastle extended a meaty hand and tweaked her ear. "Run away from me, would you? I'd a mind to find out where those stairs led to myself, but I'm getting too old for that caper. But I'm not too old for this, m'dear!"

Fate had played into Lucy's hands. As she had suspected from the way Jamieson was tipping the ale back at the servant's party, he had been too sick to perform his Christmas Day duties and the other servants had taken it in turns to make sure that hosts and guests had enough to drink. It was Lucy who had been ordered by Maud to deliver Hardcastle's hot rum punch to his bedchamber.

"Make sure you put the cup down and come straight out again. The master can be a bit, er, difficult." She winked, leaving Lucy in no doubt about what she meant. She guessed he must have tried it on with all the servants in turn, including Maud herself.

The smile Lucy gave Hardcastle as she placed the tankard on his bedside cabinet was genuine. In fact, it was all she could do not to laugh, knowing that the flavour of the sleeping draught would not be detected amid the potent spices of the punch.

She bobbed a curtsey. "Please, sir, forgive me for the other night. You took me by surprise and I was scared."

"A little virgin, I'll be bound," boomed Hardcastle from the armchair he sat in, licking his thick lips. "I like a girl who gives me the runaround – but not too much, mind. I'm not as young as I used to be, but –" his voice rose to a hearty crescendo – "I can still throw a passable leg over!"

Ugh! She felt queasy at the thought of being straddled by that podgy leg!

He rose from the chair, lifted the tankard, drank deeply, then sat down on the bed, which groaned beneath his weight.

"Undress me, my pretty," he ordered. "Then let me watch you undress yourself."

By the time she had undressed him, he would be asleep, she thought. Her fear had left her now. She was starting to enjoy this game, knowing she was not in any danger thanks to the potency of the herbs.

As she divested him of waistcoat, shirt and undershirt, grimacing at the sight of his doughy belly that bristled with dark hairs, Philip's information about the key's hiding place came back to her. Whilst folding his brocade waistcoat and placing it on a chair, she felt swiftly inside the interior pocket.

There was no key. Philip was wrong! To think she had got herself into this predicament for nothing! Somehow, she would have to trick Hardcastle into telling her where it was, before the draught took effect.

Like a wisp of smoke, an idea drifted into her mind. It remained half-formed for a moment, then solidified into a workable shape. Pursing her lips in a provocative pout, Lucy ran the tip of a fingernail across one of Hardcastle's shoulders.

"You're a fine figure of a man, George Hardcastle," she murmured, marvelling at her ability to lie so convincingly.

"I admire you," she fibbed. "You're such a successful man. How did you achieve –" she swept her glance around the room – "all this?"

"Oh, a bit of business here and there, m'dear," he replied, giving nothing away.

"What sort of business?" she inquired, hoping he would take the bait.

He took another gulp of rum.

"You must have all kinds of valuable things here. Jewels, papers … I hope you have them hidden somewhere safe, where they can't be stolen."

Was she being too obvious, she wondered? She was hoping he would boast and reveal his security arrangements, but instead, he quaffed from the tankard again and patted the bed next to him.

"Now it's your turn to get undressed, I think," he said.

Lucy gave a nervous giggle.

"Come on, don't be shy. Here, let me help you."

Lucy gasped as he stretched a hand towards her. He reached for the laces that held her dress together. He gave a tug and smiled at what was revealed. He pulled her towards him, pouting his wet lips in preparation for a kiss. Lucy sighed, cursing the damned potion that didn't seem to be working. Perhaps he needed to drink some more.

She dodged the kiss and reached for the tankard but just as she was handing it to him, his eyes rolled upwards and he gave a shuddering gasp and collapsed back against the pillows.

Dear God, she thought. Perhaps she had added too much of the sleeping draught to his drink! What if he were dead and the finger of blame pointed at her, as the last person to see him alive? Whichever way she looked at it, all her roads seemed to lead to the gallows.

Chapter Eighteen

Lucy held the waxed paper to her chilled flesh. In the guttering light of the candle she could scarcely read the closely written script, but the words *Darwell Manor* leapt off the rolled-up page as if in answer to her unspoken question.

Fearfully, she glanced at the silent bulk slumped on the bed. He did look like a corpse. Perhaps she should check to see if he was breathing. She crept gingerly towards him, touched his wrist tentatively and jumped in fright as a loud snort trumpeted from his purple nose.

At once, relief flooded her and, as regular, rumbling snores commenced, she let out her breath in a silent sigh.

In the end, finding the deeds had been easy. She had taken the key that lay in the drawer, unlocked the bureau and discovered that the inner drawer had not been locked after all. If only she had known, she could have taken the deeds the night she had bolted up the concealed staircase and accidentally arrived in Hardcastle's bedroom, and she could have been home in time for Christmas.

Oh, why had she not tried the drawer then?

Stop it, she told herself. There was absolutely no point in torturing herself with whys and what-ifs. She had the deeds now, her mission was fulfilled and in another few moments, she would leave this hateful house and travel back to Darwell Manor, although she still had no idea how.

She tiptoed up to her shared room, bundled up her few belongings, donned her thick, hooded cloak, another home-made gift from Martha, then waited until she was sure the household had settled down for the night before silently creeping out of Rokeby Hall, praying the dogs would not give her away. She was lucky. Hardcastle had fed them ale and they were sleeping as soundly as he was.

* * *

Her intention, as she started down the long drive feeling conspicuously dark against the blinding whiteness of the snow, was to walk and walk, hopefully in the right direction, until either she saw a familiar landmark, or grew so tired that she wrapped herself in her cloak and went to sleep in the shelter of a clump of bushes.

The snow-bearing clouds had been swept away by a bitter wind and the moon sailed high and frosty in an ebony sky, which was sprinkled with bright stars as sharp as glittering dagger points. A fox had passed the same way not long before, the prints of its pads not yet frozen. In spite of the cold that was already attacking her face, hands and feet, Lucy smiled to think of the creature hunting freely in the night.

Then her smile faded as she was reminded of her own hunger. Although the emphasis all day had been on eating Christmas fare, she had been far too busy to do anything other than watch other people eat. She had visited the kitchen briefly and snatched a few scraps of goose left over from the Hardcastles' table, which had momentarily satisfied her, but the exertions of this night had left her ravenous and the cold only served to sharpen her appetite.

She knew Darwell Manor was somewhere to the right, for when Matthew had dropped her at the great iron gates, they had approached on the left. No light was burning in the lodge and no dog barked as Lucy slid the heavy iron bar back and swung the gate open just enough to permit her to slip out.

As she took careful steps on the rutted and icy country road, she felt alone, vulnerable and very scared. Daisy would report in the morning that she hadn't come to bed that night. People would search for her and, finding her missing, would they not check the house to see if any valuables had gone?

You silly goose, she chided herself. Who would suspect a lady's-maid of stealing a set of house deeds? Jewels, yes, and money, too; maybe even clothes, but never a piece of paper that, as far as they knew, she would be unable to read. She felt sure it would be a long time before the loss of the deeds was discovered.

Her second fear was that one of Hardcastle's guests might have a sudden impulse to leave at dead of night. The howling of the wind might muffle the sounds of an approaching carriage and this thought caused her to turn her head constantly and peer into the whiteness behind her. Nothing stirred, except the wind soughing in the hedges and branches.

At times, her boots slipped on the icy ridges left by carriages, and at others, she sank ankle-deep into crunchy snow, the surface of which was frozen just hard enough to prick her ankles through her stockings.

In spite of her stout footwear, her toes were soon so numb that she could no longer feel them, and she recalled tales she'd been told of walkers in the snow who, on removing their socks after their return, had found that their toes came off too, snapping like icicles. Lucy had no desire to lose her toes so she kept trying to curl them and uncurl them inside her boots, until numbing exhaustion prevented her.

Soon, she was hardly conscious of moving at all. She seemed to glide, to drift like a ghost over the pallid landscape, weightless, ethereal. Soon she would dissolve and the wind would disperse her like smoke over the fields.

"Mother!"

Lucy suddenly saw Ann Swift's face a few inches in front of her own. She stretched out a hand, took a step forward and fell headlong into a drift that had piled up beneath a hedge. The sudden invasion of cold snow down her neck and up her sleeves brought her to her senses. She had been seeing visions, the kind that visited one in a fever, except Lucy knew she was suffering from the very opposite.

If she gave in to the desire simply to lie in the softness of the snow-drift, wrap her cloak around her and go to sleep, she would freeze to death. A few years ago, one of her father's dogs had done that – wandered from its kennel to be found next day buried in a drift, a dog-shaped block of ice.

No, she must carry on, warming herself if necessary with thoughts of Rory. She must really be feverish now, she realized, because she could hear Rory's voice calling her name. But he was dead and he was a ghost and maybe by now she was one, too.

"Lucy … Lucy …"

The repeated word – the word that described her but was strangely devoid of connotation now, just a meaningless sound – echoed and rang as if the very trees were chanting it. She put a hand to her face, but both hand and cheek were so cold that she could feel nothing. This must be death, this losing of one's senses and identity, this confused wandering in nothingness.

Aaaah! What was that? Something touched her shoulder, seized it hard, shook it. She was a rabbit caught by a fox, too shocked even to squeal.

"I have nothing to give you," she whispered, too terrified even to turn round and face the thief or phantom who was accosting her.

"That paper inside your bodice! Is that nothing?"

It wasn't the voice of Rory, she was certain now. But whose was it? She did not recognize it at all.

"Look at me, Lucy."

It was gently spoken but it was, nevertheless, an order. Lucy swivelled her eyes and encountered two candid green ones.

"Adam! Wh-what are you doing here? How did you know I had left the Hall?" She stood speechless, shivering as she waited for him to reply and, in those seconds which felt like hours, realized just how cold and miserable she was.

"I watched you."

Simple words, giving nothing away. How long had he been watching her, and for what reason?

With as much delicacy as if he were handling priceless porcelain, he withdrew Lucy's left hand from inside her cloak, peeled off the sodden glove and proceeded to chafe her fingers between his own large, warm hands. The pain was agonizing as feeling returned to her numb digits.

He repeated the process with her other hand and then, very gently, took her frozen face between his palms and pressed his lips against each cheek in turn, blowing softly to bring the life back into them. When this kind action was completed, he did not release Lucy's face straight away but approached her with his lips.

"No, Adam!" She jerked her head away and pulled her cloak around her with a flounce. What was the matter with her? Why did every man she met want her and try to seduce her?

And why was she so prone to desiring certain men? Was she by nature a wanton, a temptress, a slut destined to end her days in some low brothel?

"I'm sorry. Forgive me." Adam was standing before her, his hands clasped, his head bowed. "I didn't mean … I was just trying to warm you up so you wouldn't freeze to death. By God, what must you think of me?"

Lucy had never heard a man sounding so apologetic about having done something which had, frankly, brought her a moment of pleasure. She stretched out a hand, touched his for an instant then returned it to her cloak.

"There's nothing to forgive. Just tell me why you are here, and what you know."

"Let's walk. We'll both freeze if we keep standing still."

Taking her arm, Adam marched her briskly up the lane. His coat was roughly made from animal skins, sewn together with the hide outside and the fur inside, and a huge fur collar shielded his ears and face. A clump of light brown curls had tumbled over his eyes and he tossed his head like a pony, to resettle his mane.

"Just a bit further on we'll come to a gate, from which there is a track leading to a farmhouse. We'll take shelter there."

Lucy followed him obediently. Although she had no idea where he was taking her, she would be glad of warmth and shelter, and she longed for a hot drink and something to eat.

Soon, they reached the solid oak door of the farmhouse. Orange light glowed from a window. As Adam pushed open the door for her to enter, she noticed a line of hoof prints which passed the door and seemed to lead in the direction of the outbuildings.

The welcoming wave of heat which enveloped her as she stepped over the threshold wiped all questions from her mind – until she saw the figure sprawled on a chair before the fire, highly polished boots propped on the fender.

Although the head did not turn as she entered, that gleaming dark hair could belong to none other than … Lucy gave an involuntary gasp.

The head turned and Philip Darwell's cool grey eyes swept her from head to toe.

"A brandy for the girl!"

"Certainly, sir. I'll fetch it straight away."

Lucy was astonished to hear Adam accept Philip's peremptory order as if he were his manservant. After a few moments, he returned bearing a tray with three glasses, two of them brimming and one, which he handed to Lucy, containing a more modest amount of the amber fluid.

Lucy gratefully downed it and gave thanks for the instant warmth it produced in her body. The next moment she was mortified to hear her empty stomach emit a loud rumble.

Philip laughed. "When did you last eat?" he inquired.

"Not since yesterday, unless you count a few crumbs that wouldn't have been enough to keep a sparrow alive!"

Her feeble joke was an attempt to lighten the atmosphere in the room, the neglected interior of which suggested that the house was seldom occupied. The air was thick with dust and she felt a tug of tension, though whether this was between herself and Philip, between Philip and Adam, or between all three of them, she could not say.

Adam disappeared into the kitchen and soon the sounds of rattling and chopping indicated that some kind of meal was being prepared. Between Lucy and Philip, the tense silence persisted. She perched on a wooden chair, as close to the fire as she could get.

The heat, combined with the lateness of the hour and fatigue from her exertions, made her feel drowsy but the sensation of Philip's eyes on her kept sleep at bay.

"You're thinner."

The cool observation sent her drooping head jerking upwards. She was about to respond but his keen glance forced her back into wary silence. Why did he always have this effect on her? She could never relax in his presence. He made her feel supremely self-conscious and nervous, so that she stumbled in her conversation and her awkwardness turned into resentment.

Even during the weeks she had spent at Darwell Manor before leaving on her mission to Rokeby Hall, she had felt that she needed to watch and weigh everything she said, so that his incisive mind would grasp the correct meaning of her words without reading any unintentional nuances into them.

Somehow, he gave the impression that, even as he spoke, he was masterminding the whole conversation, plotting and planning several moves ahead. He must think very little of his fellow mortals, Lucy decided. Maybe that was why he had no friends, because he made people feel so small and incapable in comparison to himself.

At least, that was how he made *her* feel. Yet she was still determined not to let him get the better of her. Now that she had his precious deeds, she was free of him.

This thought gave her confidence. Reaching inside her bodice and almost blushing in the heat of his penetrating gaze, she pulled out the rolled paper and handed it to him.

"My side of the bargain is completed," she told him coolly.

She noted the elegance of his fingers as he extended a hand and plucked the deeds from her fingers. He did not say a word as he undid the red ribbon binding them and cast his eyes over the pages, as if to reassure himself that they were, in fact, the originals and not a clever forgery.

Then he turned to her, as unsmiling as ever, and announced, "Very well. I, too, will complete my side. You are free to go."

The realization took several seconds to dawn on Lucy, but finally the truth sank in.

I am no longer in bondage to any man or woman—neither horse traders, Philip Darwell himself, nor the hideous Hardcastles, she thought, beaming in joy. *I can go home now and see Mother. Oh, how I've missed her!*

Maybe, after her visit home, she would go to London; she had always wanted to taste the excitement of the bustling capital. Perhaps she would carry out her plan to trace her brother Geoffrey, the success of which would gladden both her mother's heart and her own.

"Where will you go now?"

Philip's words drowned her runaway thoughts in iced water. Surely even he wasn't cruel enough to evict her from the farmhouse that very night and watch her stumble out into the wild bleakness of the winter landscape in her pitifully inadequate clothes and not a ha'penny in her purse?

She thought back to their bargain. There had been no mention of any payment, simply her liberty for the price of the deed. Yet, if there was any human kindness or gratitude in Philip's character, surely he would help her on her way, not send her out on foot in freezing weather? She reminded herself that in his eyes, she was nothing but a thief. Why should he help her?

Just as her spirits were starting to sag, a delicious aroma assailed her nostrils from the direction of the kitchen. She felt saliva gathering in her mouth at the thought of filling her stomach with food. She had regressed into a feral creature whose first instincts were to eat and survive.

Adam appeared bearing a steaming bowl of broth in which her avid eyes could spot big hunks of rabbit meat mixed with barley, herbs and vegetables.

"Poachers' broth," he told her, handing her a slice of coarse bread as an accompaniment to the repast.

She was halfway through the wholesome, satisfying meal before she looked up and inquired, "Am I the only one dining?"

Adam glanced at Philip, then down at his feet. Lucy frowned, puzzled. Could they not answer even a question as simple as this? She shrugged. First things first. She returned to her stew, ladling it up in great spoonfuls and following each mouthful with a bite of the gritty bread.

When there was nothing left but some small bones and an inedible crust, she heaved a deep sigh and felt her spirits returning to her.

It was at this point that Philip uncoiled his long, lean body from the armchair and stood up with his back to the fire.

"I think an explanation is due to you," he stated, his face expressionless, his eyes half covered by his heavy, long-lashed lids.

Lucy gazed up at him expectantly. There was a lot she wanted to know.

"Adam here ..." He waved a hand towards him and the head groom smiled disarmingly, reminding Lucy of the very first time she had been introduced to him in the kitchens of Rokeby Hall.

He still emanated the frankness and warmth which she found so appealing and she found herself recalling their kiss in the lane. But this was not time for reminiscences, however pleasant or puzzling, and she hastily recalled herself to the present.

"Adam used to live and work in Darwell Manor. He's Martha and Matthew's son. We grew up together, he and I, until the Earl, my father, deemed it unfit for the youth of the aristocracy to mix with that of the serving classes, and separated us. Adam was sent over to Rokeby Hall, where he quickly rose to prominence in the stables."

"But could he not have gained a better position in the house? As a steward, or cellar master, or even as personal servant to Mr Hardcastle?" interrupted Lucy.

Adam answered her question for her. "What? And be constantly in the company of that dog fox and his vixen daughter? Far better to be in the stables and out of reach of that bitch's vicious tongue – and you know just how devilish nasty Rachel can be!"

Lucy wasn't sure if that last remark was directed at herself or Philip. Both of them had had considerable experience of Rachel in all her moods, perhaps Philip even more than her.

"You weren't always in the stables, though, were you, my friend?"

Although Philip's chuckling remark was an aside, spoken in an undertone, Lucy nevertheless looked wonderingly at Adam who, blushing, admitted that he had conducted a dalliance with Rachel's maid-before-last, and it had been through her that he had gained the information about where Hardcastle kept the deeds.

"Then she must have been acquainted with Hardcastle's room!"

As soon as she had blurted out the remark, Lucy regretted it, seeing the mask of displeasure that settled over Adam's usually amiable features.

"Not more so than you yourself," observed Philip cuttingly.

Lucy bit her lower lip. Surely he didn't think she had allowed Hardcastle to have his way with her? Then she realized that there was a very good chance that he thought exactly that!

"Adam has long been acquainted with my plans. I asked him to keep watch over you. Maud told him about the sleeping draught, he got message to me that retrieval of the deeds was imminent and I stationed myself here in readiness. It was he who decided you should be the one to take the tankard of punch to Hardcastle's room."

Adam took up the story. "And I crept up the secret passage and watched you through the panelling to make sure you carried out your task."

He was spying on her! Perhaps he had seen her naked flesh when Hardcastle had tried to unfasten her dress! Anger gathered inside her like a storm cloud, but just before she said something she might have regretted, she remembered the choices he had given her – retrieve the deeds or be hanged as a thief.

She took a deep breath, then asked, "Why couldn't Adam have stolen the deeds back? It would have been a lot simpler."

Philip quirked a sardonic eyebrow. "Having you do it was much more fun. Besides, he has made a good life for himself at Rokeby. I didn't want to risk spoiling it for him. Adam's final task was to lead you here, to me. I must say that he carried out my instructions to the letter."

Lucy couldn't bear the look on of fawning gratitude on Adam's face, like a dog that had been patted and praised by its master. On the two occasions when he had kissed her, he had seemed a man of spirit and initiative. Was he really a mere lackey of Philip's? Or was he playing some devious game, in the hope of advancement if there were to be an increase in Philip's fortunes? For, if Philip could afford to employ his childhood playmate, then there would be no need for Adam to spend one second longer at Rokeby Hall.

Suddenly, the whole atmosphere in the unkempt room seemed to rise up and oppress her. There was too much that she did not understand. She felt as if they had both, in their own ways, used her as a pawn in some master plan of which only a small portion had been revealed to her.

Raising her head high, she plucked her cloak from the back of the chair where it had been placed to dry and told Philip, with as much dignity as she could muster, "Seeing as you have no further use for me, I shall be going."

Then she snatched open the door and launched herself out into the cutting wind and all-masking whiteness.

Almost immediately, Adam came bounding after her. "Where do you think you're going? If you've got nowhere, then come back to Rokeby Hall with me. I'll see that nobody suspects you of the theft. I'll find a way of looking after you, I promise."

"Back to Rokeby Hall?"

Lucy's voice was edged with bitterness. Was this the "freedom" she had suffered for, the freedom to return to slavery in the service of Rachel or some other like her, or to the sweet trap of the arms of yet another man whose attentions she had never sought?

She noted the hopeful expression in Adam's eyes, and the truth struck her; he was in love with her. She was not flattered by the realization, just rather sad for him. She remembered his efforts to cheer her up at the servants' party, his tender ministrations to her freezing hands and face in the lane and the passionate kiss that had warmed her more than ten cloaks would have done. And she knew his offer to look after her would extend far further than merely keeping an eye on her.

Perhaps, had she been a different kind of girl, she could have loved Adam in return. She despised herself for feeling somehow superior to him, a feeling which had not been present in her until she had watched his subservient lap-dog behaviour towards Philip.

That man! Whatever problem she had, Philip Darwell always seemed to be at the root of it. How she hated him! How she hated the way her treacherous body responded to him.

If only he could be stripped of his cruelty, coldness and arrogance and invested with some of Adam's warmth and tenderness, then he might resemble a man who was worthy of her love, a man possessed of a mixture of strength and sensitivity, proud but just.

But Adam was demanding an answer to his proposal – for that's what it had seemed. She sensed that his remark about looking after her extended far further than just making sure no suspicion fell on her when the theft was discovered.

Rory had promised to look after her, yet look at how he had let her down! No, this was it now. She was never going to be a man's chattel again. She was no more likely to accept Adam as a husband or lover than she was Philip. Especially Philip!

"Well? What do you say?"

"No, Adam. I could never return to that ... that prison. I appreciate your offer, Adam Redhead, but I'm not a servant. I was not raised as one and I have no intention of spending the rest of my life as one."

A crestfallen look creased Adam's freckled features. Would it be too unkind, she wondered, to say what she had been about to confess – that she was not in love with him and could not envisage herself as his wife?

A peremptory voice cut in, taking the difficult decision out of her hands.

"Did I not tell you that Lucy is Martin Swift's daughter?"

Adam's mouth fell open and a look of respect entered his eyes. Lucy's father was a legend to anyone who worked with horses, as Adam did, and Philip's remark had done more to distance her from Adam than anything she could have said.

She could tell that now he was putting her on a pedestal, alongside Philip. His innate talent for servitude made her feel irritated with him. How could she ever have entertained the idea that there could have been a romance between her and Adam? She sensed that he was intelligent and resourceful enough to find a way round any kind of awkward or dangerous situation, yet here he was, mutely allowing Philip to take the lead.

Philip grasped Lucy firmly by the hand and led her back into the farmhouse. Adam marched obediently after them and Lucy was afraid to look round in case she saw any trace of disappointment on his face.

"No, do not remove your cloak," ordered Philip, seeing Lucy's hand straying towards the clasp. "We are not lingering here. I have a horse outside and will take you back to Darwell Manor before an outcry is raised and your footsteps are traced to this spot.

"Adam will return to the Hall now. If he is questioned, he will claim that he was out gathering firewood as the kitchen store was getting low, noticed your footprints, tracked you this far, but found nothing but the hoof prints of a horse and concluded that you had had a rendezvous with a fellow thief who had come to fetch you away. They will not question any further. Adam is a trusted employee and everyone would vouch for his honesty."

Adam left then, to tramp the two miles back to the Hall. Philip was already dousing the fire and blowing out the candles. In a few moments' time, they would be heading up the hill in the direction of Darwell Manor.

As for tomorrow … perhaps she would at last be able to return to Pendleton and her mother's side.

And her father's wrath.

Chapter Nineteen

"Down by the Sabden Brook
He strayed both late and early.
So strange and wild his look,
His hair was black and curly ..."

Lucy broke off her song and put down the lute on which she had been accompanying herself. She had found the instrument lying covered in dust and cobwebs in the Manor's long-disused music room and had asked Philip's permission to retune its strings and restore the neglected instrument to playing condition.

Her mother, who had been a passable musician before her marriage to Martin Swift had drained her of any form of creative pleasure, had schooled Lucy in the lute and harpsichord and had been gratified to see her daughter develop into a performer of some accomplishment.

Lucy's skills had grown as rusty as the lute strings over the last few months, but although she now had ample time for playing, she found she could not concentrate. Every note she played, every word she sang, sounded shallow, hollow and devoid of emotion. She felt locked up inside her own head, incapable of expressing her feelings, or even of understanding what those feelings were.

"You can stay here until the weather improves," Philip had told her.

Martha had been delighted to have Lucy back and life continued just as it had been before Christmas, on the surface at least. But something had subtly changed. She was not a prisoner any more, being kept at the Manor against her will. Now, she was an invited guest and her host was as gallant and charming as could be. But she knew that once the weather improved, she would be expected to leave.

Now that he had no further claim over her, Philip treated her courteously, almost as a sister. He played card games with her and they even had music sessions, with him on violin and herself on lute. He laughed, he joked, he seemed a changed man and all because the deeds were back in his hands.

The trouble was, she liked this new Philip. In fact, it was more than liking. She wished ...

But there was no point in wishing and dreaming. Philip was done with her. She had fulfilled her purpose. Soon, he would meet a well-bred young lady and start courting, and the thought of that made Lucy sob into her pillow at night and force herself to think of Rory.

Hardcastle had paid him a visit – luckily Philip had spotted his carriage coming up the drive and had had time to warn Lucy to hide in her room – and when he had departed, utterly convinced that Philip was as ignorant as to the whereabouts of the deeds as he was, Philip had knocked on her door and they had both burst out laughing like two successful conspirators.

The one thing Lucy greatly feared was that Hardcastle would spread her description abroad and she would be in constant danger of being recognized. The simultaneous disappearance of both maid and documents was too much of a coincidence and Hardcastle was convinced that Lucy was the thief.

Quite apart from that, he grumbled to Philip, Rachel was making his life a misery by moaning constantly that she would never find another maid as good as Lucy.

It gave Lucy a moment of secret pleasure to think that she could succeed at anything she turned her hand to – with one exception. There was nothing she could do to prolong her stay at Darwell Manor, particularly now that the weather had improved. And that meant saying goodbye to Philip forever.

The freezing weather lasted until the end of January but, with the first days of February, the ice had melted, the sky had cleared and snowdrops were pushing their belated way through the sodden ground. Any day now, she was going to have to be on her way.

She didn't want the embarrassment of waiting until Philip told her to leave. It would have to be her own decision and, without money, her only recourse was to return home. Back to her father's violence and drunkenness, back to his unsuitable and unacceptable marriage plans.

However, she had grown a lot stronger and more resilient since leaving home. Maybe now, she could stand up to her father and defy him not with childish protests, but with reasoned, adult argument. Martin, for all his faults, was not an ogre like George Hardcastle.

With Rory gone and Philip unreachable, the path home was the only one she could tread. She was reluctant to confess to her parents that she was returning just as she had left, without a crock of gold or a rich husband to show for her five months of absence. Without her maidenhead, too, though she had no intention of owning up to that. She was only thankful that her waist wasn't swelling.

She would never be able to tell them that, for a short space of time, she *had* had a husband, a man of whom they would have disapproved. She could never tell them of the circumstances surrounding that strange marriage. They would never understand how she, their daughter, could have loved the wild, wandering man with the strange visions and poetic words. That would always have to remain her secret.

She cried for him less often now and had even, when having cynical thoughts about men in general – her father, Philip, Adam and Hardcastle – numbered Rory among them on account of his infidelity.

Yet she had as good as killed him. She would never forgive herself for that, nor forget. If only she hadn't gone looking for Rory that morning and found him with that girl. Perhaps, if she had been ignorant of his tryst, they might have sorted out their problem, whatever it was, and might still be living together now, in blissful happiness.

But life was full of "if onlys." Now, it was *if only I could stay a bit longer at Darwell Manor.*

She strode impatiently to the window and peered out. It was a sparkling day with a clear blue sky and a pale sun as fresh and delicate as a primrose's petals. Lucy's heart should have rejoiced as she gazed out over the rolling parklands, yet the premature beauty of the new year was lost on her. She could see no happiness in her future, nothing to look forward to.

What delights faced her at home? What joy was there in watching her mother age, her father drinking even harder? She would help her mother about the house; go visiting and entertain in a small, limited way; aid her father in any way he deemed fitting for a daughter.

Eventually, though she could hardly bear to think about it, they would die and she would be left alone in the house, to grow old herself without even the consolation of a husband and family around her. For she would never marry again, she knew that. All men were flawed: Rory by his womanizing, her father by his drinking, Adam by his servile streak, Philip by his ...

Lucy simply couldn't define her opinion of Philip, even to herself. It would not form into coherent words. He disturbed her, made her uncomfortable, yet he could make her laugh, too, and move her soul with his music and sometimes she had caught him looking at her in a way that reminded her rather too clearly of the time when he almost ravished her in the stable.

He was unlike anyone she had ever met, at times so aloof and arrogant, yet at others so friendly and open. He had announced his intention of going back to join the cavalry soon and that was yet another reason why she should say her farewells and leave.

As if summoned by her thoughts of him, Philip suddenly came into view, wandering round the corner of the house in the general direction of the lake. He had a brindled hound called Solomon by his side and, as Lucy watched, he bent and fondled the animal's ears.

She caught her breath. There was something very intimate about what she was witnessing. Unaware that he was being watched, completely off his guard, Philip was showing a measure of affection towards the animal that she would never have guessed was in his nature.

He stooped, picked up a twig and hurled it as far as he could. The barking animal hurtled after it, brought it back and laid it at Philip's feet. Then it rolled over onto its back, tongue lolling, letting Philip tickle and caress its soft, pinkish-brown belly.

She could see his lips moving as he spoke to it and Lucy felt her heart move, too. They made an attractive picture, the tall, slim, striking-looking man with the glossy hair and the playful, adoring dog. Philip's fingers, stroking, rubbing, teasing... Was that how they caressed a woman's flesh, brushing the hair back behind the ears, running down the spine, sweeping over the body with such assurance and expertise?

Lucy stood mesmerized, delicious tingles rippling through her body. *No, no*, she chided herself. She couldn't, *mustn't*, think of Philip that way. What was wrong with her? She brushed her forehead with her hand. It was cool, yet the rest of her body felt suffused with a burning heat.

What kind of a fever was it that heated the blood without mounting to the brain? There must be something wrong with her. Her body seemed to be refusing to obey her mind's orders. There was a languorous heaviness in her limbs and disturbances in all her intimate parts, the way she used to feel when Rory touched her and she knew that he wanted her.

But there was nobody with her in her room, caressing her and murmuring promises of love. All she had done was take an accidental look at Philip Darwell fondling a dog. How stupid!

She left the window and sank onto the bed, trying to think of anything that might calm her and banish the aching, unwanted pangs of longing from her body. She was shocked by her physical arousal. The old worry that had first afflicted her after she'd given herself so readily to Rory, and which had returned when she found herself responding so readily to Adam's kisses, began to plague her anew.

Women were not meant to enjoy such sensations. Her own mother had told her that, in a rare moment of candour when Lucy had inquired how her sister Helen could bear to allow her husband to share her bed. Now, her mother's words came back to her in full.

"A woman allows a man to bed her only in order to produce heirs. Once the bedding has been successful, any reasonable man will leave his wife alone and seek that kind of pleasure elsewhere, with that kind of woman."

"What kind of woman?" Lucy had wanted to beg. Was she 'that kind of woman'? What was wrong with the human species, if only men were allowed to enjoy the intimate pleasures of marriage? What was wrong with her, in that she enjoyed it?

Could she be a rare hybrid, a creature with the body of a woman but the thoughts and lusts of a man? And could men see that she was 'that kind of woman'? Was this why she had found herself in so many dangerous situations, starting with the unbidden entry of her brother-in-law into her bedchamber?

The terrible throbs and yearnings were beginning to abate now. Lucy had herself under control again but was still worried. She found herself praying that these forbidden desires would never afflict her again and as she prayed, she thought of all those holy people, the monks and priests and nuns. Did they ever feel like this? And if they did, what did they do about it?

Of course, they must use the power of prayer, just as she was doing. If God could keep them from sinful thoughts and longings, surely He could do the same for her? Then she reflected that God probably had much more important things to do, like keeping the sun and moon shining and preventing the seas from engulfing the world, than stopping a woman longing for a man.

But which man? It wasn't Rory who was featuring in her thoughts now; she could have understood her bodily reactions if she had been reminiscing about his lovemaking.

Why on earth was she pining for Philip Darwell? The only time he had ever kissed or touched her had been in anger – except for that one half-forgotten occasion when he had reached out and touched her hair as she sat next to him while he traced a map of Rokeby Hall on the table top. She despised her breasts, her loins, her trembling limbs for their unruly, insubordinate behaviour.

When she and Philip dined that evening, Lucy could hardly bring herself to look at him in case the feelings started again. However, he was in a morose and uncommunicative mood, with a sullen, down-pulled twist to the corners of his mouth which defied all her efforts to make him smile.

Leaving him to gaze thoughtfully into the logs, she sought the company of Martha, who was teaching her how to spin. Fortified with home-made dandelion wine, Martha began chattering about Adam and about how she wished he could come back and work at Darwell Manor instead of having to work for that perfectly dreadful Hardcastle family.

All at once, she broke off her flow of conversation, fixed Lucy with a direct and meaningful look and said, "He asked after you, did Adam, last time he was here visitin'."

"You mean Adam comes here?" The thought had never crossed Lucy's mind. Of course he must visit them. He was their son after all, and Rokeby Hall was but a few hours' ride there and back.

"Last Thursday he came. It was his day off. 'How's Miss Lucy?' he asked me. I said as you were farin' well and he says to make sure I give you his ... regards."

Martha's slight hesitation conveyed to Lucy that perhaps his message had been something more than "regards." *Love?* She could never imagine herself marrying Adam, yet those kisses of his ... And many were the times that she had found herself regarding Martha almost as a mother.

It was strange how, before being introduced to Adam, she had not known that their surname was Redhead, having known them simply as Martha and Matthew. Did they, perhaps, view her as a possible daughter-in-law? They knew who her father was and the fact that the Swifts owned a pleasant house, a few acres of land and, doubtless, a reasonable amount of money, too.

Their son would do very well for himself if he married her. Yet Martha knew about what had passed between herself and Rory. No doubt she now thought of Lucy as slightly tainted merchandise, who would find it difficult to make a match among her social equals.

Though who *were* the Swifts' social equals? A horse trainer, no matter how expert and successful, was still a horse trainer and, as such, only slightly above the domestic servant class. She recalled her original reluctance to tell Martha the fact that she and Rory had been married and she was now a respectable widow. Well, now she *would* tell her, for perhaps it would place her in a different light. They would see that she was a girl who knew her own mind and would not hold with other people making plans for her behind her back.

Martha listened attentively to Lucy's tale, but with a growing look of concern on her wrinkled face. When Lucy had finished her account, rather than looking at her with the respectful expression she had expected, the small, thin woman leant towards Lucy and placed a hand on hers.

Shaking her head slowly, she said, "I'm sorry, my dear, but you shouldn't have believed him. That was not a lawful marriage."

Lucy's head reeled. What twaddle was the woman talking? She turned on her angrily, a protest on the tip of her tongue, but Martha's restraining hand and unwavering, sympathetic gaze reduced her planned attack to a mere, chilly, "Whatever do you mean?"

"I know this must come as a shock to you, child, but has nobody ever told you that, in order for a marriage to be legal, two witnesses must be present?"

"But there was Smithy and ... "

Of course! Pat didn't count. He was the one who was actually performing the ceremony. Martha was right. She and Rory had never been married at all. And those happy weeks during which she had shared his bed – why, she had been acting no better than that slut in the tavern!

Shame stained her cheeks crimson and her eyes flooded with tears. She hung her head and stared into her lap, watching her fingers twist nervously around each other. Then, on a sudden impulse, she snatched Rory's necklace from round her neck, snapping the thin, cheap chain, and flung it into the fire.

She regretted her action almost immediately and dashed towards the hearth, but Martha had anticipated her response and, seizing a fire iron, hooked out the trinket on its broken chain. It was warped and twisted by the heat of the flames and the chain was blackened to a sooty thread. In its ruined, misshapen state, it seemed to symbolize Lucy's wrecked dreams and lost love.

She took the tiny, spoiled thing and laid it in the palm of her hand, where it made dirty smudges. The symbolism was too overpowering for Lucy's vivid imagination to handle and she felt giant sobs well up from the pit of her very soul, and threw herself upon Martha in a storm of grief.

"There, there, child. Shush, now, it'll be all right. Don't you fret yourself, 'tis all over now. He's gone, he won't come back, and what matters most is that you thought you were married and that means you did no wrong."

"Do you really believe that, Martha?" whispered Lucy, through her tears.

The older woman nodded and continued to rock her like a baby until her sobs began to ebb like a passing storm, leaving a strange calmness in their wake.

The weeping had cleared Lucy's mind. At last, she knew what had been worrying Rory. She could understand perfectly how Rory, for all his impulsiveness and waywardness, must have found guilt lying heavily on his heart, knowing that he had cheated her.

If he had plucked up the courage to explain, how would she have reacted? Obviously, he had expected her to be furious and heartbroken, to flounce off after denouncing him as a lying, cheating exploiter of innocent young girls.

Yes, she would have felt this way, but not for ever. First and foremost had been her shining, wholehearted love for him, which nothing could have changed. As soon as he had expressed his desire to marry her legally, she would have said yes and clung to him, knowing that the truest, most important thing of all was the fact that he wanted to spend the rest of his life with her as her lawful husband.

Poor Rory. How upset and confused he must have been. Maybe he thought she had already guessed and that was why he had sought solace in another's body, thinking the situation was beyond hope.

Did she resent him for the way in which he had taken her in? She examined her feelings and concluded that she didn't. All she felt was sympathy, coupled with a strange sense of relief. The realization that Rory must have been suffering from a guilty conscience removed some of the burden from Lucy's soul. It was his own folly that had killed Rory.

Although she did not realize it until many months later, this moment marked a turning point in Lucy's life, the end of her period of mourning for her lost love. Whenever she thought of him in future years, it was to be with sympathy and gentle sorrow. The tearing, agonizing longing for him had gone for ever.

Chapter Twenty

The next day dawned as bright as the last. At nine, after she had break-fasted in her room, Philip sent a message that he was preparing horses for the two of them and that they were to take a ride up in the hills.

Lucy's spirits bubbled with anticipation. She missed the daily riding she used to do at home in all weathers and her restless, active nature demanded regular exercise. Without recourse to the mounting block, she sprang in agile fashion into the saddle, clad once again in her bor-rowed riding habit.

"How well you look today," remarked Philip, as they set out down the long, straight drive.

Lucy found herself surveying him and discovered that, in his tight cream britches, highly polished Hessian boots and burgundy riding jacket, he cut a very handsome figure indeed. His grey eyes sparkled with animation, and a slight flush of exertion from sitting his trotting mount accentuated the fineness of his complexion and the height of his jutting cheekbones.

She felt her heart skip a beat as she looked at him, and she goaded her horse into a canter so that Philip was momentarily left behind. He overtook her in a galloping flurry and the two of them raced neck and neck towards the high, wrought-iron gates, reining in their mounts at the very last moment in a noisy slither of hooves.

They were still laughing and bandying words as they ascended the winding track leading to the top of the ridge which overlooked the valley. A keen wind set her gelding's hide and ears twitching as they toiled up the last stretch of pebbly pathway and paused on the top of the hill.

Behind them stretched the patchwork of the valley which coiled for many meandering miles, connecting a dozen hamlets and villages and banded with the silver, snaking river. Ahead lay countless acres of nothingness, open moorland, growing ever steeper, until the hills became mountains and the valleys turned into the great lakes of Cumberland and Westmorland.

To their left, half a mile away perhaps, was a hump which rose some fifty feet into the air, like the back of a giant animal, crested with a spinney of dark, gaunt trees. As she looked at it, Lucy felt a sudden shudder and sensed magic in the air; old, pagan magic which had existed centuries before Darwell Manor had been built.

"Come on!" shouted Philip as he spurred his mount into a canter across the stony ground. His eager challenge dispelled the mysterious, evocative mood and Lucy set off after him, keeping a firm grip on the reins lest her mount should stumble on a loose stone or slip on a patch of muddy earth.

Their route led them across a series of hillocks and dips until Philip at last slowed to a halt in a sheltered, grassy grove. A cluster of gnarled mountain ashes, twisted and bent by the winter nor'easters, presided over the head of a clear mountain stream that fell in a miniature waterfall from the rock face, bubbled merrily through the grove and splashed among the lower outcrops of rocks.

Philip dismounted and tossed the reins over a tree stump. "Look!" he said, gesturing towards some feature at ground level which Lucy could not see without dismounting herself. When she did so, she found that the object at which Philip was pointing was apparently nothing more than a heap of stones close to the foot of the tiny waterfall.

She glanced at him in puzzlement, and then back at the stones. It seemed rather strange that such a variety of stones, some obviously not native to this particular part of the countryside, should have collected just at that spot. Something seemed to sparkle in a shaft of sunlight and Lucy looked closer. It was a fragment of green glass from an old bottle. There was a flash of blue, and one of red – more glass.

She gave Philip a questioning look and his face creased into a grin.

"I used to come here when I was a boy," he explained. "I tried to build a dam once, to trap the water and form a swimming pool, but the force of it carried away my stones every time. This is all that is left.

"I often come up here," he added. "I can pretend I am young again and all my problems just fall away and disappear, like the water dropping from the rocks."

Lucy was moved by his statement. Suddenly, as she looked at Philip, she could picture a small, shy lad in knickerbockers and stout shoes, scrambling about over the stones, or sitting beneath the ash trees pretending to be some character out of a game: a mountaineer perhaps, having just scaled the summit of the highest mountain in the world, or a fugitive king fighting to regain his lost kingdom.

How lonely Philip must have been as a boy. He kept his inner self well hidden but, when he revealed it in fleeting glimpses such as this, it touched something in Lucy's heart.

A hush had descended. Here in the hollow, the howling and singing of the wind in the rocks could no longer be heard. The distant piping of a chaffinch, the babbling of the stream, these were the only traces of reality in what had become an enchanted place where neither time nor reason existed. Surely ... *surely* Philip would kiss her now?

But he didn't, and Lucy was suddenly conscious of the restless, rhythmic movement of the horses' teeth snatching at grass blades, the slow swishing of their tails and the lingering disappointment in her heart.

* * *

That night, the feelings she dreaded revisited Lucy. She tossed and turned feverishly in her bed, trying to force her mind onto other, less disturbing subjects but, try as she might, thoughts of her childhood, of horses and music and all the other subjects she grasped at and fought to hold steady in her mind, simply evaporated. In their place came visions of Philip stroking the dog, Philip standing in the grove, Philip laughing, bent over the neck of a prancing horse or looking at her with that sudden, speculative, appraising expression.

The vivid images crowded in and obsessed her, giving her no rest but filling her with aching yearnings and uncomfortable stirrings. Why did he affect her this way when she didn't even like him? Why should a glance from him make her head swim as if she had drunk a whole glass of fine wine?

Every time she was in his presence, she tingled with awareness of him, as if a million tiny needles were pricking her all over. It wasn't fear, she realized, that made her so nervous and self-conscious when he spoke to her; it was her admiration for him, that made her want to say and do only what would raise, rather than lower, her in his esteem. Having to consider every word she spoke was a great strain.

As she lay there thinking about him, a sinful compulsion began to take control of her mind. She had no idea what time of night it was – midnight perhaps, maybe even one in the morning – but she knew Philip would be in his bedchamber, reading maybe, or perhaps even in bed, his dark locks spread across the white linen pillowcase, his face flushed pink from sleep, his lean, muscular body warm and relaxed beneath the covers.

She ached to light a candle, creep down the long corridors in the shadowy darkness, find his room, silently open the door and just gaze at him. She imagined his expression as he opened his eyes – eyes whose shade could change from smoky warmth to silver ice in an in-stant – and saw her standing there with her tousled chestnut curls tumbling over the shoulders of her white cambric nightgown. Surely his heart – and body, too – would be moved at the sight? He would not – *could* not – reject her!

The compulsion grew stronger. She *had* to go to him, even though she barely knew her way to his room and would no doubt feel cold in the draughty corridors. She couldn't dress, or even throw a shawl or cloak over her nightgown, as that would ruin the effect of spontaneous beauty that she wanted to create. Perhaps she could pretend that she was sleepwalking!

The embers in her bedroom fire were still glowing. Lucy thrust a candle into their midst and held it there until the wick sprouted a tiny flame. Then she left her room, shuddering as the chill night air penetrated her thin nightgown.

She climbed the stairs to the first floor and stealthily, silent as a moth in flight, she crept on bare feet down the dark corridor, shielding her candle with one hand lest a sudden draught extinguish its brave little flame. Several huge, framed portraits of relatives and ancestors of the Darwells frowned sternly down from their gilded frames and an ornate gold French clock, a relic of the Darwells' more affluent days, glinted elegantly from a console table.

Two doors stood open, revealing furniture covered in dust sheets. There were two more doors opposite one another, but no chink of light filtered out from either. Philip was obviously fast asleep. Perfect!

Lucy's heart beat quickly as she silently moved the handle of the first door, keeping the candle behind her so that the sudden glow would not wake him. She could make out the silhouettes of the carved oak panel at the foot of the bed and a heavy, imposing chest of drawers beneath the window, but in order to see Philip in bed, she would have to move the candle so that its light shone directly onto the pillow.

Gradually, she illuminated the room, moving the flame an inch at a time so that the pool of light it cast slowly encroached on the darkness. When the border of the candle's glow touched the pillow, Lucy stifled a gasp. There was no head resting there. The bed was empty and looked as if it had not been slept in at all.

Crestfallen, she stepped out and closed the door. She repeated her actions on the other side of the hall, but once again there was no sign of occupation. Could she be on the wrong floor entirely?

By now, Lucy was shaking from cold and fear and the bravado she had felt was beginning to leave her. Perhaps she should simply return to her own bedchamber and count herself lucky that she had been saved from humiliation by an act of fate. Perhaps Philip was in the study or the library, still poring over a book, oblivious to the time of night.

But the compulsion to see him and make her longings plain to him swept over her once more in a raging, fevered surge. Down the stairs she tiptoed, only to find the study door ajar and the room in darkness. The library similarly yielded no occupant.

She thought of the huge ballroom with its ghostly atmosphere and shuddered. Even if Philip was in there, which she doubted, nothing would persuade her to enter that empty, echoing space at past midnight, with drapes that wafted in the draughts like the billowing skirts of spectral dancers. She also knew that the faulty catch on the door had a strange way of locking unbidden visitors in.

There were other doors, but where they led she did not know, and she had no desire to explore them in the middle of the night. Apart from the servants' quarters where Martha, Matthew and the cook, deaf, crabby Eliza were taking their rest, the whole ground floor of the rambling Manor seemed deserted.

Even Solomon, the brindled hound, had not lifted its head and barked. It was stretched on a mat at the foot of the main stairs, regarding Lucy through one half-open eye. The eye closed and the dog heaved a deep sigh and proceeded to ignore her.

Lucy paused, rubbed the soft fur on its broad brow and then, remembering having seen Philip do the same thing, the burning urge to find him possessed her once more and she began to climb the stairs again.

This time, she walked the other way along the hallway, towards the rear of the house where she remembered Philip saying he had his room, as he liked to look out over the hills. As she raised her candle, debating what to do, an area of shadow in one corner suddenly assumed the shape of a man. Lucy stood transfixed, unable to scream, her vocal chords paralysed by fear.

The man appeared heavily built and dressed in something which gleamed dully in the weak, flickering light. Where his eyes should be, he appeared to be wearing some kind of slitted mask, like an executioner. He made no move towards her and she suddenly realized that he could not. The lurker in the shadows was nothing but an empty suit of armour.

The relief she felt lent her courage and without further hesitation, she walked unfalteringly towards the door on the left and pushed it open. The candle's guttering light sought the head nestling into the pillows, and found it, but the name she was about to whisper died on her lips as Lucy found herself staring into two red-rimmed, horribly distended eyeballs, yellowed like old parchment, in the center of which were two milky blue discs which hypnotized her with their crazed stare.

A crack opened beneath a nose on which the papery skin clung thinly to the bone that gleamed beneath, and a dry voice rasped faintly, "Eleanor?"

Then the eyes bulged terrifyingly and the living cadaver sat up, its livid flesh tinged red in the candlelight as if it were already upon the funeral pyre. The crack opened to a cavern and the deafening roar that burst from it sounded as if a demon had gained possession of the cadaver's soul.

"*ELEANO-O-O-R!*"

Chapter Twenty-One

"Philip ... Oh Philip, I am so terribly ... I didn't mean ..." Lucy's words, spoken in a voice that was choked with tears, were almost incoherent and her breath came in ragged gasps.

Philip looked ashen as he paced the floor, the green velvet jacket that was slung round his shoulders looking most incongruous over his nightshirt.

"You frightened him to death, that's what happened! He thought you were his dead wife come to claim his soul at last. And I'm not surprised the old man was misled. If you had wandered into *my* bedchamber dressed like that, I would have taken you for a ghost, for sure.

"But in God's name, woman, what were you doing in his room? Sleepwalking? Or looking for more deeds to steal? Why didn't you kill Hardcastle while you were about it? Instead, that swine is still alive and poisoning the face of the earth with his cheating and whoring, while my poor father ..."

He whirled round to face Lucy, his eyes flashing like slivers of steel, his lips taut with fury.

"Philip! No, don't hit me, please." Her whimper appeared to infuriate him still more as he stood over her, hands on his hips, his hair thrown back from his stark, white face. "I just got lost. I couldn't sleep. I ached. I thought that, if I could only walk a bit, ease my muscles –"

"Going for a walk? Dressed like that, with no shoes? In February? You must be mad! Or else there is some sinister meaning to all this which I have yet to discover."

"N-no, nothing s-sinister. I was … I just …"

"What were you doing going upstairs? I told Martha to warn you never to trespass and especially never to enter any rooms you had no permission to enter. You knew the extent of his frailty. Did you *want* to kill him?"

"Of course not," Lucy whispered.

This was the very worst thing that could have happened, worse even than entering Philip's room and having had him reject her. To kill his father! She had not known that he had cared so deeply for the old rogue who had gambled his fortune away.

Now, not only was she held in the deepest possible suspicion, but he would never again look on her with that light of warm interest in his eyes. What's more, she knew beyond the shadow of a doubt that she would be asked to leave as soon as the sun was up.

As if he were talking to his hound, Philip snapped, "Go to your room!"

Almost missing her footing on the stairs, so blinded was she by her tears, she fumbled her way back down to the solace of her bedroom, sobbing brokenly. She would never forget the way in which that skeletal body had levitated from the pillows, the way the clawing fingers had reached towards her, the insane look in the hideous eyes.

It had been his dying shout mingled with her screams that had roused Philip from his bed and sent him dashing into the room brandishing a sword, expecting to have to beat off robbers, or else Hardcastle come looking for his deeds.

When he had seen Lucy standing there in her nightshift, a dripping candle wavering in one hand, he had flinched in shock, then brushed hastily past her and gathered up his father in his arms. He was too late. The old man's spirit had already fled to rejoin his beloved wife's in some trysting place for faithful souls. All that was left was a brittle shell, which death had drained dry.

Trembling, Lucy had slunk from the room to allow Philip some privacy for mourning his dead father. But, rather than keep watch by his father's corpse, he had chased after Lucy, seized her arm and bundled her into his own room, where the tirade of questions and accusations had pelted her like stones.

Now, she lay huddled on her bed, her knees drawn up into her stomach protectively. Her right hand spasmodically gripped and released a corner of the goose feather pillow as the spasms of sobbing shook her. For it to end like this, before it had even begun! Before she had had a chance to tell Philip of her growing love for him!

It seemed so unjust. She was fated, doomed to wander the earth, keeping neither friend, lover, nor roof over her head, until ... until what? Until she died on the moors and her bleached bones were found, years hence, with nothing to identify them as being the mortal remains of Lucy Swift? Or until her wanton, uncontrollable desires led her to perish of some unmentionable disease in a city gutter!

She would throw herself on the mercy of the reverend sisters of some convent and become a nun, she decided. That was the only thing that would save her from her own wayward nature.

But, even as the idea formed, Lucy knew she was fitted neither by religious upbringing nor temperament to become a docile nun. As her sobs faded into weary gasps and her body started to sink into an exhausted sleep, she knew that it was her destiny to go home, back to Prebbledale and the grey stone farmhouse; back to her thankful mother and the calculating mind of her devious father.

* * *

Martha, dressed in sombre black as befitted a household servant in mourning, her usual white apron replaced by one of dull grey, woke her with a summons to join the new Earl in the library directly.

Lucy had completely forgotten that Philip would naturally inherit the title. How should she address him now? Sir? My lord? Obviously the casual 'Philip' of the previous months would no longer do at all. For a time, they had pretended to be friends and equals, but now he was elevated to a rank far above her own. She could no longer meet and speak with him as openly and carelessly as before, even if the old Earl had died in different circumstances.

It doesn't matter now, she thought bitterly. *The old Earl is dead, long live the new Earl, and could somebody please give me some assistance to travel speedily home.*

However, Philip had his own plans and they went far beyond the wildest bounds of Lucy's imagination to conjecture. As she walked into the library slowly and respectfully, wearing the homespun dress of Martha's and carrying her own old, torn dress wrapped in a bundle, all ready for a hasty and no doubt ignominious dismissal, Philip, from his seat at his father's magnificent mahogany desk, barked, "And where, pray, are you going, miss?"

"N-nowhere," stammered a dumbfounded Lucy, remembering to add, "Sir."

"I may be Earl Darwell now, but there is no need to address me like a snivelling servant girl addressing her master. We are partners, you and I, in crime if nothing else."

The way he stressed the word "crime" made Lucy look at him fearfully. Had it all come back to this? Did he view her now as he had viewed her when she first arrived at his door to deliver a useless mare? As a felon and a miscreant?

His next words substantiated her worst fears.

"There is more than one crime I could get you hanged for now."

"No!" The word burst from Lucy's lips. He had no right to resurrect this old threat. She had already paid for her first crime ... more than paid for it, if being abused by Hardcastle could be counted as evidence in her favour. The only crime of which she stood guilty now was the crime of having succumbed to her desire for a particular man, the one who now sat in judgement on her.

"Be seated, Lucy."

His calm, imperious tone both terrified and infuriated her. It would be so easy simply to tell him her real reason for wandering the house so late at night. So easy – yet so utterly impossible. She would never let Philip Darwell know how close she had come to crawling into his bed like a common slut.

Obediently, she perched on the very edge of a hard wooden chair, still clutching her bundle. Philip's keen gaze cut into hers, his eyes hard and opaque as flint.

"Never has one wrongdoer been given so many chances to redeem herself."

Whatever it was, she couldn't do it. She wouldn't. How could she perform any task for him now, knowing that all she would receive at the end of it would be, not his gratitude and pleasure, but a cold dismissal and the knowledge that he felt nothing for her but distrust and withering contempt?

Yet she knew she *had* to do it, whatever it was, because of the terrible hold he still had over her, now more than ever. What judge would ever believe that she, a girl of no means, had entered an elderly Earl's bedchamber at dead of night for any purpose other than that of crime? As for murder, creeping into the chamber of a man known to be haunted by visions of his dead wife, dressed in white like a ghost and bearing a single candle, would be all the evidence the law would need.

Philip had her cornered and, once again, she hated him for it. Yet the undeniable power that emanated from his stern presence set something deep inside her quivering. She loathed him, detested him, but she wanted him, too. It was too conflicting for her to comprehend.

"What I want you to do for me now is far less difficult than your last task, even though, God knows, the crime you have committed is far greater."

Lucy bit back the retort that sprang to her lips. She would never tell him the truth about her nocturnal ramblings. Never! Let him think whatever he wished.

"This time, the most difficult part of the task will be performed by myself."

She looked up in astonishment. Whatever did he mean? What was the catch?

"For heaven's sake, girl, drop that bundle. You look like a gypsy selling clothes-pegs."

The insult stung her and she placed the rolled-up gown on the faded library carpet with deliberate, insolent slowness. If she could not protest at his treatment of her in words, then she would do it with actions.

Philip appeared not to notice. "My father's death was a shock to me in more ways than one. After Matthew and I had laid him out, I spent the rest of the night going through his papers and boxes and I received more than one unpleasant surprise.

"I told you about my father's gambling habit, how he foolishly let that damn rogue Hardcastle rob him of all we possessed – the Manor, which you know about, of course, our fortune and my mother's jewels."

Lucy nodded and he continued: "I knew some of the jewels had gone, stolen by that ... that *vermin* over at Rokeby Hall, but I never guessed that my father had let them all go, even my mother's priceless emerald ring that had been handed down through the generations!"

He paused and stared thoughtfully down at the papers that were spread all over the table. The pause grew into an uncomfortable silence which made Lucy wish that she could escape from the room by melting invisibly into the walls. Maybe here, as in Hardcastle's library, there was a secret door by the fireplace. Lucy turned her glance speculatively towards the oak panelling, but Philip's voice recalled her wandering thoughts.

"Saturday next. That is the night of the great ball at Bidstone House which Lord and Lady Bellingdon are giving on the occasion of their younger daughter Pamela's birthday."

Lucy felt her mouth grow dry. Surely Philip would not expect her to go to the ball? Why, she had nothing to wear except one of Lady Eleanor's extremely outmoded gowns! Besides, the Hardcastles could not fail to recognize her.

As if reading her mind, Philip announced, "Naturally, the Hardcastles will be attending, especially since our dear Lord Emmett will be in

Manchester on business and will doubtless allow Rachel to feast her grasping little eyes on his esteemed and manly personage."

Despite the turmoil her thoughts were in, Lucy found she had to stifle a giggle at the thought of the unpleasant twosome the couple made, Rachel, with her pale eyes, stringy hair and flat body and the preening, lisping, effeminate Emmett, about as attractive as an earthworm.

Philip, however, did not show a trace of humour, even if he felt it. "Hardcastle will inform Adam of the time they mean to depart, so that he can ready the horses for the journey. Adam will have this information in the morning and will then send a messenger here.

"That will be the signal for you to set out on a fast horse for Rokeby Hall. I know what an excellent rider you are, so you can take Redshanks, my bay. How good is your memory?"

He shot the question at her so fast that Lucy found herself spluttering. "Well, I ... it depends what you mean. I –"

"Can you remember how to mix that unguent that your expert friends used when they wished a horse to appear lame for a while?"

The sneer in his voice as he said "expert" set her seething with indignation. "I think so," she said stiffly.

The mixing of the ointment had to be most precise, as did the timing. Apply too little, or mix it too weak and the animal would merely stumble slightly, then recover. Mix it too strong and the creature would fall to its knees, unable to rise until the effects of the paralysing drug had worn off. What could Philip have in mind?

"Excellent. Today is Thursday. You have two days in which to find the ingredients and mix your potion. Then, my little witch, you will fly on your broomstick over to the stables of Rokeby Hall and apply a good, strong dose to the hooves of two of the carriage horses. I think the ointment takes about an hour to penetrate the muscles and become fully effective?"

"Yes. That is correct."

How did Philip know this? Perhaps he had studied the activities of her erstwhile companions more closely than she had imagined.

"How will I know which horses to pick?"

"It will be the greys. They are the best lookers and the ones Hardcastle always chooses when he wishes to impress."

"How am I to enter the stables unobserved?" she asked, feeling that it was, in truth, a most risky business and fearing for her skin, if not her life, if Hardcastle or Rachel should observe her.

"It is all arranged. It will be almost dark by the time you reach the Hall. You should approach across the fields by a route which I will describe to you. A line of trees will shield you from the rear windows of the Hall. I have arranged with Adam for the gate leading to the stable yard to be left unlocked.

"He will be in the coach-house, engaging the coachmen and grooms in conversation. He will keep them there as long as he can, but I would reckon you have no more than ten minutes in which to enter the loose-boxes, pick out the correct horses, apply your fiendish mixture to two of them and get clear of the yard."

"Why two? Surely one lame horse would be sufficient? In any case, what is your purpose? Simply to prevent the Hardcastles attending the ball?"

"No, you silly goose. What good would that be to me? I couldn't give a damn if Rachel finally manages to lure Emmett into proposing. It's just the kind of thing she would do in order to upstage her friend at her own birthday party. And equally well, what care I if Hardcastle spends the whole night whoring with some silk-clad slattern? I just don't want them to do it with my mother's jewels on their pox-ridden bodies. Surely my plan is clear to you now?"

Lucy thought that it was, but she had no desire to hazard a guess. She wanted Philip to explain it himself, because she was enjoying his colourful descriptions of the Hardcastles and their extraordinary habits, so she continued to gaze at him in wide-eyed silence, inviting him to continue. Listening to him talking like this, she could almost forget that she was once more his prisoner, subject to his every order and whim.

"The ball begins at eight. Bidstone House is an hour's fast ride from Rokeby Hall. As Rachel is bound to make them late with her grumbling and her preening, my guess is that they will take the shorter but more hazardous moorland road, rather than the less direct one through the valley and round the hill. I asked you to apply your physic to two horses because I could not take the risk of your picking the one horse in the entire world which was unaffected by your medicine."

"But will they not think that something suspicious is afoot if two of their best horses go lame at the very same moment?" Lucy's doubts about the scheme were increasing with every moment that passed.

"They will not have time, I assure you. They will have something far more important than collapsing horses to occupy their minds – the appearance of a fearsome, armed highwayman!"

"You mean you are going to rob them of your own jewels? You, an Earl, act as a common thief?"

Philip gave a hollow chuckle. "I shall only be reclaiming what is my rightful inheritance. As for turning thief, it seems a very easy thing to do, which rests lightly on my conscience."

The way he looked at Lucy through half-closed lids, a calculating expression on his face, made her cringe inside. Whatever he thought, she was not a natural born wrongdoer. It did not come easily to her, as he was implying. She hated it. She feared the risk of discovery and the chance that she might forget her instructions and make some mistake.

And yet there was a certain thrill about cloak-and-dagger activities which appealed to some wild streak in her, the same streak that had caused her to fall in love with Rory – and now, very regrettably, with Philip, too.

"But when the horses recover ... what then?"

"Matthew is a countryman born and bred. His predictions about the weather never fail. He says it will be misty on the moors these next few nights, and I believe him. When I appear, I shall be intoning some jiggery-pokery which they will take for a spell. Then, when I have left with my booty and the horses have miraculously recovered, they cannot fail but to believe that they met with a magician, who cast some enchantment which caused their horses to stagger and fall at the very spot where he materialized."

A silence fell between them. Lucy shuffled her feet nervously, her mind filled with a thousand reasons as to why this latest of Philip's plans was too dangerous to undertake, for him as well as her. She had to speak out, tell him what was on her mind, even if he thought her a 'silly goose'.

"Surely your position with Hardcastle is dangerous enough already? He must have boasted to his cronies about having won this house from your father. If challenged, how will you explain the fact that you now have the deeds back in your possession?

"And as for the jewels, many people will have seen Rachel and her mother wearing them, and I cannot believe that Hardcastle and his family will not tell of their theft by this strange highwayman. You will be in possession of stolen property. You could be hanged yourself!"

The irony of her statement was not lost on Philip, who smiled wryly before replying, "I think not, Lucy Swift. You see, for all his faults, Hardcastle is a cautious man. I doubt that anyone has been told the true circumstances of how he acquired the deeds to Darwell Hall. For him to have bragged of that would have scared off the other gamblers he is planning to cheat.

"I believe he would have kept silent about the house and taken possession of it on my father's death, of which he has no knowledge yet, of course, with the pretence that he had purchased it from me. To have admitted that he had won it at cards would have been too alarming for his future dupes.

"As for my mother's jewels, I shall certainly have to avoid showing them off in future. I may even have to sell them abroad to raise money to keep the estate going. But remember that Hardcastle is hated in Cheshire, Lancashire and far beyond. Most of the well-to-do families around here have lost small fortunes to him, and were he to challenge me and accuse me of theft, and were I to denounce him as a cheat and a swindler, it would be I who would be supported.

"People do not like to admit to their gaming losses, Lucy. If Hardcastle accused me of theft, I would make him admit precisely how much he had won from my father. Others would begin to realize that it was not they alone who had lost all to the wretch, and my own counter-accusation of his cheating at cards would ring true, especially I happen to have in my possession a pack of his marked cards, obtained for me by Adam.

"It is my belief that Hardcastle will keep silent about his losses and look for other ways to wreak revenge on me. That, I look forward to eagerly, as another opportunity to crush him!" Philip smiled grimly.

Lucy had to admit to herself, albeit grudgingly, that the plan seemed flawless. If only she could be there to see the expression on Rachel's face as the two horses fell, halting the others and tangling the traces and necessitating that the whole Hardcastle family leave the coach and stand in the mud and mist in all their finery!

She felt sorry for Rachel's mother, that sad, ineffectual woman whom she had no desire to harm. Philip was correct, though. The jewels were his by right and had been unfairly won from his weak-witted father. She could only applaud his imaginative efforts to retrieve the Darwell inheritance.

However, there was one thing that she could not tell him, for fear that not only her future freedom, but her very life would be in jeopardy, and that was the fact that she had never actually mixed the numbing potion herself. She had only watched Smithy gathering herbs, boiling them into a juice and adding a white powder which he had purchased from an apothecary. She had no idea which herbs and what powder.

There was only one thing she could do and that was to confide in Martha and Matthew and enlist their aid.

As soon as Philip had dismissed her, she made her way to the kitchens where she knew she would find Martha helping the doddery old cook. As soon as she started to explain her problem to the red-faced housemaid, whose brow dripped with perspiration as she stirred a bubbling pot which hung over the roaring fire, Martha dismissed her with a wave of her hand.

"No use talking to me o' these things. Matthew's the one. He's out yonder somewhere, sweeping the path or summat. He'll know what you want."

Indeed, to her surprise, Matthew knew exactly what Lucy needed – and why. It was obvious that Philip kept little from Adam, and Adam kept nothing from his parents, no matter how secret. Lucy found herself wondering if, trustworthy though she knew them to be and much as she liked them, they perhaps knew more than was good for them to know.

But who was she to suggest that a son should not confide in his own parents? In any case, she felt she trusted Martha and Matthew more than she did Adam. It was a wonder he didn't harbour a deep-seated grudge against Philip for forcing him to work at Rokeby Hall. And yet, surely he could have taken a job elsewhere? He did not have to work at the Hall. Maybe he stayed there purely out of loyalty to Philip, in order to aid him with his plans. After all, if Philip succeeded, and wealth and property were to be his once more, would not Adam benefit also?

Matthew informed Lucy that she should leave it to him. He even offered to mix up the paste for her, but a slight niggle of distrust prompted her to thank him but inform him that just obtaining the ingredients would be sufficient. She would do the rest.

She felt certain she could remember Smithy's method, though she hoped Matthew would not think that her father, that most reputable of horse dealers, dabbled in such underhand and illegal practices.

She saw Philip only briefly the following day as he was busy making arrangements for his father's burial, which was to take place the following Monday. Messages had to be sent out to relatives and old family friends and the Manor was to expect several sombre and sympathetic visitors. He still found time, however, to run through the next day's arrangements in a manner which made her feel rather like a child having a lesson drummed into its skull by an over-strict tutor.

She felt pathetically grateful to him for smiling at her in a kind fashion once she had repeated his instructions, then hated herself for feeling that way. What had happened to her pride? Had it totally deserted her? She despaired of herself. She might want him, but she would never win him. Why could her benumbed brain not understand this fact?

The moment her next ordeal was over, she would leave and at last be free of the ill-luck which had dogged her ever since she had set foot in the Manor.

Chapter Twenty-Two

Galloping at breakneck speed over the moorland path in the dangerous dimness of dusk was a joy indeed. A wild notion came into Lucy's head simply to keep on riding, right past Rokeby Hall and out to whatever lay beyond – new surroundings and people who knew neither her nor her history and didn't care, being content to accept her as she was.

Yet, attractive as the idea was, it would mean never seeing Philip again, and that she could not bear. Better to help him carry out his plan and hope that maybe, just maybe, something would make him soften his attitude towards her, bring back that warm light that sometimes crept into his eyes when he looked at her.

She still harboured a niggling fear that, if she disobeyed him, she might find herself accused of his father's murder. In any case, she had no desire to run from him. She was mad with desire for him, and the further her horse travelled from Darwell Manor, the more she found herself longing to see Philip speeding after her.

But no figure approached her in the twilight. There was nothing but trees, rocks and gathering gloom. Ahead, in a hollow between two rocky ridges, she could see the clump of dark evergreens that marked the front boundary of Rokeby Hall.

Lucy kept to her instructions and slowly walked her horse past the line of sturdy oaks that separated the formal gardens from the surrounding land. The gate leading into the stable yard was unlocked, as Philip had promised. The messenger from Adam had reported that, as

Philip had suspected, the greys were to be used that night, four magnif-icent, powerful animals which, fortunately, shared adjacent stabling.

Lucy slid the bolt on the door of the first stall and the startled animal whickered softly in surprise as she stood beside it, running an expert hand down its flank before picking up a hoof and daubing it liberally with her foul-smelling ointment. The well-trained gelding made no fuss as Lucy treated each hoof in turn. Then, giving its long, dappled nose a stroke, she vacated its stable and entered the next.

The second horse, however, was of a decidedly different tempera-ment. It snorted and shied at the presence of a stranger and Lucy could not corner it and as it skittered from one end of the loosebox to the other. She let herself out just in time, before the nervous beast took a nip out of her shoulder.

The third carriage horse, however, allowed Lucy to do what she wished and rewarded her with a slimy lick from its gigantic tongue which left a line of equine spittle right down her cheek.

Wiping it with her sleeve, she was just stealing off to the shadow of the trees where she had left Philip's bay tethered to a branch, when she heard a door opening and the sound of men's voices spilling out in the clear night air. One of them was unmistakably Adam's.

Due to the skittishness of the second horse, her task had taken sev-eral minutes longer than she had intended. How was she to get away unseen, now that the stable staff were milling around the yard, throw-ing open the gates of the coach-house, rushing around with newly polished saddlery?

She was worried that the pungent smell of the unguent might still be lingering inside the loose-boxes. Nobody with a sharp nose could fail to wonder at the odour and she prayed that the strong smell of the animals and their droppings would cover up the alien traces.

At last came a moment when no one was in sight. Lucy crept out of the stable yard, swung herself into the saddle and urged her horse into the shadow of the massive, leafless trees.

Suddenly, her mount shied, snorting in terror as a shadow detached itself from the gloom and came to an arm-waving halt before her. Lucy almost lost her seat and had to struggle for control of the frightened animal. As soon as she had calmed it down with a pat and a soothing word, she saw who it was who had had caused the trouble. Adam.

"I kept the men talking as long as I could. You should be half a mile away by now. What happened?" he inquired.

She explained and when she had finished, he took hold of her horse's bridle, placed a hand on her knee in far too familiar a fashion, and whispered in a low, urgent voice, "Philip should never have sent a girl on an errand of this nature, especially you. You know that I care for you, and about what happens to you. How did he persuade you to come over to the Hall and put yourself in danger like this? What is his hold over you?"

When Lucy refused to answer, not wishing to incriminate either herself or Philip in any way, he continued, in the same tense, hurried whisper, "No matter. I can see that you are prepared to do anything for him. Though what Philip has done to deserve ..."

His voice tailed off. "Hasten now," he said. Stepping back, he gave her mount a hefty slap on the rump which sent it charging off in the direction of the fields beyond the trees.

Lucy hung on grimly, cursing Adam for what seemed an act of spite and jealousy. By the time she was safely out of sight of Rokeby Hall and had nothing but open moor between herself and Darwell Manor, she had come to several more conclusions about Adam Redhead and she did not like their implications in the slightest.

She could understand one man being jealous of another over a woman, but here there seemed to be more than jealousy involved. Far from acting the subservient slave to Philip, Adam was not only criticizing his former master, but displaying signs of positive enmity which boded ill for any future plans of Philip's in which Adam was involved.

Philip must be blind to trust him, she thought. There had been something in Adam's voice as he spoke the words, "What is his hold over you?" which implied the possibility of Philip's having a hold of some kind over Adam, too. There was the way he had stressed the word *you,* so slightly that it took a sharp pair of ears like hers to pick up the emphasis.

Or was he merely referring to the love affair which he imagined the two of them to be having? Perhaps the phrase had been mere sarcasm, and by Philip's "hold" over her, he meant a handsome face and a lusty pair of thighs, and was sick with envy at the thought.

If only he knew the truth! Yet if he did, he would be bound to try to pay court to her and she would be bound to reject his advances once again. Better to leave him thinking that Philip and she were in love. It was at least half true.

Chapter Twenty-Three

Matthew's weather prediction had been right. Philip took up his vantage point on a hill overlooking the moorland road in a chilly swirl of mist that grew thicker by the second. It was too dark to check the time by his father's heavy gold pocket watch but he guessed it must be somewhere in the region of a quarter past seven. Any time within the next half hour, he might hear the Hardcastles' coach come rumbling up the steep track.

His horse shifted restlessly beneath him, seeking an escape from the damp, bitter wind, and Philip's hands were numb on the reins by the time his lonely vigil was rewarded by the sound of an approaching carriage. He spied the yellow flare of the lamps, illuminating the hindquarters of the horses … But something was wrong.

Instead of the four greys he had been led to believe would pull the carriage that night, there were four chestnuts instead. What had gone wrong with his plan? The silly bitch must have mixed the ointment wrongly, causing the greys to fall lame before leaving the stables – or maybe she hadn't carried out his plan at all!

A rich stream of curses left Philip's lips. He could not believe that such a simple strategy could possibly have failed. Here were the Hardcastles, a mere quarter of a mile away, with his jewels, boxed up inside the coach, so close, so nearly within his grasp and yet so impossible to retrieve. When would he get another opportunity as perfect as this one?

He shrank back, merging into the shadows of a clump of trees as the Hardcastle's coach drew level with him, fifteen feet below. The driver's whip lashed out and curled round the flank of one of the rear horses which put on a sudden spurt so that, for a moment, the carriage jerked diagonally across the path before resuming its rhythmic forward trundle up the stony track. A streamer of mist curled around the hillside and blanketed the road. It was impossible for Philip's eyes to penetrate the thick haze, but he knew that, by the time it cleared, the Hardcastles would be out of sight around the next hill.

He patted his horse's neck and gave the impatient animal the signal to walk. Horse and rider picked their way carefully over the rocky ground and had just descended onto the level surface of the road when a tremendous crash and a barrage of shouts and curses, mingled with piercing female screams, caused them to stop in their tracks. The ears of Philip's mount flickered to and fro and Philip strained to catch the sounds through the darkness and work out their cause.

Quickly, he guided his horse off the road again and plunged up the hillside. The veil of mist shredded and parted before him and there, stationary, a short way ahead of him, was the Hardcastle's carriage, two puzzled coachmen arguing over the prone form of one of the two leading chestnuts, which was sprawled on its belly.

It was unable to rise, due to the fact that it had steered too close to a tree in the fog and a branch had snagged the traces, causing the horse to twist and fall and snapping the harness into the bargain. The shocked gelding's eyes were rolling in a terrifying manner and its flanks were shuddering with the effort of trying to untangle itself. Maybe it had even broken a leg! Philip's prayers had been answered after all.

Without a moment's consideration of whether or not Hardcastle or his attendants might be armed, he drew his pistol from his belt and, with a shout of "Ho, there!" he urged his horse towards them at a fast canter.

Harriet Hardcastle pressed her hand to her chest and seemed about to faint at the sight of the armed, masked man who was wrenching open the carriage door. The colour drained out of George Hardcastle's ruddy face as he splutteringly protested that they were carrying no money or valuables.

Philip gestured with the barrel of the pistol towards the necklaces and earrings that the two women were wearing. Harriet snatched off her earrings, lacerating one ear lobe in her haste to hand the delicate amethysts to the dangerous-looking villain who was standing there in such menacing silence. Then, without any urging, she handed over the ruby necklace and rings.

Without a word, Philip pocketed the jewels, then turned to Rachel, who was regarding him with a look of icy, imperious disdain. He moved the muzzle of the pistol close to her neck, but still she refused to hand over the gems with which she had proposed to dazzle Lord Emmett that evening to a common highwayman. Philip was forced to speak to her.

"Unfasten those trinkets you're wearing and hand them over quickly, or I shall shoot!"

He spoke in a rough, grating tone, to disguise his voice as much as possible. Rachel's eyes were fixed on him in such a penetrating look that he felt she was stripping him of his mask.

"Do you want me to kill you, pretty lady?" Philip inquired harshly, jabbing the end of the pistol barrel into her neck, just below the ear, in which dangled a flashing emerald surrounded by small diamonds, the same jewels his mother wore in the portrait which hung in Darwell Manor.

"Do as he says, daughter. This blackguard will only shoot you if you don't," ordered Hardcastle, who was crouching in cowardly fashion in the far corner of the carriage's interior, ignoring the moans of his wife who was slumped next to him, a lavender-scented lace handkerchief held to her mouth.

"Then shoot me, scoundrel," invited Rachel, with cool insolence.

His pistol still fixed against her neck, Philip raised his left hand and brought the full force of its leather-gloved power down onto Rachel's right cheek. She screamed and clapped her hand over the fiery marks that scored scarlet streaks across her sallow skin.

With one tug, Philip wrenched the necklace from her neck, stuffed it into his pocket to join the rest of his booty, then plucked each earring in turn from her ears. Rachel was wearing white kid gloves, beneath which Philip could detect the bulging outlines of the jewels she wore on her fingers.

"Your rings, too," he ordered, pressing the gun still harder against her neck. "It would give me great pleasure to shoot you. All of you," he added, cocking the trigger with a click which made Harriet squeal and press her hands over her eyes.

Philip's slap had shaken Rachel's nerve and she quickly drew off her gloves and tugged the rings from her square, mannish fingers. She handed them to him, pouring them in a jingling heap into the palm of his hand. Scarcely letting his gaze leave Hardcastle and Rachel for an instant, he selected one, a large emerald on a gold band, the mount of which was fashioned like two hands meeting around the stone, then let the rest trickle through his fingers like so many fairground trinkets onto the carriage's dark floor.

He moved the gun away and Rachel immediately sank to her knees and began scrabbling about, retrieving them. Philip noted with satisfaction that the marks he had left on her cheek were beginning to turn into purple bruises, which would doubtless ruin her chances of receiving a proposal that evening.

Bidding the company a cheery "Adieu!", he slammed the door of the carriage shut behind him. The coachmen were nowhere to be seen.

He made to mount his waiting horse, then noticed that the fallen carriage horse was beginning to make a wobbly ascent from its prone position. That moment's hesitation nearly proved fatal as a sudden, ear-splitting report from behind him took Philip by surprise.

He hurled himself sideways just as a bullet whistled past, grazing his shoulder in its passage. Thoughts pelted through his brain at thrice the normal speed. As soon as he hit the ground he kept on rolling, clutching his shoulder so that his would-be assassin, no doubt one of the coachmen, would think him seriously wounded. Wincing as his body collided with sharp rocks, he directed himself towards a thick cluster of gorse bushes and, shielding his face against their myriad thorns, burrowed into the centre of their thick stalks, where he found himself in a natural hollow with the prickly twigs spreading above and around him in a protective shield.

He could hear distant shouts, and the scrunching of feet over the hard, pebbly ground. He held his breath as a pair of boots strode over to the clump of bushes where he had taken refuge. The boots paused awhile, then turned and began to move slowly away, and Philip noticed with great interest that affixed to the gleaming leather were a pair of very distinctive silver spurs. Cavalry spurs, they looked like, although it was impossible to tell for certain in the darkness.

He squirmed forward on his belly to take a closer look, wriggling like a snake around the thick, twisted gorse stems. His eyes had not deceived him. They *were* cavalry spurs, the very pair which he had given, three years earlier, to Adam Redhead.

* * *

Lucy paced up and down, unable to rest. For the third time, she made a circuit of the rooms she had come to know so well, the library, the study, the long, elegant drawing-room, the banqueting hall, even the deserted ballroom, with Philip's hound trotting docilely by her side. Finally, she sank exhaustedly into a chair in the drawing-room and rang the bell for Martha or Matthew to bring her some food and drink to sustain her during her long vigil.

"Dear Solomon," she said, fondling the hound's silky ears. "You're not happy without your master, are you?"

The animal gave her a mournful glance from its liquid brown eyes.

"Where is he, then?" she murmured, rubbing the bristly ruff at the back of its neck. "Do you think you could find him?"

The dog shifted half an inch closer to her, as if for comfort. Sighing, Lucy removed her caressing hand and informed it, "No, I'm not very happy, either."

With a sigh, the dog sank down, rested its heavy head on its forelegs and gazed morosely into the fire. Lucy envied that ability to relax, that capacity for waiting, and wished she had some of the animal's patience.

The door opened and Matthew came in bearing a bowl of hot beef broth, some freshly-baked bread and an assortment of cheeses and cold meats. He placed them on a small table at the side of her chair, then asked meaningfully, "Master not home yet?"

"No, Matthew. I have no idea where he could have got to."

Did Matthew know about the "robbery?" How much had either Philip or Adam told him? The same uneasy feeling which had affected her after her meeting with Adam that evening stole over her again. Matthew knew something; she was sure of it. He was implying that something might have gone wrong with Philip's plan. Yet at the same time, he was not giving anything away.

Could he and Martha suspect that their son was not completely loyal to Philip? If this was the case, why had they not voiced their suspicions to Philip himself? Of course, she realized; they were Adam's parents. Their loyalty towards their son came before their loyalty to their employer.

Still, she could tell that Matthew was worried and unhappy. He lingered in the room as if trying to make up his mind whether or not to tell her something. Then, abruptly, he walked out, leaving Lucy staring unseeingly at the steaming broth.

An uncomfortable, prickling sensation in her bones warned her that Philip was in some kind of danger. Either that, or his scheme would fail owing to something as simple as Adam having persuaded the Hardcastles to take the longer, safer route to Bidstone House after all.

She had no reason to suspect that Adam wished to harm Philip physically. Maybe she was building it all up in her imagination and Adam was still Philip's trustworthy servant, in which case she was doing him a grave injustice. Yet she knew that Adam fancied himself in love with her, and that when in love, people were capable of doing strange, out-of-character things. She herself was guilty of some extraordinary aberrations from her natural behaviour.

Her common sense told her that there was no point in going out to search for Philip but, on the other hand, she knew that if another two hours passed without his return, she would not be able to prevent herself from saddling a horse, lighting a lantern and scaling the hilly track which Philip had taken earlier.

The clock on the marble mantelshelf chimed ten. Where was he? Had he himself been apprehended by a genuine robber up on the moors, who had stripped him of his jewels and horse and left him to walk the tedious distance back to Darwell Manor on foot? Or had Hardcastle or one of his attendants been armed, in which case Philip might be lying dead or injured on the lonely hillside?

She could not bear the suspense. Swallowing a mouthful of her now tepid soup, she placed the bowl beside the untouched food, left the warm room and set out for the side door leading into the stable yard, with Solomon bounding joyfully at her heels.

There were now only three horses living in a stable which had once held twenty or more: Philip's young, fast bay, the chestnut gelding which Lucy usually rode, and a docile hack on which Martha rode to market. Philip had long ago taken the useless mare which Lucy had brought him to a local horse fair, where it had brought a far lower sum than fifty guineas.

She paused and stroked the velvety nose of the friendly piebald hack, then a fusillade of barks set her whirling round to see Philip riding into the yard, looking every inch the highwayman he had pretended to be.

Lucy's first instinct was to run to him, but discretion sent her shrinking into the shadows. Watching him secretly like this gave her a strange, excited feeling such as she had felt the day she had observed him playing with the dog.

There seemed to be something slightly stiff about his movements as he dismounted from the saddle. Perhaps it was just fatigue, she thought. He removed his mask and ran a hand over his face. He paused to pat his dog, then led the bay into its stall and unsaddled it himself, rubbed it down with a cloth and fed and watered it, while Lucy cowered in an empty stall, hoping Solomon would not seek her out and advertise her presence.

She was in luck. The faithful animal preferred the company of its master and did not once come whining around her hiding place.

Having attended to the horse, Philip approached the Manor by the same side door which Lucy had used. She gave him a few minutes to get safely inside and out of sight, then followed. She wondered if he were already looking for her and decided that, if that should be the case, she would tell him that she had been in the music room, where surely he would never think of looking at past ten at night.

She re-entered the deserted drawing-room, where her discarded meal was still lying. Philip's return had released her appetite and she took a slice of the wholesome bread, buttered it and placed a piece of delicious cold ham on it, which she was halfway through eating when Philip's sudden arrival interrupted her.

She looked up in surprise as, without a word, his face totally expressionless, he deposited a pile of glittering gems in her lap. She exclaimed in delight as the firelight worked magic on their faceted surfaces and brought out the rich, warm glow of old gold, the delicate sheen of silver and the glimmer of precious stones.

"So, your hold-up was successful. Long live highwayman Philip, the peril of Pendleton Moors!" Lucy's gay words were greeted by a brief smile, which flickered across his face and faded almost instantly.

"Yes, I have the jewels, no thanks to you," he replied briefly.

Lucy's hand flew to her mouth. "What do you mean? I did exactly as you said. Matthew brought me all the correct ingredients and I mixed that ointment perfectly. So, if the potion did not work, how did you regain your property?"

"Ah. Matthew!" A look of interested speculation crossed Philip's face, but he did not venture to explain the reason for his exclamation.

"I was waiting on the hillside above the road," he continued. "The Hardcastles' carriage came along on schedule, but with four chestnuts pulling it. I deduced that you had mixed the potion wrongly and that the two greys you had, shall we say, 'interfered with', had collapsed too soon. Either that or you had not applied the potion at all.

"Rachel would have insisted on a matching team. She would not have been seen arriving at the ball with a patchwork of nags!" Philip brandished his riding whip and glared coldly at her. "So, miss, what have you to say for yourself?"

"Truly, I –" Lucy was not given a chance to justify herself because Philip, standing before her with his back to the fire, insisted on carrying on with his story of that night's adventures.

"The carriage passed and I was about to relinquish my plans and come home instead when one of the lead horses fell, the result of a lucky accident. In the resulting turmoil, I was able to persuade Harriet and Rachel to hand back my possessions."

"Do you think there is any possibility that you could have been recognized?" Lucy enquired, puzzled by his lack of enthusiasm regarding the regaining of his prized heirlooms.

"None. I wore a mask and disguised my voice well. I have no doubt but that they took me for the very creature I was trying to be, a common highwayman. I even had the satisfaction of striking a blow."

The relish with which he related this unexpected piece of information intrigued Lucy. "Oh?" she inquired. "Against whom?"

Philip narrowed his eyes and barked out a mirthless laugh. "Rachel. I thought you would be pleased to know."

Lucy's delight at hearing that the cruel, haughty girl had received a blow in payment for all those she had meted out to innocent victims such as herself, caused her to smile wryly, a smile that died the instant it formed as she remembered that she was still under suspicion. She *had* to make him believe her.

"Philip!" She stared hard at him, trying to put her whole soul into the look, noticing as she did so that his black cloak appeared to be torn near one shoulder. "I carried out your plan to the letter, but I was delayed because one of the horses wouldn't let me near it. I then had to treat another and was almost caught red-handed. I was lucky to get away at all. Adam will tell you. He waited for me."

"Adam. Hmm." He compressed his lips and looked away.

What can I do to convince him of the truth? Lucy wondered desperately. *Should I fall to my knees and beseech him?* No, she could not do that. Kneeling and cringing were not in her nature. If he refused to believe her, then that was his decision and she could only hope and pray that somehow, some way, she would be exonerated.

He jerked his head and met her eyes again. Her heart gave a hopeful flutter, but the hard, icy glint remained in his eyes and her spirits sank again. What he said next surprised her.

"I would like you to choose something in payment for having helped restore my home to me, if not the jewels," he said curtly, indicating the items still reposing in Lucy's lap. "If you see nothing there which takes your eye, I have some of my mother's less valuable, but perhaps prettier baubles upstairs. I shall bring them. They may be more to your taste."

"But Philip!" Lucy looked at him in amazement. "These jewels are so exquisite, so grand. When would I ever find the occasion to wear something so splendid?"

Just as she was reaching out to examine a sapphire bracelet, her pride reasserted itself and she drew back her hand. "No," she said. "You can keep your trinkets. If you refuse to believe that I kept my side of the bargain, then I refuse your gift as I am obviously undeserving of it."

"For God's sake, girl, just take something," he snapped. "Sell it, buy yourself some frippery, I don't care." His eyes flashed dangerously and she almost flinched and spilled the jewels onto the floor.

He was waiting. Well, she thought, if he insisted on foisting a gift on her, she would choose the very best! One item stood out from the tangled mass of glittering objects in her lap and that was a large, curiously designed emerald ring that she had last seen adorning Rachel's hand. She picked it up and held it out.

"With your permission, sir, I should like to take this ring."

"No! Not that." He snatched it from her. "I am sorry. It was my mother's and I am afraid that I cannot let it go. You can have anything else, but not that ring."

She almost wept with disappointment. There was nothing else she really wanted. Something about the ring had captured her imagination; the other jewels, even the fiery-hearted rubies, seemed lacklustre and uninteresting by comparison. In the end, she picked out a pair of delicately wrought gold and amethyst earrings.

She knew they would not fetch as much as diamonds if she were to try to sell them, but neither would they raise very much comment if she were to wear them. They would serve as a permanent reminder of the months she had spent at Darwell Manor, and of the Earl who had not just captured her but captivated her, too, and whose love she could never win.

Philip approved of her second choice and gathered up the rest of the jewels, bidding her a curt goodnight as he took them away, no doubt to be locked up with the house deeds and any other valuables he possessed.

Lucy was left sitting disconsolately by the dying fire. Apart from those dreadful days following the news of Rory's death, she had never felt so low and dispirited. She cursed Fate for having allowed her meet Philip under the worst of circumstances. She had come to him as a cheat and a thief, and was leaving as a suspected murderer and a betrayer of his trust.

Add her borrowed, ill-fitting clothes to the list and there was not much to admire and love about her, either inside or out. By now, Philip must be desperate to see the back of this awkward guest who had long outstayed her welcome.

Yet what about all the help she had given him? He would never have regained the deeds if it had not been for the aid which she, and only she, had been in the unique position to give him! As for the jewels, she had carried out his orders perfectly and could not be blamed for a last-minute change of carriage horses, which she suspected was done on a whim of Rachel's. Maybe she thought chestnut horses would set off the shade of her dress better than greys.

For Philip, she had suffered the cruel gibes and blows which Rachel had hurled at her; the outrageous mauling at the hands of George Hardcastle which still made her feel physically sick whenever she thought about it; fear and anxiety on many occasions; near death in the snow on the night she left Rokeby – and then there was Adam's embarrassing proposal, to say nothing of the danger she had endured that very day!

Surely he was aware of everything she had gone through on his behalf? Or was he really so cold and self-centred that he could use anybody to fulfil his purpose and then discard them without a second thought?

She remembered that hot, lustful look which had come into his eyes on that very first afternoon when, wearing his mother's beautiful silk dress, she had joined him in the banqueting hall. She had seen that look again on occasions such as the moment when they had been standing by the waterfall and Lucy had been certain that he wanted to kiss her but was holding himself back for some reason.

Maybe she was totally wrong. Maybe the only kind of 'wanting' Philip was capable of, was the rough sort she had almost experienced at his hands when he had dragged her into the stable after she had delivered the mare. Perhaps he had no finer feelings at all ...

And yet her intuition told her that there was a great deal of tenderness and sensitivity in his character that, for some reason known best to himself, he preferred to conceal. He was an enigma. She refused to give up and slink back to the Swifts' farm and the dreary future she knew would be hers, until she was absolutely certain that no vestige of affection for her dwelt in Philip's heart.

Her pulses raced as she realized what she must do. She had failed in her last attempt to visit him in his room, but this time there was no dying, hallucinating old man to stop her. She had nothing to lose, so there was nothing of which to be afraid.

Lucy's hands were trembling as she stood in her bedchamber lacing herself into that same exquisite blue dress which had evinced such an admiring look from Philip when he had first seen her in it. Putting on such a complicated garment without the aid of a maid was difficult, but she couldn't summon Martha for fear of her guessing what was in her mind. How shaming it would be if she were to be discovered tiptoeing up the stairs to his room, when she was supposed to be tucked up in bed in the nightgown which Martha had laid neatly out on the bed for her.

She brushed her chestnut curls until they shone, then tightened the tiny clasps of the amethyst earrings. Her neck felt far too naked without an ornament round it, as the neckline of the dress plunged so deeply. The necklace Rory had given her was too badly damaged to be wearable. She would have to go to Philip as she was and he would have to understand that she possessed no jewels apart from the earrings.

At least he can't accuse me of jewel theft, she thought wryly. Besides, she needed him to want her for herself, not for her surface appearance.

The thought of being close to Philip, of yielding herself up to him, filled her with quivers of anticipatory desire. Once again, she recognized these now familiar bodily feelings, the sensations she dreaded and yet, on this occasion, welcomed. She wanted to show herself to Philip as a passionate woman, to respond to his caresses with the wild abandon that was natural to her, not with decorous sighs and maidenly protests. She wanted to unlock that warmth and tenderness that she knew was in him; to ignite his body with her own.

Taking just one candle with which to light her way, Lucy stole out of her room and down the corridor to the staircase, wincing at the rustling of her skirts. When she reached the first landing, she paused.

Suddenly, the audacity of her actions struck her. Would she not cheapen herself in Philip's eyes by behaving no better than the slut who had seduced Rory in the inn? No, she was not going to seduce Philip; rather, she was going to create a situation where he could, if he wished, seduce her! She would tempt him with her mere presence in his room, but nothing else.

Her heart hammering like the hooves of a speeding horse, she reached for the door handle and very slowly turned it. A lamp was lit inside the room. Philip was seated at a desk, reading. He looked up in open-mouthed astonishment as the swish of Lucy's dress advertised her presence. She felt a hot blush break out all over her face and neck as she stood there in a dress which was a blatant invitation to any hot-blooded man.

Philip scraped his chair back and got to his feet, gazing at her in a silence which was heavy with unspoken thoughts and wishes. He took a small step towards her and she licked her lips nervously and felt a sudden desire to run pell-mell from the room. Why, oh why had she subjected herself to this embarrassment? She felt like a fairground freak being gawped at by curious but uncaring eyes.

No, do not weaken. Be brave, she told herself, switching on the intuition that allowed her to anticipate the reactions of a horse and hoping it worked with a man, too. *He is not sure why you are here. You must tell him, or show him.*

But what could she say? All at once she found herself in sympathy with every man who had ever been in love and, through tradition, had been faced with saying the first word, making the first move and risking heartbreak and rejection.

Yet, no matter how much she wanted to, she could not tell Philip Darwell that she loved him. But if she could not *tell* him ...

Her feet carried her forward on a wave of reckless courage. She was face to face with him, feeling as though her body and soul lay naked before his unwavering gaze. She stretched out one trembling hand and brushed the silken sleeve of his shirt – but the instant she touched him, he sprang away from her and leapt towards the window, where he stood gazing blankly out at the dark night which shrouded the Manor.

Lucy waited, her feet and tongue paralyzed. Surely he would say something? Would he not even speak her name, ask her the reason for her unexpected visit?

He did not move, just stood with his back to her, ignoring her. A rush of tears sprang up from deep within her. Stifling a sob, she turned and fled from his room, feeling that her world had truly ended. Now, at last, she knew she meant nothing at all to him – if, indeed, she ever had.

Not only Philip, but the whole of Darwell Manor was rejecting her, telling her she did not belong to its world but should return to her own lowlier one. She had aspired too high. How could she ever have dreamt that an Earl could feel anything more than either friendship or base lust for the daughter of a horse trainer?

She had found her true match in Rory, she knew that now. For all her pretensions to being a lady, her ability to read and write, to sew and draw, to grace social events with pretty talk and play simple melodies on a lute, nothing could alter the fact that she was a girl of no breeding, not fit to make a match with a gentleman of quality.

Philip was too polite to point it out to her, that was obvious, but now she knew her station. Why else had he forced her to play such menial roles in the working out of his schemes? Because he thought her fit to play the part, not only of Rachel's serving maid, but also of Hardcastle's whore. Ugh!

A shudder of pure self-loathing gripped her body and almost made her want to vomit. He had used her, and now he was finding it embarrassing to dismiss her. Well, she would spare him the trouble of saying the words. By the time the next day dawned, she would be gone.

Chapter Twenty-Four

The blue silk dress, now the subject of Lucy's burning hatred, lay on the bed in a careless heap, its pleats and folds creased and disordered. Lucy sighed to herself as she knotted the last lace on the old, stained, torn dress which she had worn the day of her arrival at Darwell Manor. She wished to leave the house with no more than she had brought when she came, with the sole addition of the earrings which she knew she would be unlikely to be able to possess for long, unless Prebbledale was much closer than she had imagined.

She was about to douse the lamp and find her solitary way out to the stables when she remembered Martha. The motherly old woman had been so kind to her that Lucy could not possibly disappear for ever without bidding her farewell, even though it was now nearly midnight.

She rang the bell to summon her, and when the bustling little woman finally entered the room, wearing a nightgown and shawl, Lucy silenced the questions which were on her lips by announcing, "As you can see, Martha, I am leaving. I regret not being able to take the lovely dress you gave me, but unfortunately I find it bears too many reminders of episodes I would prefer to forget."

She looked at Martha's glum face, and felt herself softening. "I'll never forget you, Martha, and your kindness. And Matthew, too. I wish .... wish I could stay, but ..."

What could she tell her that would convince Martha that she was doing the right thing?

Martha took the opportunity of Lucy's silence to ask the question she was obviously bursting to ask. "And where, pray, might you be going?"

Smiling wistfully, Lucy spoke the one word, "Home." Then she added, "Please tell Matthew I shall take the chestnut but I will see that it is returned as soon as possible."

Martha's eyes held hers for a moment in a searching gaze. Then, giving her arm a squeeze as if to say, *Be brave, girl, everything will turn out all right,* she left the room.

There was no moon that night but the stars were twinkling in a clear sky. Lucy was not sure in which direction Prebbledale lay, but something told her she should take the hill road. Really, she decided, it did not matter how far away her home lay, thirty miles or a hundred, so long as, by dawn, she had put as much distance as possible between herself and Darwell Manor.

And Philip.

Letting her mount pick its own way up the rough track, she allowed her mind to wander and found that, in her imagination, she was in Philip's bedchamber, eavesdropping invisibly on his thoughts. Almost immediately, she stopped herself. These were not Philip's thoughts, but her own make-believe. She would never know the way he felt about her, so what point was there in speculating?

If only she could stop aching for him like a girl who had been separated from her lover! There had never been anything between her and Philip. Why could she not wake up and realize that it was all in her head?

She was mortified to find her thoughts straying to that morning in the stable when he had displayed such violent passion towards her and had only been prevented from ravishing her by the untimely arrival of Rachel. If only he had displayed one ounce of that same passion since! If Rachel had not arrived when she did, might not one taste of her body have led him to desire another?

No. She must shut these thoughts out, banish them from her mind forever. The chapter of her life concerning Darwell Manor and all that had passed therein was over. She had to forget, for the sake of her own sanity.

"*What* sanity? Am I not already completely mad to be thinking about Philip this way?" she muttered with a hollow chuckle, not realizing she had spoken aloud until she noticed her horse flicking its ears. Sanity had deserted her. She was indeed mad – mad for a man who cared not one jot about her or her future happiness.

She reached a crossroads on the lonely path. It was too dark to read the signpost, so she let her horse plod on, not caring where it was taking her, letting the reins lie loosely in her curled fingers.

Suddenly, without warning, the whole world seemed to tip up. The signpost described a somersault before her eyes and she found herself flying through space, to land on her side with a jolt that knocked all the breath out of her. Her horse, whose rearing had been the cause of her dizzying flight and undignified landing, was standing panting by the side of the road.

Lucy could see no reason for the steady, well-mannered gelding's unprecedented behaviour but, as she lay gasping, trying to get her breath back and work out where or not she had sustained any injury, the thought came to her that crossroads were notorious among the superstitious as being haunted places where witches met and hanged men reappeared. Animals were gifted with the second sight. Perhaps her mount had seen or sensed something which her less sensitive human senses had failed to recognize ...

Her arms seemed to work all right. She moved her feet and ankles, then her legs. They, too, seemed whole. As she sat up, she felt a stab of pain in the shoulder on which she had landed, and briefly closed her eyes as she gave it a rueful rub. When she next opened them, she screamed aloud in terror and alarm, for a dark-clad man was standing in the road, staring down at her.

She scrambled to her feet but stood no chance of running away for, with two swift strides, the man was at her side, gripping her arm. As he drew closer, she recognized the familiar features of Adam Redhead.

Fear and shock made her angry. "You! It was *you* who made my horse rear and throw me. Why did you not make me aware of your presence instead of appearing like a ghost?"

"You were not riding sidesaddle like a woman. With your cloak wrapped around you and your collar turned up like that, you could have been anybody, perhaps even a highwayman," he explained. "In better weather, when there is more traffic about on these hill roads, highwaymen are a frequent hazard."

He smiled at her and she began to relax. At least Adam cared enough for her not to allow any harm to come to her. Perhaps he could set her on the right road for Prebbledale and home. Yet she sensed something was not quite right.

"If this spot is so dangerous, what are *you* doing here alone so late at night?" she inquired.

A guarded look came into Adam's eyes. "I ... I have somebody to meet," he explained, not very satisfactorily, his eyes scanning the darkness all around them.

Then, hauling his gaze back to Lucy, he asked, with a sudden note of concern in his voice, "I forgot. You may be hurt and it will be my fault. Are you all right?"

"I think so," replied Lucy, trying to laugh. "No bones seem broken."

"I am glad. Now perhaps you can tell me where you are bound at such an hour. Who was the thoughtless person who allowed a young, pretty, defenceless woman to stray alone on the moors at night?"

"I suppose you could accuse Philip Darwell of that," said Lucy lightly, and regretted her words the instant she saw the vicious expression that drew back Adam's lips in a feral snarl.

"That arrogant, callous toad!" he exclaimed venomously. "I hate that man more than I hate the Devil himself!"

Lucy felt the blood draining from her face and she stared at him, aghast. This was not the soft-voiced, fawning valet who had deferred to Philip in such a servile manner … the man she had scorned for seeming weak and feeble-spirited. This was a creature driven by bitter hatred, the reason for which she could not begin to guess.

"It was he who I was looking for, that cheating cur of a brother of mine. I meant to kill him, but he escaped me. I know he is here somewhere. Just one movement, one rustle in the bushes and I will have him!"

Lucy's eye lighted on the carved handle of a pistol protruding from Adam's pocket and felt a stab of terror. She did not understand. He said he hated Philip, and in the next breath he was talking about his brother. Philip had told her that Adam was the only son of Martha and Matthew, so who was this brother of whom he spoke?

As she stared at him, puzzled, he clutched her arm so tightly that she cried out.

"He's taken everything that is mine, the house, the jewels … We made a deal, but he has no more right to them than I. Why should *he* live a fine life in the Manor, when I am forced to slave for the Hardcastles and waste my noble blood in servitude?"

Noble? What did he mean? He was the son of servants!

'Jewels, money, let them hang. Let *him* hang! I shall kill him and then I shall have the Manor –and you as my wife!"

"No," Lucy said. "I will not be your wife. I do not care for you."

She tried to wrench her arm from his grasp but he tightened his grip and hauled her towards him, staring at her with mad, popping eyes. *He's going to kill me!* His face loomed close to hers and she raised her free hand and struck him a sharp slap across one cheek.

He appeared not to feel the blow. Instead, he gave a chuckle that sounded almost demonic. "So you like to play rough, do you, girl?" He yanked her arm and pulled her down to the ground. Summoning all her strength, she kicked him hard in the shins.

There was a sharp thudding sound and he fell backwards and landed beside her. She couldn't think what had just happened – had he tripped and winded himself? – but she knew she had to get away as fast as she could, before he came round

Scrambling to her feet, Lucy set off down the hill to where she had last seen her horse ... and had scarcely gone two steps before she came up against something solid and unmoving but unquestionably alive – the silent, terrifying bulk of a cloaked and masked man.

The scream died on her lips as a hand clamped itself across her mouth. Now she could see plainly what had befallen Adam. A heavy tree-branch lay beside his head and his light brown hair was stained dark with blood.

"Your money and your jewels, pretty lady," demanded the man, in a thick country accent which held a hint of laughter. "Come on now, me lovely lass. Your jewels and your gold, or you'll wish I'd never saved ye from that lusty scoundrel over yonder."

Lucy thought quickly. She had no money, only her amethyst earrings which were hidden in her pocket. But what would she do without them? They were her only currency. This thief must have known hard, penniless times in his life, or else why would he have taken up this way of life?

Thinking that perhaps she could plead with him and win his sympathy, Lucy pulled back her cloak to reveal the old, ragged dress beneath. "Please sir," she begged, "if you have any pity in your heart, spare a poor girl. See my clothes? I have no money, no valuables at all, not even a home to go to."

The latter was almost the truth; her father's smallholding certainly did not feel like home and in any case, she might not be welcome to return.

"I thank you kindly for what you did to save me," she added, hoping to appeal to his better nature, if he possessed one. "But now, having preserved my life and my virtue, could you not simply release me and let me go on my way?"

He laughed loudly, then thrust his hand into the small pocket inside her cloak. When he withdrew it, her earrings were dangling from his fingers, the silver gleaming in the dim glimmer of starlight.

"So ye would lie to me, would ye, ungrateful wench?"

"No! Please ... I'm sorry. I didn't mean to conceal anything from you."

Now he had discovered she was lying, what fate would lie in store for her? Whatever it turned out to be, she would accept it calmly and philosophically. She had been through too much already. Her fighting spirit was spent. She was weak, tired and hungry. She should have known better than to travel the dangerous moors alone at night.

She had brought this on herself. Two days earlier, when she had lain sobbing on her bed, she had imagined her bleached bones lying on the moor. She had inflicted a death-wish upon herself and there was nothing she could do to prevent it happening.

"I ... I n-need those j-jewels," she stammered, through chattering teeth. "They're ... they're the only thing I have. I am on a long journey. I shall s-starve if I c-cannot sell them."

Her words appeared to make no impact on the surly figure who had her wrists imprisoned in his strong hands.

"Please ... You have my only possessions now. Will you not let me go?"

"Yes, me little spring filly. When I've 'ad me fill o' those pretty lips o' yourn!"

Her lips were covered by a pair which were warm and surprisingly gentle. But the sudden sensation of cold metal against the fingers of her right hand made her gasp and jump.

He was going to kill her! She could almost feel the blade slipping between her ribs, filling her with agony so that her thoughts, her memories, all the things that made her the individual human being she was, came draining out with her blood. Perhaps, if she were to remain very, very still and not annoy him ...

There was that sensation of ice-cold metal again. He was not moving as if to cut her, however, but was pressing something against her hand. It could not be a blade. It was something much smaller.

Now he was fumbling with one of her fingers, doing something to it, trying to force something against it, over it. Was it some kind of instrument of torture, a thumbscrew perhaps?

Her hand was suddenly freed and she snatched it up to her eyes. The object around the third finger of her right hand was a large, ornate ring. In the faint starlight, she could just make out a design of clasped hands around a many-faceted stone.

No, she thought, her heart sinking. Philip had only just got his mother's ring back and now he had lost it all over again. How had this man stolen it? He had already killed, or nearly killed, Adam. What had he done to Philip? And what was he going to do with her?

Chapter Twenty-Five

As Lucy opened her mouth to scream and beg, the 'highwayman' removed his mask. She could not speak, she could not think – all she could do was feast her eyes on Philip Darwell.

I am such a fool! she thought. *I should have known.*

She should have recognized that laugh, those white teeth. Philip had told her how good his highwayman act was when he held up the Hardcastles' coach. If she hadn't been in such a fluster after her fight with Adam, she felt sure she would have seen through his disguise. Nevertheless, he shouldn't have frightened her like that and she told him so.

"I am sorry. I couldn't resist playing a trick on you."

"Call that a trick? You scared me half to death! Especially after being set upon by Adam."

"Yes. What was that all about?"

"He was out of his mind. Raving. And he had it in his head that I was going to agree to be his wife!"

"He what? Just as well I knocked him out then. Though you did a pretty good job at putting him in his place!"

His kiss still lingered on her lips and the unaccustomed weight of the ring felt strange on her finger. Had he followed her simply to give it to her, because he knew she coveted it? Or had he suspected that Adam might be up here at the crossroads?

Philip has kissed me! Was that part of the trick, too?

Then Adam's words came back to her. He had arranged to meet his brother, he said – but he and Philip could not possibly be brothers. It did not make sense.

A sudden groan alerted them to the fact that Adam had come round.

"Here, help me." Philip was kneeling by Adam's side, tying his wrists behind his back with a cord before the stunned man could recover enough to make a dash for freedom. He motioned to Lucy to secure Adam's ankles, offering her a piece of halter rope.

Finally, Philip fashioned a gag from his leather mask and, with the cheery observation, "Don't want him shouting his head off and waking the whole valley up, do we?", he slung the trussed man over his shoulder, then lifted him across the back of his bay horse, securing him to the saddle with some extra lengths of rope.

Lucy's chestnut was some way down the hillside, cropping at the bracken. Philip called its name and the obedient animal cantered up and stood rubbing its head against its master's chest.

"You'll have to carry two, I'm afraid," Philip informed it.

Bidding Lucy mount first, he swung himself lightly up behind her and they set off down the path, leading the bay with its awkwardly balanced human load behind them.

"What will you do with him?" Lucy asked, nodding her head towards Adam's inert body.

"He tried to shoot me this evening."

"No!" Lucy leant back, feeling the protective strength of Philip's body behind her.

So her earlier suspicions had been correct. Philip could have been lying dead on the hillside at precisely the time she was looking at the clock and worrying about him. The chestnut stumbled under its double load and Philip twitched the reins to pull its head up, and tightened his embrace on Lucy in the process.

As they turned a bend in the track and she spied the dark patch of trees that shielded Darwell Manor from the winter winds, the question that had been preying on her mind leapt from her tongue. "Is Adam really your brother?"

Philip heaved a deep sigh, as if she had touched on a subject that caused him distress. "My half-brother, I suppose you could call him."

"But ... Martha and Matthew ..."

"They adopted him. They are not his true parents. We shared the same mother."

Lucy let a shocked gasp escape her lips. A philandering father, especially an Earl, she could understand, men being the morally weaker sex, but for a gentle, beautiful and, by all accounts, delicate married woman to give birth to another man's child? She could not believe it.

"I realize that it sounds like a sordid story, but it is a sad one, too, if you will permit me to tell it."

They still had a mile or so to ride before they reached the Manor and Lucy was only too eager to listen to this tale which she knew would explain so much about Philip, about Adam, about the strange, haunted atmosphere of Darwell Manor.

"You have seen the portrait of my mother that hangs in the banqueting hall?"

"Yes. She was beautiful."

"All men adored her, particularly my father. I was born and Father, partly out of respect and partly I think out of fear of damaging her fragile health, refused to share her bed again. My mother was spirited. She was fond of music and dancing and loved to be admired, by men especially. When I was a year old, she insisted that a ball should be held.

"Something happened at that ball and not long after, my mother found she was expecting my half-brother."

"Do you know who Adam's father was?" asked Lucy, full of sympathy for all of them, the beautiful, wayward, neglected mother; the adoring, misguided father; Philip, the lonely boy deprived of a mother; even poor, obsessed Adam.

"I believe he was a young army officer, the cousin of one of the guests, who had brought him along as he happened to be home on leave after a campaign. Shortly after his ... dalliance with my mother, as I have no reason to suspect that it was rape, he went abroad again and was killed in a skirmish.

"My mother was not in love with him. In fact, she was full of remorse and begged my father for forgiveness, blaming her wantonness on too much drink, but his pride was hurt so badly that he refused to give it. My mother moved to the top floor of the house and she and my father did not speak to each other again until after Adam's birth, when it was obvious that she was dying.

"Seeing her so ill, and truly loving her, my father forgave her, but it was too late. After her death, he never stopped punishing himself for his unyielding attitude towards her. It preyed on his mind. He refused to remarry and became totally obsessed with her memory."

"So it was Adam's birth that killed her, not yours. What became of him then?"

"My father would have nothing to do with Adam. He refused to adopt him or acknowledge him in any way, so Martha and Matthew, being childless themselves, found a wet nurse and brought him up as their own son and took over the raising of me, too when my aunt could no longer do it.

"Then, being young and thoughtless, I made a big mistake."

He paused for so long that Lucy thought he was not going to continue. "What did you do?" she urged.

Philip sighed heavily. "One day when I was eight or nine, I let slip that if only my mother had not disgraced herself, Adam would have been my true brother and would have inherited a share of the Darwell fortune and shared my privileged life, but he couldn't because he was a bastard. My father, you see, had made the mistake of telling me the truth when I was too young to understand its significance, so I used it as a childish taunt, being too young to know any better.

"The word 'bastard' must have really stung him. From that moment onwards, our easy friendship turned into a kind of rivalry. Then, when we grew older, Adam developed a kind of fawning admiration for me which I could not bear. My father and I decided it would be best if he were sent away from the Manor.

"The position in Rokeby Hall became vacant, Adam was fond of horses and so it was all arranged. He continued to treat Martha and Matthew as if they were his true parents, because he knew that, without them, he would have been left on a doorstep as a foundling.

"I now suspect that even then he was scheming against me, though it was only today that I had proof of my suspicions. He must have thought that if I were dead, he might inherit the Manor, even though the family fortune had long gone."

"So he did not know that your father had lost the Manor to Hardcastle?"

"Not until he heard Hardcastle boasting about it. After that, it was in his interest that I should recover the deeds."

"So why use me to steal them back, when he could have done it for you?" Lucy asked, frowning. "When you said it was more fun to see me do it, I didn't believe you. I felt there was more to it. What was the real reason?"

"Because I couldn't trust him."

"But he could have done it anyway. At any time, he could have taken them and blackmailed you into paying him to hand them over. He might even have insisted you signed the Manor over to him!"

"Yes, he could. But I don't think he was bright enough to think of anything like that. The thing about Adam is that he has never been able to act on his own initiative. He needs to be told what to do. He is a hopeless leader but a good foot soldier."

He acted on his own initiative when he grabbed me up on the moor, thought Lucy. She felt that Philip had underestimated his half-brother. Having him so close, even if he were trussed up, made her feel uneasy. If Philip couldn't trust him, then who could? Certainly not her.

But how would Martha and Matthew react, seeing their son brought back to them, tied to a horse like a corpse? She feared for Martha and she felt that life in Darwell Manor could never be the same and that both she and Philip were destined for lonely, unhappy futures.

Chapter Twenty-Six

Philip lapsed into a silence which persisted for the rest of their journey, throwing Lucy back on her worried thoughts. Why was Philip bringing her back to the Manor? What was to become of Adam – and herself, for that matter? And why had Philip made her the gift of the emerald ring? Guilty conscience at the way he had treated her?

Why, too, had he seemed so unsurprised to see her up on the moor? Why had he remained in his highwayman's guise in order to meet Adam? These and a dozen more questions occupied her thoughts until their horses' hooves rang on the cobblestones of the stable yard.

"Wait here," Philip ordered her. "I will fetch Matthew and Martha to take care of Adam."

Lucy felt nervous about being left alone with Adam who, bound and gagged as he was, was making strenuous efforts to free himself from his bonds. She could not look at him, remembering the way he had mauled her. She knew instinctively that he was a dangerous man, cunning and violent.

She rubbed the arm that he had gripped so tightly, knowing she would have a bruise there in the morning. He was making grunting sounds, like a wild animal, and she was terrified in case he should suddenly escape from the ropes that held him and try to kill Philip or herself.

The appearance of Matthew and Martha put an end to her fears. On seeing them, Adam stopped struggling. He was untied from the saddle and helped down. His ankles were unbound so he could walk, but his hands remained tied behind his back. He stumbled, perhaps still dazed from the blow to the head, and Philip and Matthew supported him as they walked to the servants' entrance.

As soon as they were alone, Martha turned to Lucy and inquired, in a nervous whisper, "Has he told you?"

"You mean, told me about Adam?" asked Lucy in turn.

"Yes."

"A little. I know he is not your son, and that he was jealous of Philip."

"He loves you, you know. I think that's what finally turned his mind."

Martha was weeping. Great, silent tears slipped down her worn face and Lucy put a comforting arm around her, just as Martha had, in the past, done to her.

"They'll hang him or put him in Bedlam. Poor lad, he's not right in the head. All those years I cared for him, since he was a little 'un. We loved him, Matthew and I, like he was our own lad."

"There, there. Come on," murmured Lucy consolingly. "I'm sure Philip will not insist on anything so drastic."

"But Adam tried to kill him!"

Martha broke into fresh sobs and there was nothing Lucy could do but wait quietly with her until Matthew returned and led his weeping wife into the Manor. Lucy shivered in the chill night air. She didn't know what to do – whether to follow the two servants back into the house, or wait until Philip reappeared and settled her fate for her.

She retreated into the stable building, where the body heat of the horses and the bulky bales of straw provided some protection from the cold, damp air. As she stood there, idly stroking the muzzle of Philip's bay, its owner strode into the building, swinging a lantern.

"Oh, there you are. I thought maybe you had slipped off again, like you did earlier this evening."

There was a challenging tone in his voice which made Lucy raise her chin defiantly. "You looked for me, then?"

"Yes. I wanted to speak with you. Your room was empty and Martha, after a great deal of prompting, I may add, told me that you had taken the gelding and run off. I must say that I had my own suspicions about where you were heading, and somehow your home didn't enter into them."

"But I ..."

Philip interrupted. "It so happened that I knew that someone else was out roaming the hilltops this very evening."

Lucy gasped. "You didn't think for a moment that I ... ? That Adam and I ... ?"

She was horrified. If that was honestly what he thought, then she was done for. There was no way he would fail to give her up to the officers of the law. Suddenly, she realized why he had forced his emerald ring onto her hand – so that he could accuse her of stealing it!

"Look at it my way, Lucy Swift." His voice was firm and did not betray any clue as to how he now viewed her – as partner in crime, slut or traitor. His gaze was level, his face expressionless. Her legs felt weak and she sank down onto a hay bale.

He continued. "That night Adam brought you to the farmhouse, you left and he followed you out. I was right behind the door. I heard his offer and I did not hear you turn him down. Not in the way a disinterested woman would slap down an unwanted suitor.

"Oh yes, you put up a modest showing, full of maidenly protests. You did not wish to return to the Hall, you did not wish to spend your life as a serving maid. But I did not hear you tell Adam that you could not go with him because you did not love him, or were in love with somebody else."

During this speech, Philip's eyes had begun to flash with anger. Or was it something else, a different emotion entirely? His level tone had deserted him and an odd suspicion formed in Lucy's head. He sounded almost like a jealous lover – but no, that was impossible. Still, she kept him under acute observation as he continued his speech.

"I thought nothing more of your ... alliance, until the business with the horses. That is when I decided that you and Adam were in league to foil my plan."

"He sent a lad with a note which said they were going to use the greys. That's why I put the potion on them!" Lucy protested. "I have no idea why they decided to use the chestnuts instead. Perhaps Adam lied to me. You may think he is incapable of thinking for himself, but I think you have misjudged him. I wager he was planning something all along."

"I think you both were. It could be that Adam planned to kill me as I held up the coach, claiming ignorance of my identity. He would then collect a sizeable reward from the Hardcastles for having beaten off the highwayman and saved their lives.

"Then, after pretending to search for me – having buried my body on the moors, of course – he would return to Darwell Manor, stake a claim to the property and the title and make you his wife. You and Adam, Earl and Countess Darwell."

Lucy burst out laughing at this preposterous suggestion. Her laughter turned into near hysteria and she fought to regain control of herself. Finally, wiping the tears of mirth from her eyes, she looked up at Philip who was regarding her with some irritation.

"And what is so funny, pray? Can you not see how it all seems to fit into place?"

"B-but ..." Lucy's voice still shook with laughter. "If you really suspect me of siding with Adam and being involved in it all, why are you telling me? I should be wherever Adam is, tied up like he is, awaiting trial by a judge and jury."

Philip's stern look dissolved into something softer and he reached out and touched her hand.

"My dearest Lucy, I had only to eavesdrop on your surprise meeting with Adam on the moor and witness the way he treated you, to know there was no liaison between you. And when I saw him attack you, I wanted to kill him. It would have been so easy!

"But then I would have had blood on my hands which I would have been forced to explain. And when it came out that he was my half-brother ... well, judges never quite know how to deal with matters involving the nobility. I would not like to guess how it might have gone for me."

"And the horses? Do you still believe I told Adam not to harness the greys?"

She held her breath. So much was riding on his reply. Behind her, a horse stamped and snorted in its stall. Still Philip had not answered her question. Then at last his stern face twitched into a smile.

"Lucy, Lucy, you are so quick to jump to conclusions and so easy to fool. I must admit I have been playing with you to a certain degree." He bit his lip, a look of merriment in his eyes.

Lucy felt wounded. "That isn't fair," she said. "I have been torturing myself, wondering how to prove my innocence to you. I think you owe me an apology, sir!"

"Madam, I humbly apologise," he said, performing a deep bow which almost made her giggle.

"I have learned the truth about the exchange of horses," he said.

"And...?" She raised her head and stared at him, eager to find out what had gone wrong with their plan.

"It wasn't Adam's fault, though I am sure we both thought it was. I just heard from Martha that a few days ago on a visit here, Adam told them both that he had overheard George Hardcastle saying that greys were for ladies and chestnuts were a man's choice and by Jove he would have his carriage pulled by the chestnuts on the night of the ball. Adam was laughing, he thought it was very funny.

"Apparently, both Harriet and Rachel begged Hardcastle to let them use the greys, but he insisted it was his coach and four, and the four were to be chestnut and even Rachel's tears could not persuade him otherwise.

"So, my dear, I fully believe that you did indeed carry out my wishes. By the time the Hardcastles returned from the ball, the two greys you nobbled would have been restored to health and nobody would have been any the wiser."

Relief swept over Lucy and she sank down onto a bale of hay and asked one of the other questions that been preying on her mind.

"Why did you follow me in your highwayman's outfit tonight? And why did you not reveal who you were straight away, instead of playing out that ridiculous charade? I must admit, though, your accent was most convincing!"

"Thank 'ee kindly, mistress!"

They both burst out laughing. In the glimmering light shed by the lantern, Philip looked five years younger than he had seemed earlier that evening. The strained, tense lines had melted from his face and he looked quite boyish, although there was still an air of restless unease about him that Lucy could find no reason for.

Suddenly, the smile left his face and she steeled herself for whatever this unpredictable man was going to do or say next. Sitting down beside Lucy on the hay-bale, he placed the lantern on the floor and laid his hand on her arm.

Instantly, she felt her muscles jump and an excited thrill run through her. So her feelings for Philip still persisted, after all her attempts to eradicate them!

"I shall tell you why I was dressed as a highwayman. Firstly, because that was how Adam expected me to look. He had not seen me steal away, long after his shot had been fired. He thought I might be lying somewhere, wounded. My plan, if I did not find you first, was to leap out and surprise him and give him a piece of my mind. At least!" he added, leaving her in no doubt that there would have been a fight of some sort between them.

"And what were you intending to do with me? Shoot me?" She gave him a quizzical glance.

"No, Lucy. Not shoot you."

His grip tightened on her arm and two of his fingers strayed to her wrist and began to stroke it, absently at first, but then meaningfully, sending agonizing shivers of desire for him coursing through her veins. "I was going to give you a fright and kidnap you, and not reveal until later that your abductor was myself. But ..."

"But what?" She shifted a fraction so that she could feel her hip resting against his. What had he had in mind for her? Where had he planned to take her?

More importantly, what had he planned to do? Carry her into his bedroom and lay her gently on his bed, where she wouldn't cry out or protest but would open her arms and moisten her lips ready for his kisses? *Stop it, Lucy Swift*, she told herself sternly. *The man feels nothing for you. He's an Earl and you're nothing but a horse dealer's daughter!*

But ... the emerald ring. It was still on her finger. What was the meaning of that? Another of his jokes? Yes, that was it. She felt it, twisted it on her finger, began to ease it over her knuckle, ready to hand it back to him.

Philip looked away, the glow from the lantern reflecting on his cheekbones and making fringed shadows of his long eyelashes.

"It seemed to be taking the game too far. I hardly dared expect that you would have welcomed it. It wasn't as if you cared for me, or felt anything for me."

Lucy could not believe what she was hearing. His tone was full of doubt and hope. He was gazing at her now, waiting for a response, an expression of encouragement – or perhaps even a horrified rejection!

She seized his hand. "Philip Darwell, if only you knew!"

She stopped. How could she tell him of the hours of torment she had suffered, wanting him, loving him? Carefully, she asked, "Whatever made you think I did not feel anything for you?"

His reaction was instantaneous. Words of guilt and remorse burst from his lips as if he had been storing them up for weeks.

"After the way I treated you in the stable when we first met? And the things I made you do for me? How do you imagine I felt? Like the most unworthy, low creature that ever lived!

"I denied my feelings for you, I hid them, but I could not let you go. You do not honestly think that I thought you had murdered my father, do you? I'll admit I was upset at first and said some unforgiveable things, but after I had got over the shock of his death and calmed down, I realized none of it was your fault.

"Letting you think I blamed you was all I could think of doing to keep you with me a little longer, so that I could see you and be near you. I might have seemed callous and cruel, Lucy, but there is a fault in my nature that makes me terribly slow to realize things about people. I trust too easily. And –" he touched her lips lightly with his own – "I fall too hard."

"And so do I," Lucy whispered, kissing him back.

"It took me years to recognize the truth about Adam," he continued, once their kiss was over. "Martha and Matthew could see the terrible jealousy in him, the mean, vicious streak, and they did their best to change his nature, teach him to be kinder and more forgiving, but I was blind to it all."

He reached up and stroked her hair gently. "And I was even blinder about you, Lucy. It took me so long to realize that ... that I love you. Could you possibly love me in return?"

There was a strange singing noise in Lucy's ears, and a weightless, soaring feeling in her body, as if she were about to float right up to the ceiling. He loved her! Was this really happening?

"Yes, Philip, yes. I do love you."

He lowered his lips, Lucy raised hers. Their mouths mingled, their kiss grew more passionate.

When they broke off, Philip suddenly looked serious again. "I have another question for you," he said. "Were you really married to Rory McDonnell?"

There was a brief pang inside her, the dying spark of something that had once been hot and strong and but now was like a speck of ash in a grate, crushed by Rory's double betrayal of her. "No," she said. "No, he was never my lawful husband. I can explain everything, but not right now."

Lucy raised her arms to embrace his strong, firm body, and the emerald ring glowed in the lamplight.

"Philip?" she murmured. "This ring. I must give it back to you." She tugged it off her finger and held it out to him.

He closed his fingers round hers. "Not yet. There is something I must ask you first."

"There is something I must ask you, too!" Lucy said, her heart racing. "Why would you not give it to me when I first asked you for it? You said I could have any of the jewels I wanted, but you made me choose something else instead. You said it was your mother's, so why put it on my finger now?"

He reluctantly drew his lips from the soft warmth of Lucy's neck and replied, "It is a family custom of ours that the emerald ring is worn only by the wife of the Earl of Darwell."

"Then why have you given it to me?"

He took her right hand, gently slipped off the emerald ring and replaced it on the third finger of her left hand. "Lucy Swift, will you do me the honour of becoming my wife?"

She gasped, her hand flying to her mouth. She tried to answer, but no words would come and all she could do was gaze at him, hoping her eyes would reveal her answer ... hoping her heart would not leap right out of her chest.

He frowned. "I realize the timing is bad, with my dear father not yet buried. We will have to wait a decent while to announce our betrothal. That is, if you agree to accept me?"

Philip pressed her hand and his grey eyes searched hers, waiting for her reply. Joy surged within her and with it came certainty that now at last she was doing the right thing and that when she gave herself to Philip, it would be for the truest, most powerful reason of all: love.

"Yes, Philip," she whispered, her heart too full for speech as she planted her lips on his, opened her mouth to him and drew him down to her, allowing his hands to roam freely over her body.

At first he responded passionately, then he broke off, looked around him and muttered anxiously, "No, not here. Whatever would you think of me? We should go back to the Manor."

"Why not here?" Lucy gazed at him, knowing her desire for him was burning in her eyes.

"Because – oh God, Lucy Swift! I've desired you for so long!"

"Then why wait any longer?"

Immediately she had said it, her hand flew to her mouth. Oh, what had she done? He would think she was no better than a common slut! But she wanted him – oh God, she wanted him, far more than she had ever wanted Rory. That whole episode now seemed like a distant dream.

Philip was real, he was here and her desire and her love for him was like an all-consuming flame, one she had no control over; no means of putting out even if she had wanted to. When was he going to answer her? What was he going to do? Had she, by five thoughtless words, destroyed his respect for her and his desire?

She felt herself begin to shake. Tears sprang to her eyes. "Philip," she whispered. "I shouldn't have said that. I'm sorry."

"Ssh." He reached out and brushed her curls off her hot, damp forehead, then took her in his arms and pushed her firmly back on the hay bale. His lips closed on hers, his hands swept her body, awakening vibrant surges of desire that radiated from her loins to the outermost reaches of her body, like the intense, scorching rays of an August sun. She felt his body quivering with a need that matched her own in intensity and urgency.

"You're right, my darling," he murmured, as his seeking hands slowly smoothed her skirts away from the trembling warmth of her thighs. "Why wait one second longer?"

THE END

Dear reader,

We hope you enjoyed reading *The Earl's Captive*. Please take a moment to leave a review, even if it's a short one. Your opinion is important to us.

Discover more books by Lorna Read at
https://www.nextchapter.pub/authors/lorna-read-romance-author-liverpool-uk

Want to know when one of our books are free or discounted? Join the newsletter at http://eepurl.com/bqqB3H

Best regards,
Lorna Read and the Next Chapter Team

The Earl's Captive
ISBN: 978-4-86750-567-0

Published by
Next Chapter
1-60-20 Minami-Otsuka
170-0005 Toshima-Ku, Tokyo
+818035793528
10th June 2021